PREDATOR'S WALTZ

Also by Jay Brandon

Deadbolt
Tripwire

PREDATOR'S WALTZ

Jay Brandon

St. Martin's Press
New York

Design by Amelia Mayone

Library of Congress Cataloging-in-Publication Data

Brandon, Jay.
    Predator's waltz / Jay Brandon.
        p.   cm.
    "A Thomas Dunne book."
    ISBN 0–312–03413–X
    I. Title.
PS3552.R315P74   1989
813'.54—dc20   89–35079

First Edition
10 9 8 7 6 5 4 3 2 1

for Yolanda
with love

PART ONE

Days

of the

Hand

CHAPTER 1

Daniel

DANIEL Greer, sitting glumly beside his cash register, answered the phone on the first ring. His face lit up when he heard the voice on the other end. Anyone watching him could have seen how happy he was to hear from her, but someone only listening could have been misled by the grumble in his voice.

"No, darling, I haven't forgotten. It's on my calendar in red, it's the most important day of the year for me. I've been picking out my outfit for weeks."

He sat and listened, grinning.

"No really, I'm ready whenever you are. I'm just waiting for the kid to show up to watch the shop for me. . . . I don't know, he's always so punctual. Don't worry, there's plenty of time."

He listened again, and when he replied his voice had gone soft for the first time in the conversation. "Me too," he said.

"All right, whenever. He'll be here. If not I'll just close up. I don't think two lost hours will break me. Okay. Bye, darling."

Daniel hung up and returned to his gloomy contemplation of the pawnshop across the street. No, he thought, it won't be two hours that break me.

The boy's name was Thien, pronounced as if the *h* weren't there. He was sixteen years old but small for his age. He looked anomalous walking out of the high school on Houston's near north side at four o'clock in the afternoon: too small, too studious, too slant-eyed. He carried half a dozen books stacked atop each other. The topmost book was open and Thien read as he walked. He went two blocks in that way without noticing the men following him.

The two men were only a few years older than Thien but there was nothing boyish about them. They had an air of confident aggression. They showed no curiosity about their surroundings but remained focused on the boy. The two men were both whipcord thin. Though it was the last day of November, they wore thin nylon windbreakers. The older of the two had a jagged scar across one cheek. They were also Vietnamese.

When Thien stopped at a corner and looked both ways for cars, he caught a glimpse of them out of the corner of his eye. Until then he had been oblivious to the chill in the air, warmly absorbed in his book. But at the sight of the men he went cold. He didn't know them, but he was sure they had come for him. There was no other reason for two like them to hang around a school. They were walking not fast but purposefully, and he was standing still. He had an urge to throw down his books and run, but they would catch him in a second if he did. Instead he started across the street as if still unaware of them and everything else. A car's brakes screeched close at hand. Thien hurried on.

He didn't fool anyone. Behind him one of the men raised his voice: "If you make us run you'll be sorry." His threat was in a language the few bystanders on the cold sidewalk didn't understand, so they pretended not to have heard. It seemed to Thien that the street was emptying around him.

Shortly ahead was his bus stop. Beside it was an empty bench. When the sixteen-year-old boy reached it, he stopped momentarily and glanced back down the street as if for the bus. One of the two men pointed a finger at him. They were only thirty yards back now. He wondered what they would do to him there on the street. He knew it could be done in a matter of seconds, and afterward no one would have seen anything.

At the end of the next block was another bus stop. The bench beside that one was occupied by a fat older woman and two teenagers who could have been her grandchildren. Thien leaned out and looked down the street in that direction. Farther down, still blocks away, the bus was coming. A bus full of warmth and witnesses, heading for his home. If he could reach it . . .

He walked in that direction, picking up his pace. There was an angry shout behind him. He didn't look back. The shout had been too near. Any moment he expected to feel them close on either side of him. If he could shake them off and reach the bus stop, he'd have a chance. Maybe they wouldn't risk anything in front of the woman and teenagers, and he'd be safe until the bus came and he climbed aboard. He could lose them then. They wouldn't chase him onto a bus full of Americans.

At the corner he gave an involuntary shudder, shaking off an invisible hand. He looked back again. Now there was only one pursuer behind him. That one had a face suffused with blood and eyes that glared. He wouldn't run but he was walking fast, leaning toward Thien. His eyes promised pain.

Thien looked wildly all around him. Where was the other one? He must have gone off to the side and around, trying to cut him off. Thien didn't see him, worse news. He hurried across the street, his head swiveling. Now he was expecting a hand to fall on him from any direction.

Nothing happened. He reached the far curb safely. When

he looked back his lone pursuer was still on the other side, waiting for a line of cars to pass. Thien had a moment of breathing space. He almost ran toward the bus stop. The old woman had turned and was looking curiously in his direction. He must have been a strange sight. He hadn't dropped his books but the pile he was holding had slipped askew. He had to press them tightly against his body as he ran. It looked as if he were making off with sacred scriptures and the guardians of the temple were in hot pursuit. Thien didn't slow down. He didn't want to make himself less an object of curiosity. He was almost to the old woman now, and her grandchildren had turned to watch him too. As he drew up to them and stopped Thien almost laughed, giddy with relief. The teenagers looked bored, he noticed, not like someone watching a race. He looked behind him and saw that even his second pursuer had given up. There was no one in sight. Thien breathed deeply. In the other direction the bus was only a block away, stopped to let off passengers. Its doors closed and its loud heart revved as it started toward him. Thien's shoulders fell from their position up near his ears. He wondered what the two men could have wanted.

The metallic blue Ford slashed out of the sparse traffic and across the sidewalk right beside Thien, cutting him off from the old woman and teenagers. He leaped back, his heel caught the sidewalk, and he fell flat on his back. The car was almost atop him. It slammed to a halt and its passenger door opened. The second Vietnamese man jumped out. The first, the driver, leaned around the steering wheel to peer down at Thien. His lips parted in a lazy grin.

The passenger hustled Thien up off the ground and into the front seat. Thien still clutched two of his schoolbooks to his chest, but the others lay scattered on the ground. The man left them there. Just before he climbed into the car beside his captive, he smiled across the roof of the car at the startled old woman. "My little brother has decided not to take the bus," he said. He jumped into the car as it backed off the sidewalk and sped away.

The car was a compact. Thien was crushed between the two Vietnamese men in the front seat. "They'll call the police," he said.

"Not those, little brother," the driver said, looking in the rearview mirror. "They are just getting on the bus."

"I am not your brother," Thien said sullenly.

"Here in America we are all brothers," the passenger said jovially. His elbow was digging into Thien's right side. He said, "You almost made me have to run, schoolboy. Then I would have had to cut your little nose off and feed it to you."

Thien wondered where the man had learned that word, schoolboy. It was the contemptuous word kids at school used to describe the few serious students. The passenger pulled one of Thien's books loose from his grasp, glanced at it incuriously, and dropped it behind him onto the floorboard.

"My father—" Thien began, and stopped. My father will have to pay for those books, he had started to say. His captor thought he had meant something else. He sneered.

"We don't give shit one about your father. We are just giving you a ride to work. And on the ride, we have some questions about your boss."

Thien was startled. And then the Vietnamese thug did something that amazed him. He pulled a sheet of notebook paper from his windbreaker pocket, unfolded it, and began to read questions to him.

"There you are," Daniel said. "I'd about given up on you. Did you run all the way?" he added when he heard Thien's ragged breathing. But he wasn't paying much attention to the boy. Thien, by contrast, was regarding him intently, but Daniel didn't notice. He was standing at the plate-glass window of his shop, staring at the pawnshop across the street.

"Come over here. Explain this to me."

A few minutes later "Hah! I knew it," he said, as an old

woman emerged from the shop. She still carried the package she'd gone in with. It was unwrapped now, and he could see it was a bowl. It looked like pale-blue porcelain. There were figures etched on the outside of it, but they were so delicate that from this distance they looked like pale pencil smudges. Daniel would have liked a closer look.

The old woman hesitated. She hastily rewrapped the bowl and put it away in her shopping bag, but she still didn't move from the spot. She glanced covertly in Daniel's direction, but he didn't think she could see him in the dimness within; she was looking at the store itself.

"Come on," he said softly. "Try me if you didn't like his offer."

A young man appeared around the corner, hands in pockets, and sauntered toward the old woman. When he was almost upon her the woman's moment of indecision snapped. She clutched her bag and turned suddenly away. The young man was in her path. They collided. The old woman's shopping bag fell to the sidewalk. Daniel couldn't hear a sound, but he would have bet the porcelain bowl had shattered. The old woman's mouth opened wide. She and the young man both stooped for the bag. Both their mouths moved as they crouched there, and the old woman looked into his face for the first time. She said no more, but clutched the bag to her breast and hurried away.

The proprietor had appeared in the doorway of his shop. The young man grinned sheepishly at him and shrugged. The shopkeeper's face was hard, but the young man didn't lose his smile.

For a moment, as the old woman was just turning away, the shopkeeper had come to the door, and the three of them were framed by the plate-glass window of the shop, Daniel thought: *What is wrong with this picture?* The incongruity suddenly struck him, as it hadn't in a while. A few blocks away rose the towers of downtown Houston, glass and steel and air-conditioned defiance of nature. This street was much humbler, with small shops and sparse foot traffic, the street decaying to old warehouses a block or two farther on. What was incongruous about the scene Daniel watched was the fact that it was taking place in the middle of Houston, Texas. The nearest street signs said Jefferson and Calhoun, but the lettering on the shop window across the way said 죱 듸 죪 . The three people standing framed in the window were, like the language of the sign, Vietnamese.

As was the sixteen-year-old boy at his elbow. Thien had come to stand beside him and was observing the scene intently, as if he could see more in it than Daniel had.

"Serves her right," Daniel said. "If she'd come straight over here with the bowl it wouldn't've gotten smashed. Why wouldn't she, anyway, when the tightwad over there obviously wouldn't come up with her price?"

"Better the devil she knows," the boy said. "The old woman probably doesn't even speak English. She knows the Vietnamese pawnbroker would cheat her, but she thinks you would know some terribly clever American way of cheating her that she's never even heard of. Maybe even that she would be asked too many questions, get arrested, if she came here. You are foreign soil."

"Kid, she *lives* on foreign soil."

Thien came as close as he ever did to making a joke. "Not in this neighborhood," he said.

Daniel didn't need it rubbed in. He was quite aware of what Thien meant by that: That particular problem was ruining his business. In the last ten years a hundred thousand Asian refugees, most of them Vietnamese, had crowded into Houston. For the most part they didn't blend. They tended to cluster in certain run-down neighborhoods and make them their own. It was Daniel's bad luck that his own pawnshop had been surrounded by just such an influx. It had been a bad neighborhood already, many of the businesses closed and property values declining, so it had been easy for the Vietnamese to move in. Owners had been glad to sell out. Daniel would have done so himself if anyone had made him an offer. But no one had, so the tide of Vietnamization had swept around and past him, until his was the only American-owned business on the block. It was as if some weird urban renewal had purged the neighborhood. The block looked better than it had in decades, but it was no longer American.

And when the foot traffic on the street had changed color, Daniel's business had begun to dry up. White Houstonians still came to the street, but for the most part only to the two Vietnamese restaurants, or to poke around in the curio shops. They weren't interested in the American pawnshop in the middle of the block. Daniel still had his old customers, but his shop didn't generate any neighborhood business. There was a steady stream of Vietnamese in and out of the other shops on the street, but not into Daniel's. They stared at him as if he were the intruder. *He* had to win *their* acceptance.

It seemed he never would now that the Vietnamese man had opened another pawnshop directly across the street from Daniel's. When Daniel had seen what the place was going to be, he had gone over and tried to talk to the man, tell him it would be bad business for both of them, but it was impossible to talk to the rival. He had just stared as if the words slid right by him. The shop had opened as scheduled and of course had drawn in all the Vietnamese business, with none left over.

Daniel had tried one other farfetched tactic to get rid of the Vietnamese shop, but nothing had come of that.

He turned away from the window into the gloomy interior of his own shop. It was appropriately seedy, as a good pawnshop should be. Who would think he was getting a bargain if the merchandise gleamed like new? Who would want to slip into a brightly lighted fishbowl carrying a typewriter or camera under his arm? Goods were stacked to the ceiling on the shelves that lined the walls. Three display cases—locked, to make the cheap stuff within seem more valuable—held jewelry and trinkets. The valuable stuff, the guns, were behind the wire screen that cut off access to most of the west wall of the store. You had to ask to see those items.

"I should have sent you out to sweep the sidewalk," Daniel said. "Maybe your smiling yellow face would have drawn her in."

Thien was in fact holding a broom now, but he wasn't sweeping and he didn't seem to be listening. He was standing in the corner that held the shop's small store of books. People would often include a few books when they brought in a load of stuff to sell, after cleaning out Grandma's closets or their own. Daniel paid next to nothing for the books, and they almost never sold—who went into a pawnshop to buy a book?—but he liked having them. Gave the place class.

Daniel thought it was the books that had drawn Thien into the shop in the first place. He was a neighborhood kid, and Daniel's was the only shop on the street that had books in English. Thien had hung around the shop for weeks, leafing through the books, asking Daniel polite questions, gradually insinuating himself into the background, before Daniel had thought of offering him a part-time job after school. He had had in mind that when the Vietnamese neighbors saw one of their own working there, they might start frequenting the shop. So far that hadn't happened.

"It just occurred to me, kid, maybe you're some kind of outcast yourself. Maybe that's why you haven't drawn me any business. Neighbors think you're an untouchable now that you work for an American?"

"I am well beloved in the community," Thien said. Daniel laughed.

The boy had been born in Vietnam but you couldn't tell it when he spoke. His English had been learned in five years of American school; there'd been no occasion for him to learn pidgin. Thien was one of those smart-as-a-whip Vietnamese kids who came to America speaking no English and ten years later would graduate from high school as the valedictorian. There was nothing wrong with his brain, and ever since he had known Daniel he had even started making an occasional joke, always in that same solemn tone. Daniel saw that the book he was leafing through now was *Madame Bovary*, and he wondered how much sense Thien could make of it. The last book the boy had picked out of the pile had been *Valley of the Dolls*. He was a completely indiscriminate reader, a valuable quality if you're going to depend on a pawnshop for your reading matter.

"Daniel," Thien said, not looking up from the book. "How long have you been in business here?"

When he'd first started coming in the shop, Thien had politely asked his name and thereafter called him Mr. Greer so often that Daniel, at the age of thirty-four, had begun to feel ancient, so he had finally told the boy to call him Daniel. Now Thien exercised that privilege about once a day.

"Three years or so, to my regret." Daniel was looking out the window at the stolid old slant across the street, who was washing down his brand-new plate-glass window that he'd replaced only two weeks ago. Business must be good for him.

"And was business better before the—character of the neighborhood changed?"

"Yeah, some," Daniel said, remembering how he'd wanted to strangle the Vietnamese pawnbroker when the old fart had refused even to listen to him. It wasn't like they were Sears and Montgomery Ward, opening their respective five hundredth stores across the street from each other. They were talking life's blood here.

"How much better?" Thien persisted. "As a percentage, I mean? Do you keep—"

"What is this, an interview?"

"I'm taking a business course," Thien said hastily. He already had the lie prepared. "I thought as a project I might—"

The bell on the shop door jangled and they both looked at it. No one had come in.

"Wind," Daniel said listlessly. "My best customer."

Thien didn't reply. He was still staring at the door.

"Listen, if you want to see the books I'm going to have to—"

The bell sounded again. This time Daniel looked at it in time to see the door closing but again no one had come in.

"What the hell," he said. He walked over and rattled the knob. The door was secure in its frame. He opened it himself and let it close.

"There was . . ." Thien began, but his voice trailed off. Daniel didn't pay any attention. He opened the door again and stepped outside to see if the outside knob was tight.

There was a Vietnamese standing just outside the door. He was against the wall and hadn't been visible from within the shop. The man's presence made Daniel jump. He gave him a second glance and thought it was the young man who had run into the old woman. Of course it wasn't true that they all looked alike. This one, for example, was heftier than most Vietnamese. His face was slightly rounded and his upper body fairly thick, whether with muscle or fat Daniel couldn't tell. The man was wearing a padded jacket.

Daniel merely nodded politely and looked down at his doorknob, until he felt a hand on his arm. He looked up into the face of the man, who gestured with his other hand, indicating a path down the street. Daniel glanced that way and saw nothing.

"Speak English?" he asked.

The Vietnamese merely repeated the gesture. The grip on Daniel's arm tightened ever so slightly. Daniel glanced around and saw that the street was empty. The Vietnamese pawnbroker had gone back inside his shop. Daniel looked inside his own store and saw Thien staring at him. Daniel gave him one sharp look and then moved his gaze to the telephone. Thien was the only person on this street he could count on to call the police if there was some kind of trouble.

He couldn't imagine what that trouble might be. He looked into the unmoving face of the Vietnamese. Maybe he was a customer with no English but a valuable truckload to sell. The man started walking down the sidewalk. Daniel accompanied him. The hand on his arm fell away.

It was not a pleasant day for a stroll in shirtsleeves. The sun was out but low in the late-afternoon sky, and there was a sharp wind. Daniel put his hands in his pockets. The Vietnamese did not. He wasn't looking at Daniel.

"How far is your truck? I can't leave the shop long, I'm expecting someone."

He might as well have been talking to the pavement, for all the response he got. The Vietnamese was walking on the street side of the sidewalk, and gazing across the street. They had walked a block. They crossed another street and were essentially out of the Vietnamese neighborhood. This block looked abandoned. A block farther warehouses loomed. Daniel glanced back the way he'd come. All human life had ceased, as far as he could see. His Vietnamese companion was staring across the street as if searching for someone, but Daniel couldn't see a soul.

"Look," Daniel began, when he realized suddenly that a man was walking beside him on the inside of the sidewalk, almost shoulder to shoulder. He must have come out of a doorway some yards back, while Daniel was looking across the street. His appearance beside the pawnbroker was so abrupt and yet so casually transitionless it was as if the man had been walking invisibly beside him the whole way, only gradually shimmering into view. Like a guardian angel from a '30s comedy. And he said what a guardian angel might say.

"Mr. Greer," he said. "I've come to help with your problem."

The man was Vietnamese. He was thin, with an even thinner moustache, and sharp cheekbones. He wore a black suit with a tan shirt and matching tan tie. His hair was jet black, with no shadings of other colors. There were a few wrinkles at the corners of his eyes. Daniel would have guessed his age at forty, but wouldn't put much reliance in his guess.

"We can talk here as well as anywhere," the man said, prompting.

The round-faced younger Vietnamese had dropped back a couple of paces and was turned sideways to them. He was looking back down the street, which remained conspicuously uninhabited. Daniel wondered if Thien had called the police.

He sensed that there were others nearby, out of sight. Daniel had the strange feeling that if they went back and entered the restaurant for tea they would find it empty as well. Deference hung heavy in the air.

And then he realized who the thin man beside him must be. He was Daniel's farfetched tactic for business survival, come to call on him on the street.

A little impatiently the thin man said, "I am Tranh Van Khai. I heard you wanted to talk to me."

Khai rhymed with sky. Daniel indeed knew who he was, though few Houstonians outside the Vietnamese and the police would have.

"Y-yes, I did," Daniel stammered. "But I had no idea you'd come see me. I thought—I'd have to make an appointment—"

Khai smiled engagingly. "I'm not such a big shot that I snap my fingers and people appear before me." He snapped his fingers to demonstrate that nothing happened. Nothing did except that his round-faced bodyguard looked startled. "Especially not an American businessman such as yourself," he added.

"Oh, I'm not so . . ." Daniel trailed off. He couldn't deny being both American and a businessman.

Uninformed as he was about Vietnamese affairs, Daniel had heard of Tranh Van Khai. After his attempt to persuade his rival to open his pawnshop elsewhere had fallen flat, Daniel had begun to make quiet inquiries as to whether there was someone who might intercede on his behalf. A waiter at one of the Vietnamese restaurants, after Daniel had eaten regularly at his station for weeks, tipping generously, had agreed that there might be such a person. Daniel had wondered how he might contact this Tranh Van Khai, and the waiter had only shrugged. Daniel had thought he was on his own after that, but obviously the waiter had done more than just shrug, because here was Tranh Van Khai staring levelly at him. Daniel feared he was going to disappoint the man.

"I'm sorry you had to come out of your way for such a small

problem. It seems so petty now. You may have noticed I own the pawnshop back there . . ."

Khai nodded. Daniel, looking back, saw the shop was blocks away, out of sight.

He quickly told the history of his relations with his rival Vietnamese pawnbroker. "Obviously I can't even talk to him," he concluded, "what with the language barrier and all. I knew that you are an influential man in the community—" He didn't say "Vietnamese community" both to be flattering and because it was unnecessary. "—and I had hoped you might help me. You see, it's really not a big deal."

"Not such a small deal," Khai said. "It could put you out of business."

Daniel had to agree.

"But it is small in that it can be fixed easily," Khai went on smoothly.

"Of course I'd expect to pay you for your time—"

"As I would expect to be paid." Khai smiled and Daniel smiled back. "And I have friends who would have to be compensated."

Daniel felt uneasy. He was letting himself in for some kind of con job, he knew. Contractors and subcontractors, expenses . . . "How much are we talking about?" he asked deferentially. He glanced at the bodyguard, who was watching the street rather than Daniel and Khai. Was he watching for friends or enemies?

Khai looked off into space over Daniel's shoulder, musing. Then his eyes came back into focus and he smiled again, though his face remained serious. "Twenty thousand dollars."

"Twenty—" Daniel's mouth fell open. He was on the verge of laughing. Maybe this sharp-faced man who made him think of knives didn't understand the rate of exchange. "Are you—?"

And he fell silent abruptly, realizing what they'd been discussing.

Khai looked at him placidly, as if this sputtering were the

proper, anticipated first response in such a negotiation. He seemed to see through the layers of Daniel's thoughts.

"No, no. I'm sorry, that's not what I had in mind at all. I was only hoping you'd use your influence—"

"That's all we're discussing," Khai said softly.

"Of course, of course."

Daniel remained sharply aware that he was alone on the street with the two Vietnamese men. They were standing in front of a storefront whose broken window had been boarded up with one large sheet of plywood. The FOR SALE sign on the board was tattered. He looked at the bodyguard, whose face had gone rather flat. He was no longer making a show of staring all around the street; now he was looking straight at Daniel. His brown pants were much baggier than his boss's suit; they flapped in the wind. But his crossed arms held his jacket closed across his chest.

"Twenty thousand is much more than I thought of paying," Daniel said, changing tack. He didn't want to make any accusations. "I only hoped it could be suggested to him that business would be better for both of us if he were to relocate. I just didn't think he understood that's what I was trying to tell him."

"The suggestion alone probably wouldn't be worth much. He's a stubborn man, as you learned."

"Oh, you know him then?"

"I try to know everyone," Khai said. "We're a tight-knit community. Like a small town inside the big city."

"That's why I thought—I needed to have a friend in your community. But I don't have twenty thousand dollars. I'll have to—"

Khai looked away musingly again. "It's not carved in stone. It's a negotiable figure, to a certain extent."

Daniel took a step away from him, which brought him a step closer to the silent bodyguard. The bodyguard uncrossed his arms, letting the wind pull his jacket open slightly.

"It's so far outside my price range, though, that I'd be embarrassed even to make a counteroffer." The way to go,

Daniel had decided, was to suggest that he couldn't pay the freight. Not, certainly, that he was morally outraged that his request had been misunderstood. "I'm sorry you had to come out of your way for this. I just obviously didn't have any idea . . ."

He trailed off. He was even with the bodyguard now, still backing slowly away. The bodyguard wasn't looking at him now; his eyes stayed steadily on Khai, waiting. Daniel took another step back and was behind him, so he could no longer see the expression on the bodyguard's face. Khai, though, was staring at Daniel with eyes that were hard and black. Daniel couldn't read the thoughts behind that face.

"I'm sorry," he said again.

He took one more backward step, then turned and began walking away. There was movement behind him. His shoulders hunched, he walked on. In the distance he could see two or three people but they were small, anonymous figures, as he must be small and faceless to them. He was coming to the end of the block and wondered suddenly if Khai had someone else waiting around the corner of the building. He turned his head and looked back over his shoulder. The round-faced bodyguard had moved but wasn't coming after him. Khai was motionless, hands in his pockets. Even at this distance of half a block his sharp features were distinct. He was watching Daniel speculatively.

Daniel gave a stupid little American shrug and walked faster. He veered away from the building as he came to its corner, but there was no one lurking in the side street. He hurried across the street and up the next block. From there he was closer to his own shop than to the two Vietnamese behind him. He looked back once more, hoping they weren't following him.

The street behind him was empty. Daniel stopped. There was no car pulling away. Khai and his round-faced henchman had just vanished. There had been time between Daniel's looks back for them to walk around the corner and out of sight, but the disappearing act made him uneasy. He walked on slowly. The street was still remarkably unpopulated. He could feel eyes on him from within the other shops.

As he passed the pawnshop of his Vietnamese rival the man stepped outside. The pawnbroker was rather heavy, and tall for a Vietnamese, as tall as Daniel. He stared unpleasantly at Daniel for a moment and Daniel felt guilty. But he returned the stare with a degree of irony as well. I spared your life, he thought. You don't know how easily you could disappear.

The man showed no gratitude. Daniel slipped inside his own shop and was relieved to find no one but Thien there. The boy stared at him. "Turned out to be nothing," Daniel said lamely. He didn't notice that Thien showed no relief at all.

Daniel walked idly around the store, ending up behind the plastic-enriched glass shield that separated the counter and cash register from the customer area. He slipped his hand under the counter and his confidence grew slightly.

But you didn't just beg off from the kind of deal Khai had offered. Just hearing the offer had implicated him. He watched the window.

It wasn't Khai or any of his men who arrived next, though. It was Carol. Daniel had almost forgotten. He looked at his watch and was surprised to see it was just after five. Daylight lingered on the street but it seemed shredded. It would blow away soon, leaving cold November dusk. When Carol stepped out of her car at the curb, she was the brightest object for miles. Daniel smiled involuntarily. He was out from behind the counter to meet her as she came in the door. They were running late, he knew, but there was no hurry in her. Her cheeks were bright from the wind and her hair was flung back. She put her arms around him and kissed him, a daytime, public kiss, but for a moment it surrounded them with an invisible cone of intimacy. They had been married for a year but sometimes when she took him by surprise he still felt in the first flush of an affair, lust just turning to romance.

"You look great," he said, which was true, but what he

meant by it was that she looked out of place in his dumpy shop. With summer past, her blond hair had darkened to pale brown, though individual strands of it were still golden. She walked lightly, almost bouncing, happy about something.

"How's business today?"

"Booming," she said. "People want to get out of town for Christmas. Go to some warm beach where only the waiters speak English."

Daniel nodded, though what she said conjured up only TV images for him. He was sure it evoked specific personal memories in Carol.

Across the shop, Thien had at first turned discreetly away but then his sidelong glance had turned into an open stare. When he saw Carol turn to him he said, "Hello, Mrs. Greer."

"Hello, Thien. Found anything besides trash in that pile?"

"I'm not sure yet." Thien held up *Madame Bovary*, in which he had made visible progress if you believed where his finger held his place in the book.

Carol walked over to him, apparently not noticing how the boy's cheeks flamed when she drew close, and looked at the title. "Well, I'd like to offer you some keen insight, but you're already over my head."

"Not true, Thien," Daniel said. "She was an English major."

"Whose creed was 'Learn just enough for the final, then forget even that.' We've got to run," she added.

"I know. Thien, can you lock up? Don't stay too long. I may drop back by later on."

But it didn't occur to him to be worried about the Vietnamese boy. Daniel assumed he was carrying the contagion of danger away with him.

As he watched Daniel Greer sidling away from him, his pace speeding up as he drew farther away, Khai said to Chui in Vietnamese, "Find out all there is to know about him."

"We already—"

"That was not enough. Now I want *every*thing."

Chui nodded. When he looked up Khai was moving, almost to the corner behind them already. Chui hurried to catch up. Khai's movements were always like that: abrupt, unanticipated. You couldn't keep up with him. His thoughts were often the same way. As now. What did he care about the American pawnbroker? Americans made Chui uneasy.

They had left the car three blocks away. After they had walked two they saw two Vietnamese men ahead of them. One was their own man, Nguyen, whom they had left watching the car. The second was now a rag doll of a man, hanging limply from Nguyen's hands. When they drew closer they saw that Nguyen's thin cord was twisted around the man's neck. He was unconscious if not dead. Nguyen lowered him silently to the sidewalk. He gestured with his head, and Khai and Chui leaned out to look around the corner. There was their car, parked on a dead-end street that almost never saw traffic. The car was pointed away from them. Its hood was open. At first they saw nothing but part of a moving arm under the hood. They both jerked back out of sight as a nervous face popped up from under the hood, peered around, then disappeared again.

Nguyen gestured contemptuously at the fallen Vietnamese. "This one was the lookout," he mouthed.

Khai showed no reaction. Possibly the shadows of his eyes deepened slightly as he lowered his head. He made a sudden motion with his hand and Chui, gun drawn, hurried around the corner. Nguyen and Khai were right behind him. He ran almost silently but flat-out. When he was within a few feet of the car, he hurled himself into the air, slamming his whole body down on the hood.

The man must have heard something coming. He managed to get his head but not his hands out from under the hood just before it came down on him. His hands were caught underneath. He flung his head back and screamed, until Nguyen slapped him hard across the face. Until then the man's reactions had been automatic. When his eyes opened and he saw Khai standing next to him, the pain must have left him, as his heart stopped. The man's head lolled to the side. Shock was setting in. He began to gibber in fear. Nguyen slapped him again.

It was impossible to tell from Khai's face that he was anything more than annoyed. He seemed to be talking to the would-be saboteur when he spoke.

"This must stop," he said.

Later, after she was gone, what Daniel remembered about Carol was her ease. Nothing perturbed her. She did everything easily, without forethought. While he hesitated, she acted without looking. It made him crazy sometimes, but it was one of the things he loved about her.

She never looked as if she felt out of place, no matter where she was. Daniel didn't feel at home in the seedy neighborhood of his pawnshop or in this crowded, VIP reception, but Carol moved through both as if born to them.

She *had* been born to this. They had barely walked in when half the mob surged toward them and took her away from him. One or two halfheartedly included him in the greetings, but when they pulled away he was alone, which was what he preferred. He got a drink and roamed through the crowd trying to pretend he belonged, and knowing he was fooling no one.

The affair was being held in a bank lobby that soared five stories tall. It had the square footage of a football field. The thirty-foot-tall Christmas tree that would decorate the place for the next month was already up, but in this expanse of space it could almost go unnoticed in its corner. The tree was not the center of attention. The inanimate center of attention was the sculpture in the center of the room that provided the occasion for the party. Daniel stood and peered at it for a while, one of only three or four people doing so. The sculpture was nonrepresentational, a huge chunk of pitted black metal that looked as if it had been stretched almost to its breaking point. The metal seemed to scream. It was wrinkled and broken throughout. Daniel decided it looked like an eighty-year-old coal miner who had stepped out of a spaceship airlock into a hostile gravitational field that had sucked the air out of his body and stretched it to twice its normal height. The title didn't offer him any clue to the sculpture's identity. It was called "Desiccation."

The animate center of the party was of course Raymond Hecate himself, Carol's father. Daniel went looking for him, not because he wanted to talk to him but because he wanted to see the man in his glory. He found him in the center of a crowd, all of whom seemed to be listening to him. One of them was a television reporter with a microphone. Hecate stood out in the winter-dressed throng. He was wearing a white tennis sweater that set off his teeth, his tan, and his full head of white hair. He was in his mid-fifties, so the hair still looked premature. Propped on top of his head was a pair of sunglasses that looked like skylights in his skull. Daniel was too far away to hear what he was saying, but he was obviously delighting the crowd.

Raymond Hecate had never overcome the handicap of having been born rich. He went through life thinking some virtue of his own was responsible for that status. Even those who liked him realized there was something of the spoiled child about him. Take this business of always dressing like a golfer or a tennis player, even on semiformal occasions such as this one. It did make him distinctive. Food and drink and sun had given him a florid complexion that passed for health. But in the struggle between his appetite and his vanity, appetite was beginning to edge ahead. He tried to exercise away the pounds but didn't quite succeed. His stomach was solid but extensive. He was the kind of man who would die on a racquetball court. Soon, Daniel hoped.

In the old days, Carol had told him, her father did things lavishly but privately—bought a company while playing golf with its owner, took unheralded vacations to the Orient, threw huge parties that went unreported in the papers. Back then it seemed privacy was the greatest luxury. Now that he was not only rich but a first-term city councilman as well he did everything publicly. Like now: throwing a party that was half press conference to celebrate his donating some ugly and expensive sculpture to the city after displaying it in the lobby of his bank.

Daniel didn't push through Hecate's sycophants to join him, even when he saw Carol propelled through the crowd to give her father a big hug. Hecate greeted her boisterously, displaying her. He would be less than thrilled to share the moment with his son-in-law, though. Hecate treated Daniel as if "pawnbroker" was a genetic defect he hoped wouldn't be passed on to the grandchildren. And it seemed such a random thing that he was even in the pawn business. It was a matter of happenstance and stubbornness. When he was twenty he had dropped out of college because it seemed so purposeless, but so had everything that followed, vague years of parties and friends drifting away and odd jobs. He'd landed in the pawnshop and found it suited him. Haggling was a skill fed by indifference. Slowly he began to care about getting the better of a deal, but he could keep the caring hidden.

Mr. Jacobs, the old man who owned the shop, saw it in him. "You have the fever," he said slyly. Daniel denied it, but he didn't drift on to another job.

There was another aspect to the fever. The way your heart blossomed when the doorbell tinkled and someone walked in carrying a package. Anything could live in that package. It always turned out to be a gun or a camera or a music box, but in that first minute it could be the treasure of the Hapsburgs. You waited for someone desperate to walk in with a lifetime's jewel he didn't know he had. One night after a year on the job Daniel had awakened from a dream in which a fat old woman had put a piece of statuary in his hands and asked the standard "How much?" But he didn't hear her in his awe at what he held. It was a foot-tall porcelain figure of—what? As he began to wake the treasure began to shrink. It was exquisite but it lost definition as he lost the dream. He woke with a feeling of terrible beauty and loss, and the memory of a small perfect something dwindling away.

When Mr. Jacobs died Daniel had the chance to buy the pawnshop at a fire-sale price, and he took it. The fever had cooled in his blood by then but something else had taken hold: the desire to be his own boss. He was near the end of his twenties, which seemed very old to start over in another company. After a year or two of it he could see he was never going to make his fortune as a pawnshop owner, but after being his own boss that long he couldn't stand the thought of working for someone else.

About that time he had met Carol, which had made him wish his whole life had been different. But if he'd been just like everyone else that she knew she would never have noticed him.

But look what noticing him had done for her.

He went back to wandering through the party, skittering through the fringes of conversations. When he heard "Vietnamese" mentioned he stopped. The man speaking must have been a newspaper editor or someone else with access to undisclosed news.

"Well, did you hear that latest one yesterday? They kept it quiet for a day but it'll be in tomorrow's editions. Found three of them in the basement of a house over near Allen Parkway Village. Three men with their hands tied behind their backs and hanging upside down from a pipe."

"Dead?" someone asked.

"Damn straight. Their heads were hanging in a trough of water. They'd drowned. And the fiendish thing about it was they were tied so that they could bend their heads far enough back to just barely bring their noses out of the water. They wouldn't drown until they didn't have the strength to hold themselves out of the water anymore. Might have taken a whole day. Course they didn't last as long as they might have because they'd been beaten too."

"My God," the other man said, echoing Daniel's thought. "Who would do something like that?"

"Well, that's another funny thing. You know they used to think it was the Klan, somebody like that, like that trouble they had down with those shrimp fishermen on the coast. But now they think maybe it's the Vietnamese themselves."

"Doing it to each other, you mean?"

"Exactly right."

"But why?"

"Who knows? Maybe something they had going on in Vietnam that they just brought over here with them. They're just like animals anyway. Let 'em all kill each other, I say."

"Yes, but—"

Daniel drifted away. As the man said, who knew? But Daniel had a better idea than most. He knew what Khai was, a gang leader. There must be others like him, rivals for each other's power. In a way it was a relief to realize that. Khai would have bigger things on his mind than Daniel.

He negotiated the crowd like a white-water raftsman, following the currents but turning aside whenever he ran the risk of running aground on some friend of Carol's he had met before. He didn't realize he was looking for Carol until he found her, ahead of him in the crowd, her back to him. He slowed down to watch her as he approached obliquely. She hadn't seen him. He could imagine he was seeing her for the first time, wondering how to approach such an out-of-reach woman. He was smiling.

Carol was talking to Jennifer Hardesty, one of her oldest friends. Like Raymond Hecate, Jennifer was wearing sunglasses atop her head. Like him, she looked like a fashionable twit. Daniel and Carol had had Jennifer to their home one disastrous time since their wedding, after which Carol had tacitly agreed to meet her old friend only for lunch, for shopping, or on occasions such as this. It was clear they loved to talk to each other. Daniel couldn't imagine why. It made him nervous about his wife to know that she still so thoroughly enjoyed her rich bitch friend.

Jennifer was holding a clear plastic glass containing amber liquid. It must have been her severalth, from the sway of her shoulders. And alcohol removed any patina of politeness from the dislike in her eyes when she saw Daniel.

"Hello, Jennifer." He put his arm around Carol and she leaned into him slightly.

"Danny Boy," said Jennifer, and they just stood there. Daniel didn't apologize for interrupting their conversation and he didn't attempt to start a new one. After a long minute Jennifer clattered her ice against her teeth and went looking for another drink.

"That was rude," said Carol, but not harshly.

"That's okay, I have thick skin."

"I meant you. But it's okay, Jennifer has thick skin too."

"To match her head. Why don't we get out of here?"

"Aren't you enjoying yourself?"

They started walking. Daniel still had his arm around her shoulders, and his fingers began lightly stroking her arm. She slipped her arm around his waist.

"We've already put in our token appearance. Isn't that all you said we had to do? I thought we could go eat at some low Mexican dive I know and make it an early night. We have a busy day tomorrow."

Carol's eyes were no longer scanning the crowd as they neared the door. She was looking down, smiling. "I think you mean for us to have a busy night first," she said.

"What?" he said innocently. He inclined his head toward her, she whispered something, and they went out the door laughing. They didn't look back to see Raymond Hecate's eyes following them, or the glare on his flushed face.

Nor did they notice the two Vietnamese men across the street who became more alert when Daniel and Carol emerged from the bank.

* * *

Later that night, after their argument, after Carol had gone off to bed, Daniel sat up on the couch for almost an hour, watching television with the sound almost inaudible. He was thinking about how much he had changed in the year they'd been married. He had gone into it not expecting it to last. For the first few months he had acted not cool toward her, but holding a certain reserve for himself; not making any lasting commitments.

He didn't know when he had lost that reserve, but he had. It had changed not only his feeling toward her but toward everything. He'd turned so sentimental: Beer commercials could leave him misty now.

He padded down the hall and looked at her face on the pillow, surprised as always to see her still there. He turned off the lights, undressed in the dark, and slipped into bed beside her, touching her as if she might have faded away in those few moments.

She hadn't yet.

CHAPTER 2

Meanwhile,
Business as Usual

"COME on, don't be such a weenie. Nobody's going to do anything to you."

"I was thinking of you," he said with dignity. She just laughed at that, but it was true. It wasn't just that the bar she was trying to drag him into looked exclusively Asian. It also looked exclusively male. He didn't see any other women inside, not even waitresses.

"Come on, it'll be fun. We go to the same places all the time."

Because he liked those places, he wanted to say, but he didn't. After all, she was his fiancée now, he supposed he had to indulge her sometimes. They had been out celebrating their engagement, so he was already a little tipsy. Maybe the alcohol emboldened him.

"It's cold out here," she said, prompting him. They were standing on the sidewalk in this dim end of downtown, peering through the plate-glass window, half covered by curtains. The men didn't look threatening. They looked dead, in fact. He couldn't even see them move. The place looked like an opium den.

"All right," he said, "it'll be fun."

As soon as they stepped inside, the Vietnamese men at the bar looked up at them. Their eyes didn't change at all: They stayed flat, black, and hostile. The man in the doorway wanted to step back out into the cold. He realized immediately they'd made a bad mistake.

When Daniel left with his wife, Thien realized it was the first time he'd ever been alone in the pawnshop. Daniel had given him a key and taught him how to turn the alarm system on and off, but it seemed to Thien he'd regretted that trust immediately. Thien never arrived early enough, even on Saturday, that Daniel wasn't there, or Jeff, the part-time clerk, and Daniel never left early and let Thien lock up. Even today he had said he'd probably come by later. Thien knew what that meant. Checking up on him.

But who could blame him? Trust didn't come easily to anyone. Thien continued to sweep for a while. When he passed the front door he locked it. If a customer came he could open it, but he wanted some warning if the two who had kidnapped him after school returned. He went behind the counter and looked under it at the little shelf just at hand level for a man standing at the cash register. He laid a hand on the black handgun Daniel kept there. Its handle was smooth from handling. For a moment Thien felt again the envelope of safety he'd imagined he would find when he came to work for a white businessman. But the feeling was illusory. He looked out the window and stiffened.

Dusk had fallen hard but the streetlights hadn't yet come on. They, like the late-afternoon shoppers, weren't used to the early dark yet. Dusk had cleared out the streets. The man slipping along the side of the building across the street stood out. Thien knew him by sight. He wasn't one of the two he had encountered earlier, but he owed the same loyalty they did.

Thien laid his hand on the gun again. He wondered how many more were slipping around the side of *this* building. He thought of the pain his family would feel.

The man across the street came to the corner of the building and peered around it to see that the sidewalk in front of the Vietnamese pawnshop was empty. Thien flinched slightly when the man reached into his pocket.

But it wasn't a gun the man brought out. If it was a weapon at all it was a very sophisticated one; it looked much too small to be a bomb. The man looked around the corner again, this time craning his head farther so that he could see into the pawnshop. A moment later he emerged from hiding, walking swiftly along the sidewalk. When he reached the front door of the Vietnamese pawnshop, he stooped and pushed his package through the mail slot. He hurried on.

Thien kept his head down, waiting for the explosion. Nothing happened. After long moments the Vietnamese pawn-broker emerged from his shop. He was holding the package in his hands and glaring up and down the street. There was no one to be seen. The middle-aged Vietnamese shifted his glare to the shop across the street. Thien imagined he could see him inside. He tried to look innocent.

After another long moment the man went back inside his shop. Nothing more happened that Thien could see. He shook his head in puzzlement. Glancing at his watch, he saw that it was six-thirty, half an hour past closing time. His father would be waiting. Hastily he closed up the shop, turning the sign on the door from OPEN to CLOSED and hurrying down the dark street in the direction from which the young Vietnamese man had come before he had slipped the package into the other pawnshop. Thien wondered what that had been about.

The streetlights came on suddenly. Their light seemed more threatening than the dimness had been. They spotlighted Thien as he hurried down the street but left patches of darkness in shop doorways and the mouths of alleys. He slowed as he approached corners, then hurried past them. The shops were closed or closing. In this neighborhood even the shops that weren't Vietnamese-owned had Vietnamese employees. One or two spoke to Thien as he walked by, but no one joined him.

He stopped outside the lighted square of a dry cleaner's window. The store was already closed but he saw two people inside—a middle-age Vietnamese woman behind the counter and a young Vietnamese man who joined her behind the counter as Thien watched. The racks of clothes made a cozy nest for the two of them. The young man wore an easy, unpleasant smile. The merchant was nodding and nodding and pointing toward the back of the shop. The young man made no response at all, but when the woman turned the young man let her go. He glanced out toward the front. He might have seen Thien, or he might not. He turned away casually and sauntered after the merchant, his shoulders brushing the clothes on the racks.

Neither of them reappeared in the two minutes Thien stood watching. He finally turned away and picked up speed, his heels clattering on the sidewalk. He didn't meet the eyes of the few other pedestrians.

Three blocks farther on was the drugstore Thien's father managed. Thien rushed into it and slammed the door behind him. At once he began speaking in Vietnamese, calling in a loud voice as he loosened his jacket. No one answered. He started down the aisle toward the pharmacy counter at the back, calling to his father again, then stopped abruptly, silently cursing himself. He was so careful on the street but lost all sense as soon as he was home, as if he were safe there.

A young Vietnamese man had stepped out of an adjoining aisle to stand beside him. He wore a red windbreaker and white tennis shoes. He was grinning at Thien. It was one of the men who had kidnapped him that afternoon. Thien felt hollow from his chest down into his legs.

But they weren't there for him. Windbreaker's partner stood behind the pharmacy counter with Thien's father. They both looked at Thien but then turned back to each other. They were by the cash register and both their hands were on it.

Thien's eyes sidled to the man beside him, hoping his attention was also on the two behind the counter, but it wasn't.

Windbreaker was still grinning at him. He put a hand on Thien's shoulder. "Are you following us, little brother?"

Thien stood rigidly, staring at his father. He looked up from his negotiations, saw Windbreaker's hand on his son, and came around from behind the counter. The young man holding Thien just grinned at him, waiting. The cash register bell sang out and the older man stopped dead. Thien's father had a high forehead and a prominent vein in each temple that throbbed when he was angry. The veins were all that moved in his face now as he stood there. Windbreaker's other hand, the one not on Thien, had gone inside his jacket.

Thien's father turned away, head lowered. He returned to the other young man, who was rifling through the cash drawer, and spoke softly. The young man ignored him. He was pulling bills out and stuffing them in his pockets.

When he was through he came out from behind the counter, ignoring everyone, and sauntered down the aisle, brushing Thien. His partner gave a last painful squeeze of Thien's shoulder and turned to join him. Thien stood there. His father was still behind the counter. They looked into each other's eyes for a long moment.

Thien turned and hurried down the aisle, so quietly that the two who had reached the front door didn't hear him until he spoke. They whirled. When they realized who it was their grins returned, angrier because he'd seen that for an instant they had been afraid. One of them reached for him, holding him by the back of the neck and squeezing.

"You like pain, little brother? You must like pain. We can help you."

Thien tried to ignore him, looking at the other one. "I want to join you," he said.

"Join us in what?" crooned the stupid one holding his neck. The other just shook his head angrily. "Wait till you grow balls," he said.

Thien said steadily, "I have." They laughed at him. They were both six inches taller than he, and they were no giants.

"Let me talk to Khai," Thien insisted.

They made wide eyes at him. "Tranh Van Khai will have you ground into paste just for speaking his name," one of them said, grinning. The other squeezed his neck harder. Thien tried not to flinch.

They were bored with him, ready to be out the door. "What can I do?" Thien asked.

"Impress us," Windbreaker's partner said. "Teach us how brave and mean you are."

They stood there for another moment as if waiting for him to do so, then they laughed with each other and pushed out the door. Thien's shoulders slumped. He stood there looking out into the black night. He could feel his father behind him and could already hear his reproaches.

"Better to be one of them than to be afraid all the time," Thien said.

He managed to talk his fiancée into taking a table by the window, as far from the other customers in the bar as possible. He was sure it had been a mistake to come in, but he thought they could have one drink and clear out. They weren't going to be held back by a crush of camaraderie. Theirs were the only voices in the place. The Asian men didn't speak. He wondered if they'd been talking before the two of them had come in. Maybe it was their ritual just to gather at the end of the day and drink silently, thinking murderous thoughts. Maybe ritualistically killing the nearest white people when they finished getting drunk.

The American gulped his scotch. He'd had to go to the bar to get it. No waiter had approached him. His idiot fiancée had wanted a piña colada but he'd managed to talk her out of that. She was drinking gin and tonic now, and smiling at him as if she were having the time of her life. She was a crazy girl. He'd known that, of course, but he'd found it charming. Now that her flightiness had turned life-threatening its charm had faded.

He was overreacting, he knew. In the back of his mind he

was already turning this into a funny story. "So she insisted we go into this little bar, and as soon as we walk in I see a sign saying Vietnamese Murder Inc. is meeting here tonight. 'Honey,' I say, 'maybe if we just turn very quietly . . .'"

But as she said, this was their city, no place was off limits. He leaned on the table and started talking to her again.

Because they were sitting by the window, they were the first to see the car. The view out the window was down a long deserted side street, a street of warehouses mostly. Not much of a view. When something moved out there, it caught his eye and he glanced out. A car had turned from somewhere and its headlights were aimed directly at them. It was still three blocks away; the headlights weren't an intrusion, they were just something that drew his eye for a moment.

"Maybe we could have our reception here," she was saying.

He laughed. "Right, and for entertainment we can have strolling bands of muggers. You want to have all your wedding presents stolen before we even get 'em home?"

She rolled her eyes at him, drained her glass, and held it out, rattling the cubes. He groaned inwardly. He didn't want to make another trip to that bar, where the men wouldn't even move their shoulders to let him get close enough to give the bartender their order. Maybe he could convince her to move on now.

She was looking out the window. He followed her gaze. The car was still coming straight toward them. It had picked up speed. He couldn't see past the headlights to the driver. He couldn't even see if it had a driver. His fiancée was shading her eyes with her hands.

"Funny, it looks like it's not even going to turn, doesn't it?"

He was glad she was the one who'd said that. After she'd already accused him of being a weenie, he didn't want to act afraid of strange cars too. But it did seem to be speeding up rather than slowing for the turn.

It wasn't until he saw the driver's door open and someone roll out onto the pavement that he allowed himself the luxury of panic. "Oh, shit," he said, and stood up. He remembered to grab for his fiancée's hand to help her out too but she was already up and scrambling away from their table and the window. Men at the bar turned to look at the commotion. He started to shout but it was unnecessary. They were scattering too, after only one quick glance out the window. He was running, holding the girl's hand. He turned to look back and could see almost nothing but headlights. The car had jumped the curb just outside the bar. That pushed its front end upward, angled straight toward the plate-glass window. It came like a wild animal after prey.

The window shattered into a million pieces. The man dived over the bar for cover, dragging the girl. They landed on other groaning, cursing bodies. The sound of the car's engine was amplified as it smashed inside the room. It sounded as if it were still coming for them.

When the dust began to clear, they peeked fearfully over the bar. The car had knocked the table where they'd been sitting across the room. The car was wedged in the broken window now, half in and half out. Its engine had died but they could hear the ticking sound of its cooling.

Everyone sighed. The American man even smiled at the Vietnamese next to him and the Vietnamese smiled shakily back. "Are you all right?" the man asked his fiancée.

She said, "Of course I'm not all right," but she was grinning with relief too.

Just when they thought it was all over the car shuddered and slid back out of the window, its balance giving way. More glass fell into the street. The patrons of the bar gathered outside, around the car, and were surprised to find that the crash wasn't the worst of it. The worst of it was the man who'd been dragged behind the car. At first they thought he was a run-over pedestrian, but when they looked closer they saw it had been deliberate. The man's ankles were chained to the car's back bumper.

Horribly, he was still alive. He must have been dragged for blocks. There were no clothes left on him and almost no skin. But he was groaning in shock. He was alive. The Vietnamese leaned over him. It was almost impossible to recognize him, but they saw he was one of them. One of them finally saw something that made him guess who the victim was. It was the gang member who'd tried to plant a bomb in Khai's car.

"What are they jabbering about, honey?"

"I don't know, I think maybe they know him. Don't look, it's too horrible."

"Don't worry about that, you couldn't pay me to look. Let's get—"

They were all gathered around the car. They weren't conscious of the tiny sound—it just sounded like the engine cooling—but when it stopped one or two of them glanced up.

"Let's—" said the man.

The only survivor, who was standing seventy feet away when the car exploded, said later that it looked like the whole engine went straight up in a pillar of flame. In fact, it went outward in all directions. In an instant the car and engine were transformed into thousands of bits of metal, lethal shrapnel. In effect it was a giant grenade.

It took weeks to identify some of the bodies, but it was only a day before the news was out that two of them had been native-born Houstonians, the first innocent casualties of the war.

The Vietnamese pawnbroker whose shop stood across the street from Daniel's was a fifty-eight-year-old man named Linh. His shop was already closed for the day, but he was reluctant to leave it. He thought that if they were going to contact him it would be there at the shop, not at his home. He was still hoping for some word.

Perhaps for that reason his ears were sharper than usual. He heard the tiny *thump* of the package dropping to the floor. At first he thought it was a footfall at the front of his shop. He reached instinctively for his shotgun. But in the dim light he could see that the shop was empty. Outside in the street a young Vietnamese thug was hurrying away. Linh didn't know him, but he knew his look. He was one of *them*.

He hurried to the front of the shop, scooped up the package, and opened the door. He stepped out onto the street, into the twilight-laden wind. There was no one around. He glared in all directions. He glared at the pawnshop across the street for good measure, but it looked already closed, like his.

Linh went back inside and locked the door behind him, still listening for the sound of a car approaching or running footsteps. He had been waiting for them for two days. But as he walked back to the counter, his attention focused for the first time on the package in his hands. It wasn't the envelope he'd been hoping for, not a letter with a demand. It was too small for that. It was a rectangular box half the size of a box of kitchen matches, wrapped in brown paper. As he turned it over in his hands his heart began to speed up. He had heard stories as a child in Vietnam. But those were stories with which to frighten a child. Surely not here . . .

He pulled at the brown paper and it came off in one piece, falling to the counter. The box inside was made of bamboo, with a hinged lid. The pawnbroker waited a long moment before opening it. He could hardly stand to touch it. His heart was hammering.

When he saw the contents he began to cry. Later he would pound the counter and swear and scream, but for the first long moments there in the gathering gloom of his shop all he could do was cry.

CHAPTER 3

A Way of
Turning Up

THE next morning, Saturday, Daniel woke feeling something was wrong. His eyes snapped open as if the angle of light were unexpected or a familiar sound had been silenced. For a moment he thought Carol was gone. But she was there, curled into a ball against the coldness of the bedroom. The king-size waterbed in which they slept was so big and so malleable that each could form his own little valley during the night. Under the thick blue comforter Carol had almost disappeared.

A very diffuse light filled the room like mist. There was no headboard, their heads were within a foot of the window behind the bed. Daniel pulled back a corner of the curtain and saw that the window was covered with frost.

The bed almost filled the small room. When he crawled out he had to hug the wall and then thread his way carefully between the bed and the dresser. He padded down the hall, staying on the carpet runner to avoid the cold hardwood floor, turned up the thermostat, and hurried back into bed before sleep deserted him. The motion of the bed woke Carol. When her eyes opened they appeared already focused, and she gave him a hard look as if she were still mad, but she snuggled close to him. As the house warmed into life around them they murmured under the covers almost wordlessly, a hum of forgiveness lost in the hum of the furnace. Their faces smoothed as they fell back asleep, into a more restful sleep than they'd had all night, because now they were holding each other.

What they'd had the night before couldn't be called a fight. Just a matter of clashing preoccupations. His mind had been on his meeting with Tranh Van Khai. Hers had been on the friends she'd left behind at the reception. She was reminded anew of what Daniel expected of her: that she give up her whole past in exchange for life with him. It wasn't a bleak life, but it wasn't complete either. They had almost no friends. It was unfair to ask her to live a life of such isolation.

About the time Daniel realized his mind had been far away, he realized Carol hadn't been talking either. What was she thinking about?

"Nothing."

When he pressed her and she snappishly repeated her answer, he guessed the truth. "Would you like to go back?" he asked.

"Not now. It's all over now." She stared off across the threadbare Mexican restaurant as if she were looking for people she knew and frowning because they were late.

He tried to strike up a normal conversation, but it was about his business and she seemed uninterested. So they had sat in cool silence over cooling food. At some point each realized that the position he had staked out was not quite his own, but by that time it was too late. It wasn't the kind of fight that could be called off. It had to dissipate overnight.

Consequently they were being very tender of each other's feelings this morning. They made breakfast together, talking away last night's silences, and continued to talk while they ate. Normally Daniel would have read the morning paper about then, but today he set it aside after just glancing at the headline: GANG VIOLENCE KILLS SIX. He didn't read the story to learn that the gangs referred to were Vietnamese. In most Houston homes that morning the Vietnamese gang warfare emerging from the shadows was big news, but not in the Greer household.

The day had warmed considerably by the time they went outside. Frosty dawn had turned into cool morning.

"We don't have to do this," Carol said.

"No, I want to."

"We don't have to stay long. I just want to see what it's like."

"Who knows, I might pick up some customers. Wander around, let 'em see I'm willing to make friends . . ."

They were on the freeway aimed at downtown. The cold front that had come through during the night had swept the sky clean. Against that vibrant blue backdrop the towers of downtown Houston looked like the Emerald City of Oz. It was a self-consciously modern city, nothing gothic about it: All the most visible buildings had gone up in the last twenty years. A day this clear was relatively rare. The buildings gleamed as if basking in it.

In the neighborhood of Daniel's pawnshop parking was already at a premium. A blue van occupied the "Employees Only" space in the alley behind his shop. Daniel cursed mildly and drove on. "Now remember where we're parked," he told her after he squeezed into a semilegal space farther down the alley. "Because I'll probably forget."

She took his hand as they walked up the alley. The mostly brick back walls of the stores they passed were grimy and worn, and odors clung to them. There was grime underfoot as well, decaying gunk that could have started life as anything.

"What's the name of this holiday?" Carol asked. Her tone was light and chatty. They both knew Daniel was making a concession in coming today, but he was being nice about it, especially after last night. She was going to be nice as well.

"Suck-in-the-Tourists Day. I'm sure it's something they just made up."

"Cheer up. Maybe it'll bring you some business."

"Yeah. They'll spend all their money on egg noodles and come in to hock their Timexes."

They came around the corner of the building at the end of the block—a dry cleaner's that was closed today—and Daniel said, "My God."

For two blocks the street had been closed off to automobile traffic. Overhead the streetlights and power lines were festooned with paper streamers, balloons, and long kites decorated as fish or dragons. In the middle of the street there were pushcarts and booths, and most of the stores were open as well. But what had caused Daniel's exclamation was the crowd. The street was jammed with people on foot from storefront to storefront. Their flow was mainly counterclockwise, but that flow was disturbed by dozens of individual eddies and currents and lines at some of the booths.

"I had no idea it would draw such a crowd," Carol said, and again: "We don't have to stay long."

But Daniel was fascinated now. He walked slowly into the throng, still holding her hand, staring around bemused not at the vendors but at the patrons. The crowd was mostly Occidental, though Asians were well represented. All the pushcart and booth vendors were Asian, usually several at a stand, a whole family working the business. Even little children had some sort of function they performed with serious expressions, carrying trays or sorting utensils.

Carol and Daniel joined the crowd, walking slowly and being jostled occasionally. Someone bumped Daniel's shoulder and hip, and when he turned to look there was no one there. He felt for his wallet and found it still in his back pocket. He kept his hand there. His other hand clutched Carol's. She turned another direction and their arms stretched before the connection was broken. Daniel hurried to catch up to her.

All street festivals are basically alike. Only the foods

change. This one had Vietnamese trappings and the music coming from loudspeakers was unfamiliar, but there were still booths selling American beer, with men in cowboy boots lined up in front of them. Confetti eggs had no place in Vietnamese tradition, but there was confetti underfoot. Some such familiar elements inevitably infiltrated every fair. Or perhaps the cultures were blending before one's eyes.

This festival may have drawn a bigger crowd than Daniel had expected because it was so late in the season. Thanksgiving had come and gone; the time for street fairs had passed. This one drew everyone who was unwilling to let autumn pass without one more celebration. Maybe the story of last night's gang violence had cut down the attendance. On the other hand, maybe it drew the morbidly curious.

"Let's go in here," Carol called above the crowd noise. Her face was flushed from the heat of the crowd and the cook fires they'd passed, but there was enough breeze to blow her hair back from her face. She looked beautiful—and happy as a child.

She dragged him into a small shop on the opposite side of the street from his own pawnshop. He would have been delighted if his shop were drawing half as many customers. The narrow aisles of this one were clogged. Everything for sale looked extremely flimsy to Daniel, baskets or figures made out of straw and bamboo. He was afraid to touch anything. The place was a shoplifter's paradise too: The figures were so small and everyone's coats so bulky. But Daniel glanced at the shopkeeper, an old man with a stringy white beard, and saw his eyes darting as if he could see everything. Daniel also saw a small Vietnamese child keeping an eye on the customers. Looking around, he saw others he had at first taken for shoppers but who were probably members of the owner's family. The old man's eyes lighted momentarily on Daniel and a small, ironic smile seemed to shape his features. Daniel wondered if the old man had recognized him.

Carol was close at his side, oblivious to all but the flimsy treasures. Pressed close in the alien swarm—even the white

people were alien—he could feel they were in a foreign city.
Maybe that was the pleasure she drew from the cheap trinkets—
the feeling of adventuring through a bazaar.

"Hot in here."

"Look at this," she said, holding up a carved devil mask.
"Do we know anyone who'd like this?"

"God, I hope not." Daniel gave a mock shudder. Carol held
on to the mask, though her eyes traveled onward. "Let's get
something to eat. Breakfast was a long time ago."

A few minutes later Carol followed him reluctantly out of
the shop. "I'll have to come back later."

"How come you never showed any interest in investigating these stores on normal business days?" Daniel asked.

"I was interested, I just never had the time." She looked at
his amused expression and slapped lightly at his arm. "All right,
it's that now I feel a desperate sense of competition with all these
other shoppers. Is that what you think?"

"That's what I think." He led her out into the street where
they wandered for a while sampling the food at the booths:
imperial rolls made with rice paper rather than dough and so
lighter and crispier than Chinese egg rolls; marinated fruits,
some relatively unfamiliar, such as kumquats; a Vietnamese
poorboy made with fresh-baked French bread and stuffed with
both meat and pâté. Daniel was familiar with most of the food
from excursions to the two Vietnamese restaurants in the
neighborhood, but in the fresh air, freshly made, they seemed
like a new experience. "This is delicious," they kept saying to
each other. "Taste this."

It was midafternoon, the sun was already declining, but
Daniel felt uncomfortable in his jacket. He was also tired of
fighting the crowd. "I want to go check on the shop again," he
told Carol, meaning his own pawnshop. He had glanced into it
once when they'd first arrived.

"Good," Carol said. "I'd like to do some shopping without
you looking over my shoulder."

"So I can't stop you from buying something ridiculous?"

"I just don't want you watching. Christmas is coming, you know."

An expression of horror crossed his face. "All I want for Christmas is that you *not* buy me something here."

"You never know, there might be—"

"I know I have enough bamboo crap to last a lifetime."

"You see why I don't want you along?" she said sternly, but smiling.

"Why don't you check out the other pawnshop?" he suggested. "They probably have wonderful stuff in there. Junk even Vietnamese couldn't stand to have in their own homes."

Carol just nodded. Her thoughts had already left him.

"All right. Meet me back at the shop in—an hour?"

"And a half," Carol said, not looking at her watch.

Daniel sighed. "All right. You remember where the car's parked, in case you want to put something in the trunk?"

Carol nodded, still distracted, half turned away from him. Daniel pulled her closer and said, "I love you."

Her eyes and smile focused on him again. "I love you too."

They'd only been married a year; they said the words every day still, but with a wide variation in feeling. Today it was more than perfunctory. She kissed him lightly and turned away.

For just a moment as Carol disappeared into the crowd he was gripped by fear for her. The crowd looked sinisterly indifferent as it swallowed her up. Everyone seemed to be glancing slyly in her direction. Daniel didn't want to let her go.

The feeling passed. A few minutes later Daniel had forgotten it. He was making his way back to his shop, but in no hurry. He stopped for a beer and carried the can through the crowd. It had thinned out slightly; walking was less of a struggle.

He reached the sidewalk and almost stepped on a Vietnamese boy who was looking down, shepherding an even smaller girl. The boy lifted his face and gazed at him with mysterious intent. Then he realized it was Thien. Daniel found himself delighted to see him. "Hello, Daniel," Thien said, as if he'd been expecting to run into him.

He indicated the younger girl, who was probably five years old, but tiny. How could her parents let her loose in this crowd? "This is my sister Alice," Thien said with some pride.

"Alice?" Daniel thought his American ear must have turned a Vietnamese name into something more familiar.

"She is American," Thien explained. "Born in this country."

"Hello, Alice."

"How do you do," said the little girl, with the same concentrated expression that seemed to have been doled out to all Vietnamese children.

Daniel stood chatting with Thien for a few minutes, feeling the glances of passersby. He enjoyed the feeling that he belonged in this neighborhood, wasn't just a tourist at a festival. So small a link to the Vietnamese community, Thien was, but for a moment he gave Daniel a sense of place.

"Do you need help in the store?" Thien asked suddenly. Without waiting for an answer, he bent to his tiny sister and said, "Go to Mama. See? Go to Mama." Daniel craned his neck, curious to see Thien's mother, but there were several women who would have qualified in the direction in which Thien was pointing. The little girl made her way unerringly through the crowd to one and hugged her skirts. The woman looked too young to be Thien's mother.

Together Daniel and Thien threaded their way through the crowd. The boy came to Daniel's shoulder. At the door of Daniel's shop a Vietnamese man only a few years older than Thien was lounging. It seemed to Daniel, with his newfound sense of belonging, that the young man looked familiar. But that was silly. Daniel didn't know any Vietnamese except Thien. The young man's eyes slid over the crowd and settled on Daniel's face as if he too had experienced a moment of recognition, but then he looked away. His gaze settled on Thien as well before he drifted off from the door of the pawnshop.

Coming in from the street festival made the shop look even dimmer and dustier than usual. Also emptier. One young couple

was idly making their way around the shelves, looking as if
they were surprised and uncomfortable to find themselves
there. At the counter a young woman glanced back furtively
at Daniel. She had streaky blond hair and a drawn face and
looked old before her time. She went back to conferring in
whispers with Jeff, who lounged inside the cage looking
uninterested, the proper pawnshop clerk's expression. Jeff
was a part-timer Daniel employed only a few hours a week
and didn't entirely trust. He looked scraggly this morning, as
if he'd been dragged out of bed abruptly before he was ready.
When he wasn't working in the store Jeff was a college
student, now in (Daniel estimated) his seventh year at the
University of Houston.

Daniel went inside the cage and rang up NO SALE on the cash
register to see how much money was in it. Something less than
a fortune. The bills looked worn, like family heirlooms. He
closed the drawer. Beside him, Jeff straightened up slightly and
the customer lowered her voice even further. Daniel saw that
she was trying to sell a bracelet that could have been silver and
turquoise or could as easily have been tin and glass. He hovered
nearby to see that Jeff didn't offer too much for it. Daniel's
presence seemed to make both of them nervous, and they failed
to come to terms. The young-old woman turned away and
looked at the young couple browsing, as if she were thinking of
dealing with them directly, but then she hurried out of the store
without speaking again.

"Any drift from the fair?" Daniel asked.

"Mostly they just look in the windows and walk on."

Daniel nodded.

"Those two there've been here longer than anyone else all
day."

As if they heard Jeff's remark and felt stigmatized, the
couple went out without looking back. Daniel felt briefly
annoyed. Jeff was a good buyer, as stingy as if the money were
his own, but at customer relations he sucked.

"Why'oncha take a break, Jeff? Go see some of the fair."

"What'd I want with any of that junk?" Jeff responded, but he picked up his jacket and walked out, giving Thien a suspicious look on his way.

The American man and the Vietnamese boy sat there in companionable silence for a while. Thien picked up a broom but didn't do anything with it. He was gazing out the window at the crowd of people. Daniel wondered what he saw.

"Is it strange to see so many of your people at once? Like being back home?"

"When we came here," Thien said instantly, as if he'd been waiting to be asked precisely that question, "I thought we would be all alone. I thought we'd fall into America and have to blend. I thought we would have to be Americans. I didn't understand there would be so many of us we could—make little Vietnams anew."

"You seem fairly well blended to me," Daniel said idly. "You've been here what, eight years? Half your life."

"I was seven when we left. My father had been a government official in the old government. He called himself just a clerk but I think he was more. He was deathly afraid the Communists would find out who he had been. When Saigon fell he escaped with us to the countryside, but the fear never left him. Once in a while he would hear that another of his old colleagues had been killed or imprisoned. Besides, my father was no farmer. When he could live like that no longer he decided to escape."

"By boat?"

"First we had to get to the coast." Thien was looking out the window as if seeing the story enacted there. His voice was almost entranced. "We lived miles inland. We left in the dead of night one night, seven of us, all the family members we had together. We had one old horse but most of us walked. We avoided the roads. But in Vietnam you could not avoid the soldiers. Everyone was a soldier. Two of them stopped us. You could see it was the delight of their night. They grinned at us like—"

"Like wolves?" Daniel tried to help.

Thien shook his head. "Like cruel boys who have caught something helpless. They asked so politely where we were going. My father told them we were helping a relative move. So we would be returning? the soldiers asked. Oh yes, my father said. The soldiers whispered together and said that we could go. It seemed I started breathing then for the first time since they had stopped us. But then they said something more. They said one of us must stay with them until the rest returned.

"There was no argument. We had no deal to strike. We could only do what they said. They had rifles and pistols and we had nothing. I remember one of the soldiers touching my mother's face. I wanted to throw myself on him but my father's hand was on my shoulder, his fingers digging.

"I have often wondered since—" Thien's voice turned musing. It was much older than a sixteen-year-old's voice. It didn't rise with emotion as he told the story. In fact it seemed to grow deader. "I have often wondered if the story would have been exactly the same if they had chosen my mother. Would we have gone back for her or would we have gone on? Would my father have been more than a clerk after all? But they didn't choose my mother. They chose my father's sister-in-law. Her husband had been killed years earlier, in the war. She had a sour tongue, but all the soldiers saw was her pretty face. They said they would just detain her against our safe return. My aunt began speaking to us, saying something angry, but they shut her up. One soldier was already pulling her away into the darkness, and the other hurried to catch up, leaving us alone. We had paid our toll. We don't talk about my father's sister-in-law now. Maybe she is alive."

Questions rose to Daniel's tongue but he stifled them. He was staring aghast at the Asian crowd in the street. His perception of them had changed abruptly. They all seemed touched with death. What kind of horrible loss did each one's presence there represent?

Thien's voice changed again. Now it sounded like a child reading a moral from a story. "In America, I thought, we would not have to make such a sacrifice. When I came to school here and read your history, I thought it was the most wonderful thing I had ever heard of. Here people *choose* to make sacrifices of themselves, and willingly. And in times of crisis they band together, like the Founding Fathers. No one gets thrown to the wolves."

"That's right," Daniel said earnestly, but his voice sounded hollow even to himself. Perhaps because his throat was so dry.

"In school that's right," said Thien. He was looking across the street at the Vietnamese pawnshop. It wasn't open for business on this busy day. By now Thien knew what had been in the package Linh had received. Everyone in the neighborhood knew.

Impress us, they had told Thien. How do you impress men who could do a thing like that?

Daniel stood up. He felt stiff, as if Thien's story had lasted for hours. Outside the shadows of the stores across the way stretched halfway across the street. Daniel felt suddenly anxious to see Carol again.

A man came in and bought a gun: "Something small the missus can handle, but with stopping power. Too many crazies around." A few more drifted in from the fair, and he actually did a good afternoon's business, but he was glad to turn the store back over to Jeff when he returned. "Want to stretch my legs," he said.

Thien went out with him, but left immediately to rejoin his family. Everywhere Daniel looked it seemed to him he saw Vietnamese families, working together. No wonder they had such a reputation for solidity, if they had lived through such stories as Thien had told him. A little economic adversity and children growing into adolescence would be nothing compared to that.

He was ready to take his own wife and go home. Maybe it was that thought that made him think he saw her. He stood on the curb looking over the heads of the crowd, the sea of faces. One of them stood out for a moment. Carol's, he was sure. She was coming toward him, her face lifted, smiling at some triumph. He was raising his hand to wave to her and he thought she looked up, straight at him.

But in the next moment she disappeared. Her head bobbed down and didn't resurface, exactly as if she had drowned in the crowd. Hours later he remembered that moment—the way she had been there and then vanished. The way his heart lifted and fell. At the time he thought only that he must have been mistaken.

Daniel crossed the street. A couple of the shops were closed already, and a few of the food stands were empty and draped with canvas. It was five o'clock in the afternoon. The sky had lowered and turned threatening. There was a bite to the wind as well. The people still in the streets had buttoned their jackets. Daniel stood and watched a Vietnamese family close up their food stand, unrolling canvas and tying it down. The wind fought them for control. The woman, wearing a thin dress and a scarf on her hair, looked cold, and the three children paused in their work to hug their arms. One thing that had attracted so many Vietnamese to Houston was the climate, hot and humid most of the year, like home. As winter came on they looked more displaced.

Daniel wandered the streets for a while before going back to his own shop. Jeff had already closed up and gone home. Daniel unlocked the door and went in to wait for Carol. The shop was so dim it made him nervous, and he turned on all the lights. Walking through the Vietnamese crowd had made him think about Khai again. If Khai wanted to find him, this is where he'd come looking. The thought made Daniel uneasy. He would have locked the door again but he wanted Carol to be able to walk right in when she arrived, not have to stand out there to be studied by anyone who might be watching.

Instead he went inside the cage, one more layer of protection between him and the outside world. The cash drawer of the register was standing open, empty. It made the machine look broken, the aftermath of a robbery. The sight would have startled him if it hadn't been a daily commonplace.

His gun was in its place under the counter. It was a heavy black .45 revolver, with a long barrel. It was supposed to look menacing and did. Its main function was to intimidate would-be robbers. He checked to see that it was loaded, then looked thoughtfully at the hardware in the case behind him. Jeff had taken the guns down from their pegs on the wall and locked them in the long wooden case on the floor, so they weren't visible from the street or even from the shop outside the cage. Daniel unlocked the heavy padlock and looked inside. One of the guns was a pump-action shotgun. He lifted it out of the case and inspected it. He had shells, but stopped short of loading it. Let's not overreact here. What, after all, had happened? He had asked for help, found out the price was too steep, and turned it down. Khai wasn't going to send an army in here with guns blazing over that. Daniel might have unintentionally insulted him, but it wasn't a killing matter. Khai was a businessman—he had made that clear—and there was no profit to be made here. Daniel put the shotgun away and locked the case.

He wished Carol would come back so they could get out of there. It was dusk, and the neighborhood seemed dank and ugly. He wanted to go someplace nice for dinner and forget about this.

He wandered to the front window. There were still a few merchants open for business, unwilling to give up the last few dollars they could make, and maybe fifty tourists in the street, unwilling to give up on the festivities. He didn't see Carol among them. The hour and a half they had agreed on had passed, and more. He couldn't imagine what treasures could be keeping her this long. Maybe she was in the alley, putting something she didn't want him to see in the trunk of the car.

He thought again of Khai's offer. The high price had made it clear that it was an offer of murder. Khai hadn't specified that and Daniel hadn't wanted him to specify, but he was certain. It hadn't been the thought of murder, though, it was the twenty thousand dollars that had accounted for the quickness of his refusal: No no no, that's not what I had in mind at all. But what if the price had been only five thousand dollars, or five hundred? Would he have been so quick then to refuse, or to ask questions to clarify exactly what the offer was? The solution, after all, would be rather abstract from Daniel's point of view, because he didn't know his Vietnamese rival at all, probably couldn't pick him out in a crowd. If he moved away or just disappeared, the effect on Daniel's business would be the same. He'd never see the man again in either case.

These were undoubtedly the speculations Khai had thought he had seen behind Daniel's protests. He would probably return with a new offer. Daniel tried to shake off his thoughts. No, this wasn't what he'd wanted, at any price. He wished he had never gone looking for someone to "intercede" on his behalf.

Where the hell was Carol? He was irritated with her now. But of course she had no way of knowing how the darkening neighborhood was making him jittery. He found himself pacing the narrow aisles of the shop and decided to go out. Carol had her own keys. He scrawled her a note—"Carol, wait here, I'll be right back"—and put the exact time on it: 5:45. He taped the note to the door and went out, locking it behind him.

The crowd in the street had shrunk to a couple of dozen aimless people. A few other men were also looking around, ready to go home. He didn't see Carol among them. As Daniel crossed the street the last food stand was closing. The shuttered stands had been pushed to the sides of the street or removed altogether.

Only two stores were still open. Daniel went in the first, a small, cluttered place that he could see at a glance did not contain his wife. The second open store was larger, with a couple of side alcoves he had to check. He drew a quick glare from the Vietnamese woman behind the counter when he bent to glance under the louvered doors of the clothes-changing stall, but it seemed unoccupied.

"My wife—" he began, but the Vietnamese woman shook her head immediately. He went out again.

The only other places still open were the two restaurants at opposite ends of the block. The first was called the Golden Door, which made it sound more like some kind of porno palace than a place to eat. Perhaps that contributed to the restaurant's lack of success. At any rate, there were few diners. There were no women dining alone at any of the tables, and none of the couples included Carol. A couple of men turned to glare at Daniel as he looked around, and so did the owner, who first tried to hand Daniel a menu and then scowled as he turned and walked out again.

The other restaurant, the Far East, was a slightly fancier place and more crowded, though it was equally empty of Carol. Daniel had to walk through the tables to make sure. The maître d' followed and kept trying to seat him. In a far corner was the waiter who had told Daniel about Tranh Van Khai. He watched Daniel with an expression that looked deliberately inscrutable.

Back out on the street, night had fallen. The wind had grown stronger. It blew a paper cup that seemed to pursue Daniel as he crossed the street. He returned to his own pawnshop, which was now the most brightly lit store on the street. He could see from the note still taped to the door that Carol wasn't inside, but he opened the door and called her name anyway. There was no answer. The shop was silent except for the faint hum of the fluorescent lights.

The only other place he could think to look was their car. Accordingly, he walked down the block to the end and around the corner. The alley was dim. Two or three individual stores had lights over their back doors, but there were no streetlights back there. His footsteps echoed off the backs of the buildings and his heartbeat speeded up. He felt a strong desire to run, either toward the car or better yet away from it, out of the alley, but he forced himself to walk deliberately, looking around. There were plenty of hiding places in the alley besides shadows. There were garbage dumpsters as tall as he was, a delivery van parked overnight, a few unlighted doorways. Daniel quivered not only with the tension of not knowing who might be there, but also of what he might find. He peered hard into the shadows. The wind blew debris in the far reaches of the alley, coming toward him.

His Toyota was halfway down the alley. It was brown and blended into the darkness, but he thought he could make out a shape where he had left it.

If a random mugger was going to hide and wait for a customer, the best place would be the car, because it made sense that someone would return to it. On the other hand, the alley wasn't a very lively place to wait for trade in the mugging business. That wasn't what concerned him. Sure enough, no one was waiting near the car. He opened the door so the interior light came on, and saw that it was empty. As an afterthought he opened the trunk as well, but it held nothing unusual.

He would have liked to move the car around to the street but decided to leave it where it was on the slim chance Carol would return there first. He didn't want to leave her alone in the dark alley, searching for a car that wasn't there.

But another worry was growing in his mind, other than that she had run into trouble. He shook off this thought just as vigorously as he tried to ignore the images of her body lying in an alley such as this one, slowly losing blood.

He allowed himself to hurry out of the alley. The echo of his footsteps sounded like pursuit. He ran faster, dreading a voice raised behind him.

When he emerged from the alley the street seemed blessedly, almost painfully bright. He came to an abrupt halt, feeling foolish, but still looked back over his shoulder. The alley looked no less sinister for his knowledge that he had traversed it safely.

A man and woman passed him, hunched in their coats, glancing at him suspiciously and sidling away. He took some comfort in that. If he could inspire nervousness himself he must not look as much like a victim as he felt.

Deciding to check the restaurants again, he stepped into the street. That was when he heard the car engine he had ignored in his abstraction. From the corner of his eye he glimpsed the car bearing down on him. He froze in its head-lights.

Daniel recovered just as the driver of the car seemed to become aware of him. The horn blared as Daniel jerked back out of the path. The car swerved out toward the middle of the street. He heard a man cursing. The car missed him by no more than a foot. When it was past he saw the brake lights flare and thought the car was going to stop completely, but then the red lights dimmed and the car sped on out of sight.

Shaken, Daniel looked down the street in the direction from which the car had come. The barricades at the end of the block were gone. The street fair was officially over now, and the street had been reopened to traffic. The driver of that car probably hadn't realized the block had ever been closed.

Daniel walked back toward his own shop. The near-miss with the car had left his heart racing again, making him feel light-headed, hollow. Adrenaline with no purpose to serve made his hands shake. The doorknob rattled loudly when he opened the door of his pawnshop.

"Carol?"

There was no answer. The door swung closed behind him and he didn't stop to lock it back. He crossed the shop and went through the doorway in the far wall, beside the door to the wire cage. The back of the shop held only a tiny office and an even smaller bathroom. Both were empty. He turned on their lights to make sure, and left them on when he came back out into the shop.

"Well," he said aloud, hands on his hips, looking slowly around. The shop felt different after dark. He always closed earlier than this and had been there this late only a few times. He remembered feeling like this on those occasions—alien, as if the shop had a different purpose after hours and he no longer belonged in it.

Another half hour passed, minute by slow minute. Daniel kept passing from fear to anger. If she was doing this to him out of pure thoughtlessness, he was going to be furious. Maybe she had run into friends, gone to have a drink, forgotten he was waiting. He called home on the crazy chance that she had gotten another ride there for some reason. The phone rang and rang. He pictured the empty house, dark and silent except for the shrill ringing of the telephone.

He remembered seeing her face in the crowd. Had she looked at him? Had she seen him before she turned and disappeared? He pushed the thought away.

The only places she could be now were the two restaurants. He went out again and crossed the street, this time looking carefully before he stepped into it. The street gave him another bad idea. Maybe Carol had stepped unthinkingly into it as he had earlier, into the path of a speeding car, driven by someone who didn't see her in time. She could have been hit and dragged under the car for hundreds of feet. You read about that happening all the time. If no one saw it happen and if the driver didn't stop she could still be there, lying in the gutter a block or two away, bleeding to death or already dead. Daniel peered down the street in both directions. The only places open for business were the nearby restaurants; the rest of the street was unpopulated for blocks and blocks. He started walking, then running, out of the circle of the streetlights into the echoing blocks of boarded-up storefronts and blank-faced warehouse buildings. There was nothing in the street. A shapeless mass in the gutter made his heart stop, but the wind scattered it as he approached: newspapers blowing away.

He bent to peer under the one parked car, but there was nothing to be seen. He went for three blocks in that way, studying the street and the gutters, then ran back and searched for three or four blocks in the opposite direction. There were streetlights on every corner, casting enough light for him to be sure there was no body in the street. Two or three cars passed him while he walked. Traffic was light but steady. Someone would have seen a hit-and-run, or seen the body afterward. He felt slightly reassured.

She wasn't in either of the restaurants. Both proprietors seemed to be expecting him this time, as if he were a cop making rounds. He even questioned the waiter he knew, but he hadn't seen Carol. Daniel didn't know if his description was sufficient to distinguish her from any other blond white woman the waiter might have seen that day. The waiter didn't seem to take the questioning very seriously.

He returned to his own shop, slowly, because it was the last place to go and an admission that he couldn't find her. The note he had left for her looked forlorn hanging on the door. A corner of it had already begun to curl up as if it were an artifact that had hung there untouched for years.

For the next hour he just jittered—sitting, rising, pacing, staring out the window. Gradually he was giving more thought to the other idea that had occurred to him: that Carol had left him. That last night's reception had left her old life calling her, and their coldness to each other afterward had been the last straw. This morning's kindness had only been a way for her to slip away gracefully, with that ease he so admired. It hadn't been much of a fight but maybe it hadn't taken much, after she'd seen her old friends. He never had believed that she would try very hard to save their marriage if trouble came. A year of living together had brought them closer but hadn't entirely assuaged his mistrust. They were too different to belong together: That was something he knew and she wouldn't admit, but she must be aware of it too. Maybe she hadn't worried about their differences as much as he did because she wasn't as troubled by the thought of breaking up. Maybe it was something she just intended to play along with as long as it amused her and no longer. Last night's party had reminded her how much nicer her life had been before him. It seemed to him now, sitting alone in his shop with black night encroaching on every side, that even after a year of marriage the two of them had not coalesced into a couple. The main threads of their lives were still separate: separate work, separate friends.

But would she have left him this way, knowing he would

wait there and worry? It didn't seem likely. But maybe she gave him credit for knowing when it was over. Maybe she expected him to give up and go home and when he did he would find half-empty closets and a farewell note.

In a way these thoughts were comforting. They offered a much more pleasant alternative to the other images that had been assaulting him: of Carol in the backseat of a car being driven out into the country, struggling and pleading but with no one to hear; of men with knives and ropes and loose, malicious grins; of Carol crying silently, trying to be brave, her only hope that Daniel was doing something to save her.

He shook himself out of his trance and looked at his watch. It was eight o'clock. He had been sitting on this stool for half an hour, sunk into hopeless inaction. There was one thing he should do, at least, should have done an hour ago. He found a phone book and called the police.

When the police dispatcher came on the line Daniel had to clear his throat. He hadn't spoken for hours. He thought he must sound like a nervous criminal himself, calling in a bomb threat.

"I want to report a—I don't know what, a missing person, I guess."

"Yes, sir. And what is your name?" The dispatcher sounded like a middle-age man. His voice had a brisk efficiency designed to calm the frightened and to elicit as much information in as short a time as possible. Daniel felt slightly reassured just by the official tone. He gave his name and address and the shop's location.

"All right, sir. Now, who is the missing person and when and where did you last see him or her?"

"My wife. I don't know exactly when she disappeared. She was supposed to meet me hours ago and she hasn't shown up."

There was a short pause and the question was repeated. "And when did you see her last?"

"About—it must've been three-thirty, four o'clock."

"Today. Just this afternoon." The dispatcher's voice had gone a little flat.

"Yes." Daniel explained the street fair, emphasizing the very small area in which Carol had disappeared. "But it's all over now," he concluded. "Everyone's packed up, all the stores are closed. There's no place for her to—"

"Sir," the dispatcher interrupted. "We can't accept a missing persons report until the person hasn't been seen for twenty-four hours. That's just standard. You understand, before a whole day has passed there are just too many other explanations—just a missed connection, or the person visiting someone else, or . . ."

Or that she's left me and I just don't know it yet, Daniel filled in for him silently. He understood the policy, all right. He wasn't yet sure himself if she was really missing. "But it's not her missingness I'm worried about." His voice was rising both in pitch and volume. He was losing the police, just as surely as if his phone connection were fading away. "It's what might have happened to her. This is a bad neighborhood after dark. She wouldn't be out there on purpose. The only way she'd still be gone is if she's hurt, or someone's taken her. If you wait a whole day before you investigate—"

"We'll take steps before then, Mr. Greer. We'll alert our officers in the area to the possible kidnapping or—"

"Kidnapping, that's right. That's what it must be. Her father is Raymond Hecate. Did I mention that?"

There was a pause. "No, sir, you didn't. I'll send a car to look over the neighborhood."

"Tonight? Now?"

"Yes, sir. In the meantime, why don't you try your home?"

"I've called there, no one—"

"Yes sir, but I mean go there to check. You never know—"

He was suggesting the good-bye note and the missing clothes Daniel had thought of earlier. What was funny was how well the dispatcher's suggestion meshed with Daniel's own suspicions, but it had nothing to do with him. The dispatcher would be obliged to make the same subtle suggestion to anyone who called in such a report: Maybe your wife has just left you.

Even in the happiest marriage, if one spouse turned up missing, that's what an outsider would think. That's how they'd have to proceed.

"I will then," Daniel said.

"Good. And give us another call tomorrow afternoon if you haven't heard from her by then."

"Yes, all right."

Before he hung up the dispatcher's tone turned kindly again. "I wouldn't worry about it, Mr. Greer. They have a way of turning up."

Daniel read the newspapers. He knew the way some of them had of turning up: naked in a field, bound and gagged and three days dead. He was not comforted.

But the police dispatcher had set his mind more firmly on the other track. He looked out at the empty street and the images that came to him now were of Carol somewhere else in the city, safe, having a drink with someone, wondering if he had found her note yet. She'd be thinking of him, her memories already slightly skewed and beginning to solidify into their final form, the memories that would occur to her occasionally years from now, of a youthful experiment that failed. He gave her credit, she'd be sad tonight. She wouldn't be ready to laugh it all off.

Tears blurred his vision. He found paper and pencil and left her a new note on the glass case, just saying he'd gone home. That was the best thing to do. She obviously wasn't coming back there. He hadn't convinced himself she had left him volun- tarily—though it was, all things considered, a comforting idea— but home was still the best place to go. If she had been in an accident and taken to an emergency room, the hospital would try to contact him at home.

He had one last ugly duty, though. When he left the shop this time he took a powerful flashlight. The alley wasn't nearly so frightening when he entered it this time, and that wasn't just because the flashlight's beam dispelled the shadows. He would have almost welcomed someone attacking him, physical danger

coming at him head-on. Deep in his mind, beneath the speculations and rationalizations, was the reptile brain that doesn't
speculate, that knows what it knows. In that part of his mind
he was certain someone had hurt his wife. Banked down there
as well was an animal fury clawing for release. The heavy
flashlight wasn't just a torch; it was a club. His hand was white
from gripping it. Yes, a mugger would have been welcome just
then.

But the alley was quiet. Daniel approached the first dumpster he came to. There was a small stirrup on the side, designed
to catch the lifting arm of the garbage truck that came by
periodically. Daniel steeled himself for a moment, then climbed
up and peered inside.

The dumpster wasn't half full. It held mostly paper. A
sprinkling of glass glittered in his flashlight's beam. Luckily the
restaurants were on the other side of the street and used
different dumpsters, so the smell from this one wasn't too
terrible. He climbed up over the edge and eased himself down,
afraid of what his feet would find. Crouching, he swept the
papers aside. Glass tinkled. Heavier objects slid aside. Tenta-
tively he pushed at it harder.

There was nothing. He kicked through all the trash until he
was satisfied there was no body, then he hauled himself out and
went to the next one. He had to check them all. That's where
you always read about victims being discarded, and one of the
dumpsters would have been the logical place to dispose of Carol
if someone had killed her here in this alley when she came to the
car. But his search revealed nothing. He trudged back to his car,
bits of paper clinging to his shoes.

There was no message from Carol there. The engine roared
to life, breaking the silence. Daniel put the car in gear, and just
as he did he had a terrible sense that he was abandoning her. He
kept his eyes in the rearview mirror as he drove slowly away, as
if he might see her running after him, calling out. His brake
lights lit the alley garishly. He paused for a moment at the
mouth, then pulled out into the street, leaving her behind.

* * *

There was no note waiting for him at home. The house appeared unchanged since he and Carol had left it this morning. He called her name hopefully, but if she'd been there she would have turned on the front porch light. He snapped it on as he came in.

The front room, at the left end of the house next to the garage, was a small living room, maybe fifteen by twenty feet, perfectly nondescript until Carol had started arranging it. Plants grew from a clutter of stands just inside the front window beside the door. The antique coffee table in front of the sofa was where she would have left a note, but the only thing on the table was the morning's paper.

The living room extended back to an even smaller dining room, the window of which looked into the large backyard. The doorway in the dining room led to the right into the kitchen. The back door was there, and another window into the yard. The kitchen was a bright room even at night. It had been rather grim when they'd first bought the house, with stained walls and scarred floor. But the new linoleum they'd laid themselves had brightened it considerably, and painting the walls and cabinets pale yellow had completed the transformation. Daniel went hastily through the empty kitchen out the other door, into a hall that ran the width of the house. Doors in the hall gave onto a bathroom to the left, a bedroom on the right, the master bedroom also on the right, on the front corner of the house, and finally the hall ended at the third bedroom, which was the back corner. Daniel went through all the rooms snapping on the lights. Light seemed to throw the silence into bold relief, making it something active rather than passive. Daniel deliberately made more clatter than was necessary.

He ended in the master bedroom, the room filled with their waterbed. That had been their only major purchase together so far. They had both been over thirty when they married, they had their own furniture, but Carol had said they needed a new bed for a new marriage.

He opened the closet door. Rods on each side of the closet held hanging clothes, packed in tight. He stepped inside and pulled the string that turned on the bare bulb. Clothes filled the space all the way back to the wall. He stepped on something firm but yielding and jumped back hastily, but it was only a shoe. The floor of the closet was littered with shoes, as always. Nothing seemed to be missing from the closet. Suitcases were stored on the shelves above his head, and they were still there.

Next he went through the dresser drawers and then the bathroom. Not even her toothbrush was missing. He was searching almost frantically at the end, to find *any*thing she might have taken, anything to tell him she'd been there since this morning. But there was nothing. If she had walked away, she hadn't come back there first.

Soon he was standing in the doorway of the master bedroom. They had painted this room themselves too, a gray that seemed bright in the morning but dim and cozy at night. Squinting, he could picture the room as it had been when they'd first moved in, empty of furniture, newspapers spread on the floor, and Carol laughing with a dab of paint beside her nose.

He stumbled out of there and back down the hall. From the kitchen he could hear a thumping noise. When he walked into the kitchen a high-pitched whining replaced the thumping. Through the glass louvers of the back door he could see Hamilton staring in at him. He hadn't been fed today. Hamilton Burger—Carol had named him, more or less, after the district attorney on *Perry Mason*—Ham for short, was the Doberman Carol's father had given her when she had announced her engagement. Unspoken but obvious had been the implication that she was moving into a dangerous neighborhood with an unreliable character. In the year and a half since then the dog had grown from a cute puppy with legs too long for him into a ninety-pound beast with a chest a foot wide and a frightening growl. Inside he was still a baby, but only his owners knew that. Even Carol's old man wouldn't go near the dog anymore, on his rare visits to the house.

Daniel opened the back door and Ham put one diffident foot inside. He wasn't a house dog and knew it. But he must have been starving. Daniel knelt and scratched between and around the dog's pointed ears.

"She'll come back for you," he muttered.

He fetched the hubcap-size food dish from the back patio and half filled it with Gravy Train and warm water, then added a can of Alpo on top. Hamilton's whines rose in pitch as he watched this operation, and when Daniel finally set the food in front of him on the patio, the big dog ate as he always did, as if this were the last food in the world and someone was planning to snatch it away from him at any moment.

In the next two hours Daniel picked up the phone four times. Each time the dial tone assured him it was still working. The last two times he started to dial Carol's parents' number but hung up instead. When he finally did call the Hecates he was almost relieved when there was no answer. He didn't think she would have gone home to them, and if they'd received a ransom note they'd be home, waiting for a call.

Finally he called her friend Jennifer. The only reason she was home on a Saturday night was that she was obviously having a party. The noise almost overwhelmed her voice when she came to the phone. Daniel was embarrassed. There were probably a lot of Carol's old friends there, so in a matter of minutes there would be a rumor circulating that Carol had finally left that dork she'd married.

On the other hand, maybe Carol was already there among them. He didn't ask Jennifer that directly, but told her he and Carol had been supposed to meet somewhere and had failed to connect, and he wondered if Jennifer had heard from her.

"Tonight? No, uh-uh." Which was the answer he expected in any case. "And I've been right here by the phone too. Why don't you just go home, guy, she'll show up there."

"Will she?" Daniel said.

The background noise diminished as if Jennifer had closed a door. "That's kind of a funny response," she said after a pause.

He and Jennifer had never been anything approaching friends, and he didn't trust her now to tell him the truth even if she had heard from Carol. In turn he couldn't bring himself to tell her the truth. But he came close: "If you hear from her, Jennifer, tell her— Just tell her to call me at home."

"I will," Jennifer said, and paused again. "Listen, is something— Have you tried calling her parents?"

Daniel didn't even answer that.

"Yeah, I guess that was kind of a joke. Well, if she turns up here—"

"Thanks," Daniel said, and that was all he said before hanging up, because his throat was tightening up.

For the next hour he paced, and had a drink as well. It turned out to be a strong one because his hand wouldn't stop pouring. He kept picturing Carol back in the neighborhood of the pawnshop. He knew how unlikely that was. Even if the worst had happened, that meant she'd been taken somewhere else. But he kept picturing her stumbling down that damned dark alley, bruised and bleeding, her purse gone so she didn't have keys to the shop or change for a phone. He paced faster, until momentum seemed likely to burst him right through the walls of his house. When he couldn't stand it anymore he raced out to his car and went speeding back toward the pawnshop. It was a fifteen-minute drive he did that night in ten by running red lights and speeding on the freeway. If a police car had started pursuing him, he would have led it to the pawnshop with him. That was probably what kept police at bay: his desire for them.

The area around his pawnshop was dark and deserted. The two restaurants had closed, leaving his own shop the only brightly lit building on the block. Light still poured out its plate-glass window onto the sidewalk. From the street he could see his last note still lying on the countertop with no new note near it. He stopped there only for a minute, then drove to the end of the block and around into the alley. He put his headlights on high beam and slowly drove the length of it. The beams were like spotlights, throwing a sharp line high on the walls of the buildings on either side. Always he seemed to catch movement out of the corners of his eyes, as if something lurked there just outside the circle of light, some slithering creature that moved faster than the car or higher than the beams of the headlights could reach. Daniel rolled down the window so he could hear better. The night air drifted in, cool and yet pungent. He drove five miles an hour, slower than a fast walker.

At the end of the alley he turned, drove to the next alley, and slowly down it as well. This one held the dumpsters where the restaurants dumped their trash. When his headlights hit the first dumpster, tiny eyes gleamed back at him before the rat leaped back down inside. Daniel stopped the car, leaving the headlights on, and walked up to the dumpster. He was muttering to himself. He slammed his hand against the dumpster and screamed.

"Get out of there!" he shouted. "Get out, get out, get out!" He slammed the dumpster's side again and started kicking it as well, still screaming. Rats came swarming out, over the sides and leaping into darkness. One almost landed on his arm. Daniel was hardly sane. Revulsion rose in his throat, threatening to make him sick, but rage overcame it. He kicked at the skittering swarm of rats running past him.

When the exodus had ended he grabbed the rim of the dumpster and pulled himself up to peer over the edge.

Dead eyes stared back at him.

Daniel screamed. He pulled himself higher and fell over the edge into the dumpster. He screamed again when he landed on something that gave under him. He scrambled to his feet.

The eyes he had seen weren't dead after all. A huge rat, bolder than the rest, stood its ground and stared back at him. It wasn't alone either. Daniel could feel stirrings through the trash in which he stood knee-deep. Something brushed his leg.

He found a stick close at hand and brandished it at the rat, but the rodent barely shifted its weight. It was a giant, the size of a small cat. Daniel growled at it inarticulately. He began sifting the trash with the stick, probing delicately, wincing when the stick encountered something heavier.

There were bugs in the trash as well, roaches and smaller insects driven to a frenzy by Daniel's movements. They swarmed through the dumpster, unable to distinguish his legs from the trash. He kept stamping his feet to dislodge them.

The stick turned up nothing larger than empty industrial-size tin cans. Daniel was sick with disgust, but he was grateful as well. There was no body in the dumpster. His mind had gone blank because he could no longer stand the pictures it had been showing him of Carol's body in this tiny hell with the rats and the bugs and the rotting food. When he climbed out of the dumpster, he was sobbing without being aware of it. The rat went back to eating.

The other dumpsters in the alley weren't quite so bad. He seemed to have encountered the king of the rats in that first one. Daniel didn't come across one that big or that fearless again. He also found a better stick, one long enough that he could probe through the trash without climbing down in it. He was thorough, though. When he was finished he was certain there was nothing unusual in any of the dumpsters.

Neither his screams nor his headlights had brought anyone to the alley to investigate. He was all alone in a dim world. Civilization seemed to have retreated from this corner of the city. It was just as well no police came; Daniel would not have been coherent. He walked jerkily and kept brushing at his clothes and stomping his feet. He looked like someone coming down from a bad drug experience. His eyes were red and his throat hoarse. He kept clearing it as if he had something important to say.

He returned to his car and drove out of the alley. Gradually he grew calmer as a layer of numbness grew over his fear. He drove for half an hour, crisscrossing the same blocks over and over, until it was painfully obvious there was no life here. He ended up back parked in front of his own pawnshop. It looked clinical with its harsh lights, like a place where illegal medical experiments would be conducted in the heart of the night. Daniel stared in its windows, hating the place. If he didn't own that damned shop they wouldn't have come there. Carol would be safe now, sleeping, oblivious to the danger she'd escaped.

He drove slowly home, tears streaming down his face. Houston was vast and streetlights were a joke. Darkness prevailed. He could spend his life searching and not cover a fraction of the city's terrain.

His own neighborhood exerted a slight comforting influence. It was a middle-class area of one-story two- and three-bedroom homes. The neighborhood was called Oak Forest, but it was pine trees that dominated, some of them soaring two and three times as high as the houses. It was a pleasant unpretentious neighborhood and Carol had always claimed to like it, but he had never gotten over the feeling that she was slumming, not only in the neighborhood but in her choice of husband.

He began to think again that she had left him on her own. His mind grasped at the possibility. He pictured her in comfort somewhere, sad but alive. That began to seem likely—more likely than that she had disappeared without anyone but him noticing.

His heart leaped up when he opened his front door. It was such a commonplace act that for an instant he was sure she'd be there waiting. But the house was still silent and empty. For the next half hour he called hospitals. He also had another drink. It had been hours since he'd eaten, and the liquor went straight to his head. None of the hospitals had admitted anyone like Carol that night. He called the police again as well, and learned nothing.

When he hung up from the last call, he found his glass empty. He shuffled to the refrigerator and twisted a plastic tray of ice cubes to free them. The ice cubes cracking free of the tray made a sound like small bones breaking. Daniel leaned his forehead against the cool freezer door. He was past crying. The liquor began to numb him and his mind cooperated. He was exhausted emotionally as well as physically. He sat on the couch and his eyes struggled to focus on the clock. It was still twelve hours before he could report her as a missing person. What machinery that would set in motion he didn't know.

What if she never turned up? What if there were going to be more nights like this, a chain of them stretching into eternity, hope and grief slowly fading? How long would he have to wait until he could be sure she was safely dead, free from suffering?

He had resigned himself to sitting there all night waiting, but the next time he rose to fill his glass he set it down instead and stumbled down the hall. He took off his filthy clothes and stuffed them into the laundry hamper. He stared vaguely at the shower, but the phone might ring while he was in it. Instead he crossed the hall to the bedroom. The sight of the empty bed made his throat tighten again. When he put his hand over his eyes a wave of dizziness swept through him. He almost fell.

He decided he would lie down for a few minutes and rest his eyes. There was an extension phone on a nightstand beside the bed, so he wouldn't risk missing a call. He lay down on his back on top of the covers on the side nearest the door, her side. The bed rippled slightly, absorbing his weight, shaping itself to his body. His forearm was flung up, covering his eyes. It blotted out the whole terrible night. His chest rose and fell more and more slowly. Within a minute he had fallen into a drunken, restless sleep that gradually deepened.

He was perfectly safe that night. It wasn't until later, after he'd made himself troublesome, that they came to kill him.

CHAPTER 4

Carol

CAROL loved the street fair. She loved the crowds, the smells, the apparent bargains. It was like being a tourist in her own city. The day was perfect for it too: crisp, cool, with a promise of change in the breeze. Autumn air smelled adventurous. It reminded her of something as well, though she couldn't put her finger on it. The decorated street was unfamiliar, but she had been somewhere like this before. Every autumn she felt the same way. Nostalgia scratched at her memory.

She was glad when Daniel walked away—she couldn't shop with him tagging along impatiently—but she began missing him immediately. She was sorry for last night's coldness; it made her thoughts toward him all the warmer today. She remembered yesterday when she had dropped in on him in his shop. From his expression it had been clear he'd forgotten she was coming. When she saw Daniel unexpectedly like that during the day, took him by surprise, he could almost have been an acquaintance or a lover from years ago. Their marriage was a year old but he still looked at her sometimes as if he were surprised to see her. Carol was happy, but Daniel didn't believe that, or at least didn't believe he was the cause of her happiness. He couldn't step outside himself and see what made him lovable to her. That he liked sitting at home and playing old records. That he was kind and hard-working, without expecting too much to come of the hard work: just a slightly nicer house, money for a child, an ordinary life. That he cared about her. She could sometimes feel concern radiating from him.

The problem was his insecurity. He was still puzzled that she loved him. That was what made Carol draw away sometimes, her knowledge that deep down he didn't trust her. Didn't quite believe in their love.

Even if she hadn't been distracted with thoughts of her husband, Carol probably wouldn't have noticed the man following her. It was too crowded. Occasionally she was conscious of a stare, but she was used to that.

He was a skinny white man who needed a shave. The blue jeans jacket he wore had its cuffs turned back to expose the black hairs curling at his wrists. He or the jacket or both had gone too long without cleaning. He had the look and the smell of a man who spends no regular time in the company of women. He appreciated his view of Carol, though. A grin kept twitching his lips, threatening to dislodge his cigarette.

There weren't that many shops and they weren't that big, but every time Carol went into one the place seemed to open up like a Chinese box. Merchandise filled shelves and counters. So much of it was in miniature. You could pack a lifetime's accumulation of treasures into a three-by-five space. She marveled at the delicacy of the carving on some of the figurines. If Daniel took the time to look at them, he'd appreciate them too. She was determined to find him a Christmas present that he would just love. She wanted to embarrass him when she told him its source. "Remember that day at the fair, when you begged me not to buy you anything? . . ."

Once in a while it seemed to her that one or another of the Vietnamese merchants was paying particular attention to her. She wondered if they knew Daniel and had seen her with him, or seen her going in his shop some other day. She smiled and nodded. They nodded back. Daniel could fit in here if he tried, Carol thought. These were not unpleasant people.

She was unaware of the passage of time. The man following her was not. The shadows grew longer and he stayed in them. The crowd had thinned out a little but not nearly enough. It might have to wait until tomorrow. The man had started out enjoying his work, but now his little eyes were turning mean. He cursed under his breath as the bitch went into another shop and dawdled through it.

Carol finally found the perfect gift. She coveted it herself. It was a figure of a woman in old-fashioned Asian dress. Carved in ivory, it was small but substantial. Somehow holding it in her hand was very soothing. The carving was beautiful. You could see the expression on her face and the strands of her hair. From the slight pinch of her nostrils you could tell she was inhaling. Carol almost felt her move.

The proprietor was pleased with her purchase. He should have been, for the price. But he seemed particularly glad that the figurine had found Carol. "Good luck," he said. Carol thought he was wishing her well and thanked him, but he shook his head and indicated the ivory woman.

"She brings prosperity," he elaborated.

Carol closed her hand over the goddess. Perfect, she thought. Daniel could keep her in his own shop. She thanked the merchant again and went out into the street.

She realized suddenly that it was later than she'd told Daniel she would be. She had made other purchases, including one of those horrible devil masks as a joke. Her sacks felt heavy. She plunged into the crowd in the street. People bobbed and swayed around her. Most seemed satisfied with the day and its conclusion. A few were grumbling.

She saw Daniel standing on the curb, surveying the crowd. Looking for her. She almost lifted her hand to wave to him, but then remembered the packages. She didn't want him even to see that she'd bought anything. The goddess had to come as a complete surprise on Christmas morning. Carol ducked her head behind the tall man in front of her. Daniel might have caught a glimpse of her, but no more. She cut obliquely through the crowd. Luckily there were still enough people to hide her, but the crowd was thick only in the very center of the street. Thirty feet away she walked out of it. Only a few stragglers were nearby, walking away with their heads down. Down the block she saw people heading for their cars.

When she turned the corner she left everyone behind. The alley was ahead. Carol was walking fast, hurrying to put her bags in the trunk of the car and get back to Daniel. She wasn't aware of how isolated she was until she turned the next corner, into the alley, and caught a glimpse out of the corner of her eye of the man behind her.

He scared her for a moment just because he was unexpected and because he was looking straight at her. She shrugged it off. It was still daylight and there were people around. He was just another fairgoer headed home.

In the alley, though, there was no daylight and no people. Shadow fell from one side of the alley to the other. The few lights back here hadn't come on yet because the sun was still up. But there was no sun here. The buildings blocked it out completely. The air felt cold. She couldn't see to the far end of the alley.

And there didn't seem to be anyone else around. The lucky few who had found these parking spaces back here close to the fair had been those who had come early. Most of them had gone home early too. There were only a few cars left, and no one in them.

Carol looked back over her shoulder and saw the man there at the mouth of the alley. He was just standing, looking back the way he had come. His head swiveled as he looked the other direction down the street. Then his eyes were on her again. He entered the alley.

She allowed herself to worry, without embarrassment. The man looked menacing. He hadn't come with anyone else to the fair. And now he was following her, apparently purposefully. He hadn't turned into the alley heedlessly like someone just walking to his car. Carol walked faster herself. The packages rustled in her arms.

The alley grew darker the deeper she plunged into it. Dumpsters loomed out of the dimness. She stepped on something round and her foot almost went out from under her. She stumbled ahead. She could hear footsteps behind her but didn't turn to look again. The footsteps weren't hurrying as hers were.

Carol shifted her purse in front of her so she could get into it and find her keys. She wasn't going to stop to put her packages in the trunk. She was just going to get into the car, lock the door, and wait for the man to walk away. Undoubtedly that was what would happen. This had happened to her before, worrying about someone following her, and then the man would just walk on by. She'd had these little moments of panic and nothing ever came of them. That was no reason not to be cautious now, though.

The Toyota was twenty feet ahead. It seemed to have just appeared there. She was grateful to see it. The old car looked like a friend. She was under its protection now.

The man behind her seemed to sense that too. When she turned around the car she looked back and saw that he was thirty yards back, too far away to catch her before she got into the car. He still wasn't hurrying either. She had been right, there was no threat here. Just a man walking to his car farther down the alley. She wasn't taking any chances, though. Her car key was already in her hand. She unlocked the driver's door, opened it, and spilled her packages inside. She sighed with relief as she started to step inside herself.

The hand that gripped her ankle was rough and thick and very strong. Carol was too startled to scream. She gasped. In another moment she *would* have screamed, but by then the man in the alley had caught up to her. He came up behind her and put one arm around her waist, the other hand across her mouth.

Now two hands were gripping her ankles as well. Carol struggled, shaking her head back and forth and trying to get her hands over her head and into the face of the man behind her. He shifted his grip to pin her arms to her sides. One of his arms was right under her breasts. The other arm still crossed her chest so the hand was on her mouth. She tried to bite his finger.

"Hurry up," the man growled.

He stepped back, dragging Carol with him, and the hands holding her ankles released their grip. A face appeared on the ground. It was broad and flat and bearded. The man dragged himself out from under her car with difficulty. He was so big he almost upended the car.

"See, babe," the other man was whispering in her ear, "we know more about you than you think. We know your car, we know where you live . . ."

She kicked backward and caught his shin. He grunted and shut up. He bent forward heavily, bending her too. Carol kicked back again. This one was a glancing blow to the other leg, but it hurt him too. His grip loosened. She pushed her elbow back as hard as she could, finding his stomach. He exhaled heavily again. Carol tore herself free.

She turned and looked at him. She wouldn't forget that face. She put her hands up and went for his eyes with her nails. He was too slow to get his hands up but he lowered his head so she couldn't get at his face. Instead she kicked him, harder than she'd ever kicked anything in her life. She was trying for his crotch but he turned so that it only caught his thigh. He'd have a bruise to remember but he wasn't crippled. He fell aside and Carol ran past him. She inhaled to scream finally.

She was off the ground. Her feet were still moving but they were no longer under her. She was rising straight up in the air.

The other one had caught her from behind. He was strong, much stronger than the first man. The air rushed out of her. Her captor slung her around so she was again facing the first man. He had recovered enough to stand up and grab her legs, one in each hand, one on each side of his body. He looked at her face and knew what she was thinking.

"That's right," he said. "Soon, baby. Maybe right here in the alley."

She drew her legs in, jerking him forward. He lost his leer. "Would you hurry the hell up with that stuff?" he said again.

The big one holding her shifted and then a rag covered her nose and mouth. She tried to twist away but he pressed her back too hard against his own chest. The fumes blinded her. She struggled for air but there were only the evil-smelling fumes. She could feel herself going limp. The man holding her legs dropped them and stepped forward, grabbing the waistband of her pants. His fingers were inside. She tried to pull away but there was nothing there. No body, no world. And finally no Carol.

"Anybody behind us?"

Ralphie was hunched over the wheel, driving as if being pursued. Carefully, though. The bitch was in the trunk, knocked out from the chloroform, and Ralphie knew Houston cops. They'd search the car just for the hell of it even if they only stopped him for speeding. Ralphie had never been stopped for something minor without getting hassled. For some reason cops didn't like his looks.

The bearded one looked back at the crowded streets behind them for a minute, then turned back without saying anything. Ralphie hadn't yet heard him say a complete sentence. The guy was nice to have at your side for something physical, but he sure as hell wasn't company.

Ralphie got on Interstate 10 and headed west toward Katy. If you wanted to find someplace truly isolated in the big city, you practically had to leave town. He tried to blend into the flow of the traffic but there was no such thing. The guy behind him wanted to do eighty, even if he had to go through Ralphie's bumper to do it, while the guy in front of him insisted on going no more than forty-five. And one lane of the damn freeway was closed, as usual. Houston was arranged so that by the time they finished fixing a freeway it was time to start over again.

"Know any place along here we could stop?" Ralphie asked. "That's some good-looking stuff we got in the trunk. Shame to waste it."

"Shame to *get* wasted over it," the big guy said, surprising him.

"Aw, those guys don't give a shit. Look, there's a little park right over here off of T. C. Jester. Nobody—"

"It's Saturday, everybody's *in* the park. Just drive."

The guy was turning articulate at the wrong time. "What're you, a pansy?" Ralphie said. "You one of those guys that went to prison and enjoyed the social life? . . . All right, all right. What're ya gonna do, punch me out while I'm driving?"

"You gotta stop sometime," the big guy said.

"Whoo, I'm terrified. I'm wetting my pants."

The big guy went back to staring moodily out the windshield, and Ralphie just drove. At the North Belt exit he turned off and found the street he'd been told about but had never heard of before. After a few blocks it grew depopulated swiftly, almost turned into a country lane. They came to a field. He drove straight into it. It must not have been a park because, as the big guy had said, the parks were full today but this place was dead empty. It was sunset by now anyway. In another half hour it would be full dark.

Ralphie hoped the others would be late, give them time to damage the goods a little first, but there ahead of him was a gook standing all alone in the field. Their employer. "Shit," Ralphie said, and pulled up next to him. They got out of the car. The guy was big for a gook, a little taller than Ralphie, though of course he looked like a dwarf next to the big guy. Ralphie wasn't worried, but he kept his eyes open. This was always the tricky part, getting paid.

"You have her?" the gook asked.

"Of course we have her. Think we'd show up here without her? No problems, nobody followed us."

"Oh, really?" said the gook, because just then here came another car. This one was backing across the field, until it was trunk to trunk with Ralphie's. Another Vietnamese got out. This one was normal-size for one of them, a dink. And skinny as mesquite branches. The bigger gook said to this one ironically, "Did anyone *else* follow them?"

The dink shook his head. He opened the trunk of his car and waited.

"Show him," Ralphie said, handing the keys to the big guy. He trudged away.

"She is unconscious?" the boss gook asked anxiously. "We don't want—"

"She's out, don't worry about it. Let's see the color of your money."

"All right." The gook pulled a thick wad of bills out of his pocket. Ralphie relaxed a little. He really had the money. "Now, you were already paid half—"

"Yeah, yeah." Ralphie looked back over his shoulder. Both trunks were open and they were moving the girl from one car to the other. Ralphie wondered how they'd take it if he offered to knock fifty bucks off the price if they'd just leave him alone with her for ten minutes first. Naw. No chance. He sighed. Well, he'd have money in his pockets after this. The streets wouldn't be safe from him.

He turned back to watch the one who'd hired them counting out bills. The big guy came and stood beside Ralphie, watching. The other gook was still back at the trunk of the car.

"Don't trust me to give you your cut?" Ralphie said to the big guy.

"You are certain you were not followed?" the gook said. He turned his head sharply to look across the field. Ralphie followed his gaze.

"Relax. There's nobody. Just give us the bread and let's get the hell out of here."

The big guy started making sounds like he was trying to clear his throat. The boss gook handed Ralphie the wad of bills. Ralphie took them in both hands, grinning. It looked like more money even than they'd been promised.

The big guy now was wheezing like a four-pack-a-day man. "What the hell's wrong with you?" Ralphie said. The guy was distracting him from his pleasure in the money. He was counting the bills from one hand to the other.

The big guy bent at the waist, his hands at his throat. He leaned against the car, still making noise.

"What're you—"

"He is choking to death," Chui said calmly. Now there was a gun in his hand. And Ralphie had nothing in his hands but goddamned money.

"And you are next," Chui said. He fired. The first two into Ralphie's stomach, just for pleasure. After he went down to his knees, Chui stepped closer and fired a more careful shot into the back of his head. He bent and held the wrist until the pulse stopped. He looked at the other one, who was on his back, eyes bugging out of his head. Nguyen's thin wire was imbedded in the flesh of his neck. The man's hands were at the wire but they were no longer moving. It was an exotic way to kill a man— Nguyen favored those—but couldn't be traced to them.

Chui stooped to retrieve his money from Ralphie's lifeless hands. He searched the man's pockets and found the first payment. Fool. "Take them," Chui said. He got into Nguyen's car, now with the girl in the trunk, and left Nguyen to dispose of the bodies and the car.

Montrose is the most interesting neighborhood in Houston. Once fashionable, it had declined badly but now was fashionable again, though evidence of its years in decline still were visible. There would be an isolated block of fine old homes built soon after the turn of the century, two- and three-story minimansions with columns and wide verandahs. In other blocks tiny houses would predominate, with an occasional burned-out wreck no one had ever had the money to rebuild or tear down. And sometimes the mansion and the wreck would be next-door neighbors. Montrose was also a center of gay life, nightlife, and a high-crime area, where most nights drunks were rolled and elegantly furnished town houses burglarized. Regularly one of these activities would end in murder. And deeper into the neighborhood there were narrower, darker blocks over which the rapid growth of Houston seemed to have washed and then receded like a tide, leaving an occasional block isolated. Families had moved out but gentrification hadn't set in.

It was to such a block that Chui drove, slowly. For the last half block he turned off his lights. The street was dark. To his right was an empty lot and on his left two, small frame houses, also empty. Beside the vacant lot a large culvert emptied into a drainage ditch. The culvert was a concrete pipe big enough for a man to walk into. Chui backed the car up to its mouth and got out.

The woman in the trunk was still unconscious. The sight of her worried Chui anew. American. Americans were bad business. But it wasn't his decision. He carried her into the culvert, set her down safely, then went out and moved the car away before returning to carry her farther. Inside the culvert was blackness and the sound of water dripping. Chui was careful to shuffle his feet, taking small steps. Rats lived there.

After a certain distance he stopped, though he could still see nothing. He put out his hand, brushing his fingertips against the slimy wall of the pipe, until the wall ended and he gripped instead an iron bar. Fumbling in the dark, he found a lock and inserted a key. The gate opened with a creak. Chui hurried through it, carrying the woman over his shoulder, into the side tunnel behind the gate. This one was a wider tunnel that entered the culvert at a right angle. Once inside it, Chui lit his cigarette lighter and held it high. The gate of iron bars closed behind him, locking automatically. Chui hurried along the corridor, the woman heavy and shifting on his shoulder. This corridor was drier. After a few yards it turned, so that he was out of sight of the gate and the culvert, and from that point on the tunnel floor sloped upward ahead of him. Chui eased the woman to the ground and went looking for the buzzer that would sound in the house.

* * *

"All safe?" asked Khai.

"*We* are safe," said Chui. "Nguyen is disposing of the temporary help." It had been necessary to hire the two American men. Chui understood that. If anyone saw the kidnapping, they must not identify the kidnappers as Vietnamese. Chui understood that sometimes they must work with Americans. It was the woman herself who made him uneasy. They could solve their problem without her. But Khai didn't think so. And one did not argue with Khai.

"Must we keep her here?" Chui asked.

"I like it less than you," Khai said. "But Tang's men are everywhere. I want her near me." As the gang war had escalated, Khai had developed the beginnings of a siege mentality. He seldom left the house nowadays, and he liked everyone close at hand.

They were still standing in the tunnel, near the entrance to the house, which was simply a large ragged hole cut in the rock wall. The hole led through a fake wall that could be slid aside into a closet on the first floor of the house, near the kitchen. When Khai had come into the tunnel he had closed the closet door but had left the fake wall open and out of sight. Now another man opened the closet door from the house side and came toward them, stopping in the tunnel entrance, filling it. The man was American, the only one in the house. Khai took no notice of his sudden appearance.

In the dim light of the tunnel, the body on the ground was barely visible. It may have taken the American's eyes time to adjust, or he may have just been staring at the body, wondering at its implications. At any rate, he stared in the direction of the woman for a long two minutes before crossing past Khai and kneeling beside her supine body. Chui glanced at him a trifle uneasily.

His name was John Loftus. He was a tall man with sunburned arms but a pale face. Loftus was well muscled, but looking at him one could easily see the skeleton he would someday be. Bones were prominent in small knobs on the tops of his shoulders as well as at his collar and wrists. The skin of his face was white and taut, and he had that blond shade of hair and eyebrows that is almost invisible a few feet away, so that the shape of his skull was apparent. When he opened his mouth vertical creases appeared in his cheeks.

Khai was mulling over Chui's protest. "Perhaps we could keep her here in the tunnel. If we—"

"No," John Loftus said.

He was as much Khai's man as any of them. Being an American here gave him no enhanced status; probably reduced it, in fact. But once in a great while he could still speak with the authority of the sergeant he had been; the voice of a noncom who follows dumb-ass officers' orders without protest for months, until the day he thinks one of those orders will get him killed. Then it's the officer who had better listen. Khai looked annoyed but didn't immediately snap out a response.

John Loftus had knelt beside the woman's body. Chui had pulled her blouse up over her face to serve as a makeshift blindfold. Underneath the woman wore a sheer bra paler than her white skin. Loftus had pulled the blouse back to look at her face. He let it fall back into place, covering her breasts and leaving her face exposed. Still kneeling, he had turned to look at the Vietnamese men.

"No?" Khai said softly. The calmness of his tone made Chui glance sideways at him. Clearly Khai was wondering at Loftus's motive in interfering with the disposal of the white woman.

But Loftus's tone was strictly business. "Leave her out here so if anyone finds the tunnel the first thing they'll find will be her?" He stood. He was half a foot taller than the other two. In the dimness of the tunnel he seemed even bigger. "If she manages to scream anybody in that drainpipe could hear her. Kids probably play in that pipe. I did when I was a kid. You want her that close to the outside world?"

Khai looked at the woman thoughtfully. "My father is asleep upstairs," he said slowly. "I do not want him disturbed with this business. More important, I do not want her to see any of us. If we release her I do not want her to say 'Vietnamese held me in a large old house—' "

"Keep her in my room," Loftus said. "No need for her to see anyone else. I'll keep her blindfolded and gagged. The only voice she'll hear will be mine." Loftus had his feet planted and his fists on his hips. He was wearing a white undershirt that emphasized his skeletal nature, but the muscles of his arms were tight, highlighted by a thin sheen of sweat. "I'll take all the risks."

Chui started to protest that the risks would be all of theirs, if they entrusted the woman to Loftus, but Loftus's voice rode over his. "What d'you think?" he said to Khai. He gestured at the woman's body. "She'll be waking up soon."

Khai was stroking his chin. He nodded. He appeared to be lost in thought, but in fact he was carefully watching John Loftus's face. When he nodded he saw a grateful expression quickly cross the American man's countenance and as quickly disappear. "You make sense," Khai said. "Take her then."

Loftus nodded briskly. He crossed between Khai and Chui and stooped to lift the woman. She hardly seemed a burden in his arms. He passed the two Vietnamese men again without another word and disappeared into the house with her.

Chui began protesting in Vietnamese. Khai stopped him. "Let John Loftus run the risk of identification. He is right about that. When it is over it may be necessary for someone to take the blame. Who better than the man whose face she has seen?"

Chui nodded, of course. Khai put a hand on his shoulder and they followed Loftus into the house.

It was no accident that Khai lived in this mansion equipped with a secret tunnel to the block behind it. Khai and his father had lived in a mansion in Saigon every bit as large as this one, though lighter and airier. It too had had a bolt hole Khai's father himself had ordered built, as an eventuality not against a Communist takeover, which he had not foreseen, but against changes in police administration, which happened regularly. Sometimes negotiations with the new administration were protracted and difficult, and the police chief would seek to accelerate them to a happy conclusion by sending minions to arrest the elder Khai in his home. The tunnel had kept him out of jail more than once, even saved his life when the police were acting under the orders of a rival. When they had come to America, where Khai's father knew nothing about the police and trusted them accordingly, he had insisted on finding a headquarters similarly equipped. Khai had found it in the crumbling old mansion in Montrose, which had stood empty for years before Khai purchased it.

The mansion had been built in the '20s, during Prohibition, by a bootlegger with gothic tastes, who had stood in the identical relation to Houston police as Khai's father to Saigon police and had held their reliability in equally high regard. Just as important, the bootlegger's personal stash had to be brought into the house, and not through the front door. Hence the tunnel from the street behind, ending in the bootlegger's closet, which served as his wine cellar.

When the two Vietnamese emerged from the closet, Chui asked, with an unattractive edge of eagerness in his voice, "What about the other one?"

"Ah, yes," said Khai. He had forgotten the other. It seemed so trivial now. "We are becoming a house of women, are we not?"

"Is tomorrow the second Day?"

"Tomorrow? No. The next, I think. We don't want it to pass too quickly."

"No," agreed Chui.

"There must be time for the information to pass."

"I think it has," Chui said.

"Really?" Khai found this flattering.

"Everyone knows. Everyone waits."

"Let them wait another day, if you think best. I leave it to you." Khai dismissed the whole operation. He had much larger schemes at hand now.

Chui, though, was looking forward to seeing the Days of the

Hand played out. In the old days of Saigon, he had heard, it had been a time-honored practice, though one not performed for many years because it had been that long since a merchant refused to pay protection. But here in America an occasional one like the pawnbroker Linh was unfamiliar with the old ways and had developed an inconvenient independence of spirit. After other tactics had failed Khai had decided that the Hand would be the ideal device for bringing such a one into line. It would do the pawnbroker no good but would serve as an invaluable learning experience for others.

The operation of the Days of the Hand was simple: Leave the recalcitrant merchant in place but kidnap his wife. They would keep her for a while, sending easily detachable parts of her back to her husband's shop: fingers primarily, sometimes ears or toes for variety. The pawnbroker would never go to the police, out of a wan hope that his wife would be returned to him, alive if not quite whole. Still, news would leak out within the community. His fellow merchants would see the effect on the stubborn fool as the packages arrived with their delicate cargoes bespeaking growing pain and disfigurement. The husband would grovel. Before the end he would beg to be allowed to pay protection. But it was too late for him already. On the last day of the lesson he would come to the shop in the morning to find a fingerless hand nailed to the door. The next day the pawnbroker himself would be gone as well, and no one would ever again think of not paying. The procedure was elegant in its simplicity, Chui thought. He was honored to be participating in its fulfillment.

They had Linh's wife and had already made the first delivery. Having secured Khai's blessing to make the second, Chui walked away, toward the stairs. Khai shook his head as he would have over an overeager child, and went off to his study and the pleasure of his contemplations.

To say that to the Vietnamese, newly come to America, Houston was like a jungle would be inaccurate. A jungle would have been comforting by comparison. Houston was a giant city, exposed to the sun and reflecting everything in the glass buildings. It offered no place to hide. There were one hundred thousand Asians in Houston. Many of them didn't speak English, didn't have any skills America wanted, didn't understand or care about anything they saw on the TV news. The urge to re-create the countries they had lost was irresistible. To cling together, to find a base and build a world they understood, barely impinged on by the one they did not. But to cling to the old ways was to allow old evils to flourish. It wasn't only honest men who had escaped from South Vietnam. Men of wealth and power, however obtained, knew that the new Communist rulers would resent that power and confiscate that wealth. They had good reason to flee the new regime. And once established in America, some of them had seen the opportunity to revive their enterprises. Khai was only one of several who began charging Vietnamese merchants for protection.

The new Asian society was even more vulnerable to organized crime than it had been at home, because the community here was so ingrown and afraid of the world surrounding them. The immigrants had no place to turn for help. The devil they knew was preferable to the white-skinned devils they did not. In the scramble to find a place for themselves, there was no time to try to fight the old enemies.

It didn't even occur to most to try to fight. They lived with a system their ancestors had lived with. A Vietnamese businessman might try to escape paying the graft only in the way his American counterpart would cheat on his taxes: not openly, as if it were his right to be free, but sneakily, fearfully, telling no one. There was no organized resistance.

There was, however, the occasional maverick like the pawnbroker Linh who refused to pay. Khai knew that Linh had not been a merchant in the old country; he had been of a higher class. Maybe that accounted for his stubborn refusal to pay. He wasn't familiar with the system. But that could be no excuse. Linh's attitude was dangerous for everyone. Others knew that he didn't pay protection. They watched to learn if there would be consequences.

The old man was terribly stubborn, though. Harassing his customers, even smashing his shop window, had had no effect on him. He had told Khai, "I will spend everything I have to replace a thousand windows before I will pay you a penny." To Khai's face he had said that, and other merchants had heard about it. It was then that Khai had initiated the Days of the Hand.

At almost the same time, he had heard that the *American* pawnbroker was asking to see him. By that time Khai had other worries on his mind. He had almost forgone the meeting with Daniel Greer. Now he was immensely grateful he had not. Always see to the small matters, he reminded himself. One never knew when a small matter might offer a solution to a larger problem.

The larger problem was that the gangs in Houston had grown fat. Inevitably, they had begun to prey on each other. At first their conflicts had amounted to little more than pushing and shoving over fringes of territory. But Khai controlled far and away the richest territory. The others would not give up. Rivalry had erupted into war between Khai and his largest competitor, Tang. War was dangerous and bad for business. It called the attention of police to their profitable enterprises. Everyone feared that, but intemperate Tang still pushed. The attempt on Khai's own life had been the last straw. He had retaliated creatively and now wanted to end the war before Tang could arrange an even more vicious reprisal. But how? Tang himself was inaccessible to Khai.

Then had come Daniel Greer. Khai was delighted with the results of that interview. He had never before given any consideration to the American pawnbroker. He was not Vietnamese, he was not subject to Khai's influence. But now Khai saw a chance to use him. He would kill Linh, as he'd already arranged, and on top of that charge Daniel Greer for the favor. That was the mark of a good businessman: to get paid for doing what one planned to do anyway.

Khai was an ambitious man whose ambition had taken a great leap forward there on the dirty city street. He saw now the possibility of exerting his influence over Greer. He need not limit himself as he'd always assumed. If he could exercise his power over American businessmen as well as Asians, the whole city would be open to him.

It had actually been *lack* of ambition that had been holding Khai back. He hadn't raised his head out of the muck to look around. When he did he discovered that not only did Daniel Greer have a wife, but the wife had a rich father. A rich city councilman father. It was beautiful. All sitting there waiting for Khai, once he had the initiative to look for it.

He was smiling when Chui came to see him in his study, but the smile disappeared when the door opened. Khai was all business.

"Have John Loftus call Daniel Greer. We don't want him going to the police."

"He has already tried," Chui said. "He is not home. Maybe still looking for her."

"Have him keep trying. See that the man stays quiet."

And then Khai forgot about Daniel Greer. Raymond Hecate was more important. He began to smile again.

PART TWO

In the
Shadow
of the
Towers

CHAPTER 5
Monday

"WHY the fuck didn't somebody show me this as soon as it happened?"

Detective Steve Rybek was waving a police report under the nose of the civilian clerk who had delivered it to him a minute earlier. The clerk looked bored.

"The computers were down, Steve. The dispatcher can't remember everything. He sent a patrol car to cruise the neighborhood, but they didn't see anything. It wasn't until the uniformed officers filed their report that—"

"Everything that happens in one of those neighborhoods is supposed to come straight to me."

"And it has. There it is. You've got it in your hand. It only happened two days ago."

"Two *days* ago." Rybek rolled his eyes and looked around as if hoping to find a higher form of intelligence with which to communicate. "You know how much heat I've taken in the past two days? You know how much sleep I've had? First they start blowing up white people, now you tell me they're kidnapping white women?"

The clerk, who was a white woman herself, looked undistressed. "It's just a routine missing person. Probably got nothing to do with Vietnamese."

"Oh, thanks for that insight, Sherlock. I guess I don't even need to look into it, since you can just mystically *know* what's behind it. They oughtta make you the detective."

The clerk just stared at him, a civil servant unintimidated by abuse. Rybek walked away muttering loudly enough to be heard, "What's the point of *having* a goddamned task force if no one *tells* the goddamned task force anything?"

He drove to the pawnshop in his unmarked car, thinking as he drove what a joke that was. The car was "unmarked" only in that it didn't have a giant shield and "Houston Police" on the sides. But it was the same make and model as the marked police cars, and its license plate said TEXAS EXEMPT. It wouldn't take a criminal mastermind to puzzle out what would drive such a car. Besides, the idea of any cop slipping unobtrusively into a Vietnamese neighborhood was ludicrous. The city actually had two Vietnamese police officers now, but neither was assigned to the Vietnamese task force. Only a month out of the academy, they were assigned to regular street patrols. Maybe after they had some experience they'd be some use in handling Vietnamese crime, but in the meantime there were only white and black and brown officers trying to win the trust of yellow people, which was a laugh riot.

Rybek cruised through the neighborhood before finding a parking space. He knew the area as well as you can know a place whose inhabitants won't tell you more than the time of day. He knew most of the businessmen, how long they'd been in Houston, how many times they'd been burglarized, who they paid for protection. He wondered what an American business was still doing in this neighborhood anyway.

Rybek filled the doorway of the pawnshop. The owner glanced up at him nervously. Rybek had that effect on people. He had a vague hope that middle age would distinguish him with graying temples or something like that, but in the meantime he was mired in his mid-thirties and still looked like a thug. He was of average height, which made his shoulders seem all the broader. Rybek looked like a wrestler not many generations removed from Eastern Europe. He and Lech Walesa would not have seemed out of place at the same family reunion.

"Can I help you?" the pawnbroker said.

"You can take your hand out from under that counter without blowing my leg off. I'm a cop."

He opened his wallet to show the badge and advanced with it, but he didn't expect that to be his ticket to a joy-filled welcome so he wasn't surprised when the owner's face stayed hard and his hands stayed under the counter.

"You Daniel Greer?"

"That's right."

"I'm Detective Rybek." He stuck his hand out so the guy was forced to bring his hand out empty and shake with him. Neither of them evinced any pleasure in the contact.

Like most cops, Rybek considered pawnbrokers at best semilegitimate fronts for gun dealers and fences. Check a stereo in a pawnshop and find a serial number that's been scraped off. Too bad the guy didn't run a perfectly respectable business that would welcome cops hanging around—say, a doughnut shop— but that couldn't be helped.

"Saturday night you reported your wife missing, Mr. Greer. Is she still missing?"

Daniel started to speak and ended up licking his lips instead. He tried again and came out with "I'm not sure, to tell you the truth."

Rybek looked at him steadily. "Have you heard from her?"

"No."

"Heard from anyone? A ransom demand?"

"Oh, no. Nothing like that at all."

"Okay, I have to ask, have you checked with her parents, see if she just went home to Mom and Dad?"

"I checked with a friend of hers who'd be the first person she'd call. She didn't know anything. I don't think Carol would go home to her parents. Anyway, I haven't talked to them. I'd rather not worry them until I know something definite. They and I . . ." His voice trailed off.

"Yeah," Rybek said with a trace of sympathy. "I saw their address. Kind of a dream come true for them to have a pawnbroker for a son-in-law?"

Daniel almost smiled. "Their very words."

Rybek was leaning on the counter and looking out at the street. They both were. "You have any children?"

"Not—no."

"Okay. She disappeared from right around here, right?"

"Yeah. They were having a street fair— Listen, I seem to be repeating myself. Are you just checking on my story?"

Rybek was still looking out the window. He had seen more interesting street life in his time. There was hardly anyone outside. Two young Vietnamese men had appeared across the street, standing there idly, but they seemed to have nothing to do and no interest in anyone. They didn't look across the street. They didn't seem to look anywhere in particular. The two were dressed similarly, in black dress pants, jackets, and cowboy boots. One of them wore a leather jacket with fringes.

Rybek turned back to Daniel. "I have a special slant on this. I'm with what we call Special Crimes, specifically looking into crimes that take place among the Vietnamese. Which you're not, obviously, but I get reports on anything unusual that happens in a neighborhood like this one."

"You think Vietnamese had something to do with this?"

"I don't have any idea. But the circumstances make me curious. So do these Saigon cowboys hanging around on the corner over there."

To Daniel the phrase sounded both knowledgeable and bitter, not like something the cop had made up on the spot. He wondered but didn't ask if Rybek had been in Vietnam during the war. It would be embarrassing. Not like asking if someone had done something shameful, but a painful question, like asking if someone had lost a friend or lover. If the answer was yes Daniel couldn't pretend to understand the cop's feelings and he'd feel like a clod trying to do so, a tourist in someone else's memories. Daniel hadn't been to Vietnam, though he was the right age for it. So he just stood there and nodded his head knowingly.

"You know them?" he asked of the Saigon cowboys.

Rybek shook his head. "But I know the type. I've been investigating the gangs for almost a year now. There's too many to keep track of, and they keep changing. But those—"

"Gangs? Like a mafia? I've heard rumors, but—"

"Mafias'd be more like it. There's no one dominant one. But, hell yes, they're out there. Wherever you have a large, cohesive ethnic group you have mafias." For a moment he sounded like a sociology text, except for his peculiarly heartfelt tone. Daniel thought he must have done some passionate study of the subject. "These were thriving from the first boatload. They brought it with 'em like laundry businesses. Besides, it makes sense that they'd prey on their own kind. Who'd you rather steal from, hard-working gook families that half of 'em own their own businesses, or nigger junkies that don't know where their next fix is coming from?"

Daniel paid little attention to this mini-lecture. He was thinking of what he needed to say to make the detective back off the investigation.

"I—I'm really not as worried as I was Saturday night. I think maybe I overreacted. I have a feeling she's . . . okay."

Rybek looked at him steadily. "Has she done this before?"

"Gone away? Well, just for—overnight, maybe, once or twice."

"Uh-huh," Rybek said. He looked idly out the window again. "Well, I'll tell you what. Here's my card. I'll be trying to check from the Vietnamese end, but that could take a while. If you hear anything, let me know."

"I will, but—"

Greer's tone changed abruptly. He had sounded almost breezy so far, but Rybek had seen that reaction before; it didn't mean much. But now suddenly the pawnbroker seemed clenched tight, eyebrows to toes. He probably wasn't even aware of it.

"I think she's probably alive and well," Daniel finished. "Don't you?"

"I think she is," Rybek said, looking him in the eye. "After this much time without a trace. She'd have turned up by now otherwise."

That was a complete lie. Sometimes a body didn't turn up for months. Sometimes never. The earth is full of unfound bodies. But the guy looked relieved, which was the purpose of the lie.

Of course, her still being alive would raise other specters in the guy's head soon enough.

"We're not going to give up on it, Mr. Greer." Rybek's tone had hardened. "This isn't some goddamn Third World country, not yet. A white woman can't just disappear without somebody doing something about it."

The pawnbroker looked away, then turned back and nodded and shook hands again, more warmly this time. Rybek hoped he had sounded convincing, because he did mean that one.

Daniel watched the cop leave. He wished he had said something stronger: No, *do* give up on it, Officer. Don't look for her. But he hadn't been able to bring himself to say that. What if the cop decided he wanted to hear it from Carol herself?

Daniel could still hear the voice on the telephone. It had awakened him from a troubled sleep in the very early hours of Sunday morning. A quiet, husky voice telling him not to worry, his wife was fine.

"Let me speak to her," Daniel had said, wiping sleep from his eyes.

"No. Just listen. Don't call the police."

"I already have."

The voice had made a heart-stopping pause. But finally it

went on. "Then don't call them again. If you hear back from them tell them everything's swell. It will be if you just keep quiet."

"What have you done with her?"

"She's fine," the man's voice had said again. "Nobody's touched her. You just don't do anything until you hear from me again. Go to work like normal. Look like a happy man."

"What do you want from me?"

"Nothing yet. Just no interference. Understand?"

"But—"

"You're starting to annoy me," the voice had said. "And there's only one person here for me to take it out on when I get annoyed."

"All right, all right. Don't— I won't do anything. Should I start trying to get some money together?"

There had been another pause. This one seemed to signify amusement. "You don't have enough," the voice had finally said. "Just keep quiet."

"I will," Daniel had said, and the phone had gone dead in his hand.

Now he was afraid he hadn't kept quiet enough. He should have told that cop his wife was home safe and sound. But what if the cop had checked on that?

Daniel found himself gripping the counter as if he would strangle it. That was all he could do.

Back at the station house, Rybek continued his speculations aloud to his partner. "Why *would* they keep her this long? A tall white woman who'd stand out among them like Judy Garland in Munchkinland? Why would they run the risk? Why would they take her in the first place?"

"Remember snuff films?" his partner said musingly. "I heard a rumor that the Vietnamese are reviving the genre right here. Maybe they've got a casting agency."

"Shut up," Rybek said.

His partner shrugged. "I did hear it." A little while later he interrupted Rybek's loud questioning again to say "Hey, did you ever think maybe the husband just offed her himself? That happens, I hear."

Rybek said, "How'd you get to be such a prick? You take a correspondence course?"

But he'd already been thinking the same thing himself.

When Raymond Hecate got on the elevator on the fortieth floor, he had too much on his mind to notice the delivery boy who got on with him. Some guy wearing a white T-shirt and carrying something. Hecate turned his back on him, punched the button for one of the parking levels below the lobby, and thought about the car he was descending toward. Raymond Hecate was not the kind of man to employ a chauffeur. Even if he was a billionaire he'd still drive himself. He'd never settled for one of those geezermobile Lincolns or Cads that other rich men in Houston drove either. His car today was an XKE. Hecate still loved it, still loved the looks it drew. But he was thinking about moving on. If every Joe Schmo ice-house clerk recognized what you were driving, it wasn't exclusive enough. Hecate was starting to think Excalibur. The trouble was if you got too exotic people might think it was one of those kits built around a Volkswagen engine.

The elevator continued to plummet. People got on and off. Half of them spoke to him. He'd give them the big grin and backslap, on automatic pilot, but he was glad when the elevator began to empty. Nearly everyone got off at the lobby, no one else got on, and the last passenger who had called him by name got off at the first underground parking level. The doors closed again, leaving him alone with his pleasant automotive thoughts.

As the elevator doors opened on his level, he took one step when the arm came from behind and the hand toward his face.

"Get the hell away from me," Hecate said irritably. It wouldn't have occurred to him to be frightened.

"Don't you even recognize your daughter?" said a voice.

Hecate realized that the hand before his face was holding a photograph. Without even looking in the direction of the voice, he took the picture and studied it. It was Carol, all right. She was blindfolded. It was too much of a closeup to pick out any details of the background. She was holding something in her hands, displaying it.

"That's today's *Chronicle*," said the voice. "You may recognize the headline."

Hecate felt an involuntary thrill race across his shoulders and down his arms. He had expected this moment since before his daughter was born. In fact, it was almost insulting that no one had ever kidnapped her before. He stayed very calm. "All right," he began. "What—"

He looked for the first time at the source of the voice and jerked back. It was the kid in the white T-shirt. His head was completely obscured by a Ronald Reagan mask, one of those that fits over the whole head. Hecate had to look up to see it. He was awfully tall for a kid. Maybe not a kid at all. Hecate didn't have the slightest memory of his face.

"Let's get away from the elevator" came the voice, muffled by the mask. He took Hecate by the arm and led him into the recesses of the parking level. Hecate jerked his arm away and marched. His face was grim. No despair in it, only determination. When they reached a wall he turned and stared into the eyes behind the mask.

"This is the only time you'll ever see me," the kidnapper said. "I'm just here to bring the message. I don't know where she is or who has her. This'll be the only contact. You do what they want, you get your daughter back: She just turns up at home one of these days. You don't, you never see her again either."

Hecate was thinking he could take him. The guy was taller and his T-shirt revealed a body that worked out, but if Hecate got in the first punch, put his fist right through this guy's belly back to his spine, it'd be all over. Hecate stood there calmly with his arms folded, letting the guy play out his spiel.

"And how much is it you want, and where?" he asked.

The mask turned side to side. "Not money. We want somebody arrested."

He handed Hecate another photograph. This one showed a stolid Asian in his fifties. The hand turned the photograph over to show the information on the back: a name, an address, more.

"Chou Lee Tang?" Hecate said. He was flabbergasted. Now he thought it was a joke. One of his cronies had put the kid up to this. Some damn Democrat, he guessed from the mask, except he didn't know any Democrats. "What the hell? Who the hell is he?"

"He's a Vietnamese gang leader. He's responsible for the car bomb that killed that couple this weekend. More too. You won't be sorry when you have him in jail."

"And what the hell makes you think I can arrange something like that?"

"Maybe you can't. That would be a bad break for both of us. Because that's the price to get the girl back."

"City councilmen don't pull any weight with the police, you know."

"Forget city councilmen." The voice behind the mask was persuasive, more a collaborator's than a kidnapper's. "If I was a man who'd lived in this city all my life, rich as Mick Jagger, and had enough pull to get myself elected to office besides, I'd have some kind of contacts that could get it done. I'd know what strings to pull."

Hecate stared at the wall for a moment. His voice came more slowly. "What happens after he gets arrested?"

"Nothing more from you. But if I was you I'd manage to take credit for it. Because after that the gang violence stops. No more Houstonians get killed. We can even provide you with evidence Tang was behind it. You think there'll be any glory in it for the city councilman who stopped the gang war?"

Hecate had a faraway look in his eye, like a bewildered man, but his mind was racing. He was on his own ground now, making a deal. Everybody comes out of it thinking he's a winner. But the big winner would be Raymond Hecate. He could see now who was behind this. Not a specific person, but he could find out. Other things aside, it wouldn't be bad to have such a man on your side in the future.

Raymond Hecate had a marvelous capacity for believing that whatever he wanted was the best thing for everyone involved. He was riding that facility now like a champion steeplechase jockey, hurtling over obstacles. He had to do it for Carol, of course. But Carol had already moved off into an alcove of his thoughts. He was thinking about his own future. The only way to end the gang violence was for one side to win it. Hecate liked winners. He was always a lifelong fan of whatever team had most recently won the Super Bowl. Of course, no one would know that he had backed this particular winner. They would just know that he had put a stop to innocent Houstonians being caught in the crossfire. And afterward he would have a line into a large, profitable subculture. Raymond Hecate knew about strings, all right.

"All I care about is my daughter," he growled.

"Of course."

"If anything happens to her, nobody'll be safe from me. Not you either, Mr. Go-Between."

"You don't have to talk tough, Mr. Hecate. Nothing's happening to your daughter. She's sleeping like a princess."

"She fucking well better be."

Raymond Hecate put the picture of Tang in his pocket and stalked off to find his car. John Loftus waited until he was out of sight, then turned the corner and opened the door of the seldom-used staircase. Beside the door was the door of a trash chute. He dropped the mask down it, straight into the furnace below. In the staircase as he climbed he opened the briefcase he carried. Inside was a white dress shirt with a tie already loosely knotted around its collar. He pulled the shirt on over his head, tightened the tie, and tucked in the tails. He slipped on the jacket from the briefcase as well. When he emerged from the staircase into the lobby of the bank, he was one of hundreds of men in downtown Houston wearing a suit and carrying a briefcase.

When he emerged onto the sidewalk Raymond Hecate raced past him in his XKE. The light was barely green behind him and Hecate was already speeding. Loftus grinned after him.

"Get 'em, Tiger," he said. He was thinking of the old man's little princess.

Thien had been in the shop for two hours and Daniel Greer hadn't spoken as many words. He watched the window like a hunted man. Thien was more than curious. Something was in the offing. The neighborhood was astir with speculation. As yet there had been no retaliation for the car-bombing of Tang's men Friday night. Khai's men had all but withdrawn from the streets. They were waiting. The curious thing was that Daniel appeared to be waiting too. But he couldn't possibly know what was happening. What did he know, or suspect? What was his role?

"Is Mrs. Greer picking you up today?" Thien asked.

Daniel whirled on him. "What?"

"Mrs. Greer. Is she picking you up today as she did Friday?"

"Oh. No. She's—already home, probably. I haven't, uh—" He gave up trying to make a sentence and just shrugged.

Thien nodded and turned away. What did this mean? It was after six, past closing time for the pawnshop, yet there Daniel lingered. He had not picked up the phone to make any calls. Thien was usually in the store in the late afternoons. He tried to remember when Daniel had not either called his wife or received a call from her before closing time.

Knowledge was the only power Thien had. He studied his world as thoroughly as he studied algebra. He knew which men worked for Khai, which for Tang, which merchants paid whom, the dates of collections. Thien's family was one of the many at the bottom of the pyramid, helpless, preyed upon. They had no champion. Thien could not be their savior—not, at least, through physical strength. But he watched, he learned. He waited for his chance to penetrate those layers above. He had been serious when he had told Khai's thug he wanted to join. He had seen no other way up.

When he started hanging around the pawnshop, he had hoped that Daniel Greer might somehow offer a solution. Now he wondered if instead Daniel had been pulled into the problem. Thien's background, while acquainting him with murder and extortion, had not familiarized him with more mundane domestic problems. Families stayed together no matter what. When he saw a worried man missing his wife Thien didn't think of arguments and separations.

He looked across the street at the other pawnshop. Linh was there, waiting, beginning to crack. He had been all through the neighborhood asking how he could contact Khai. He had begged for help. People shied away from him as if his touch were fatal. Now Linh had retreated to his own lair.

As had Daniel Greer, Thien realized.

It was dark by the time Daniel stirred himself. The world matched his thoughts. He seemed startled to see Thien.

"What are you doing still here? What'll your parents be thinking?"

"And your wife."

Daniel turned away from him to find his coat. "That's right. We'd both better be getting home."

He ushered the boy out, turned on the burglar alarm, and locked all three locks on the front door as Thien watched. The air was brisk but not brisk enough to carry away all the odors from the restaurants. The atmosphere was foreign to Daniel, home to Thien.

"Good night," they said, parting on the sidewalk. Thien looked back to see Daniel turn the corner. Thien wished he had a car.

Knowledge is power. He went to find a phone book and look up Daniel's home address.

CHAPTER 6

Carol

SHE had slept and pretended to sleep for so long she was no longer sure of the waking world. Especially when dusk filled the room so that she could no longer see its edges, she could imagine herself in a hospital bed or even the bed she'd slept in as a girl. She only half opened her eyes, afraid it would turn real.

At least her headache was gone. How long had she slept from the drug and how long had it taken for the drug's aftereffects to wear off? She could be days from home now.

She lay atop a worn coverlet on a narrow bed, on her back. Her arms were stretched up and back and handcuffed together through one of the brass rails at the head of the bed. She had already tested the strength of that rail and found it greater than her own. Later, in the dead of night, she would see if it could be loosened. For now she just lay quietly, wishing dreams would enfold her. She hadn't cried. In some ways she was her father's child. But it wasn't her father she was thinking of. It was her husband. If she did cry, it would be from thoughts of Daniel.

The door opened softly, as if he didn't want to disturb her. The first time she had seen him she had screamed. It had been twilight, like now, and he had looked like a monster. In the dim light it had looked like real flesh that sagged at his jowls and neck, real oversized teeth that thrust toward her. Not only had the man been unrecognizable, but so had his mask. She would never be able to look at Jimmy Carter again without a twinge of that first fright. She wondered if the mask was a collector's item.

"Dinner," he said. He set the tray on a night table and bent over her to unlock the handcuffs. Carol stared up at his jeans and green T-shirt. The hair on his arms was blond.

"I have to go to the bathroom," she said.

"I'll arrange it," he said. "Eat first."

That was just what he'd said the last time: "I'll arrange it." As if a trip to the bathroom required enormous preparations.

Dinner was potato chips and a sandwich, bologna on white bread. Lunch had been soup out of a can and saltines. Carol offered neither criticism nor thanks. She existed as minimally as possible, almost pretending not to be there.

The man in the mask sat watching her as she chewed. His forearms rested easily on his thighs. So far he had spoken as little as she, but there was something creepy about him. His stare made her feel her blouse was unbuttoned.

Before she finished eating he went out. By the time he stepped back into the room her plate was clean. "All right," he said, and she knew he was referring to the bathroom, because they'd done this routine already. She got up and walked toward him but he stopped her before she reached the door. He twirled his finger in a circle. Carol stood there for a moment, thinking about refusing, but what good would it do? She turned around and presented her back to him.

Being blindfolded made her feel that a silent crowd surrounded her, reaching, their fingers almost touching her skin. Her shoulders hunched inward and she was torn between stretching her arms ahead of her to feel her way and wrapping them around her chest. The man in the mask had a hand on her elbow. She resented his touch, but it was her only guide in the dark world.

After a short passage he pushed her forward and the door closed behind her. She removed the blindfold immediately. The first time she had done that she had found that he was in the bathroom with her. He planned to stay. "No," she had said firmly. "I'll turn my back," he had offered. "I can't," she had said, refusing to elaborate. Finally, reluctantly, he had left her alone in the bathroom. She had immediately gone through all the doors and cabinets. They were empty. It was like a bathroom in a cheap motel. They had anticipated her.

And there was no window. This time she didn't bother to search. When she emerged she had put the blindfold back in place. He adjusted it. He took her elbow but she stood her ground for a moment.

"Could I have a shower this time?"

Again she felt that silent crowd. She stood up straight, forcing her shoulders back. She felt his disapproval. She was causing trouble.

"Tomorrow," he finally said.

Back in her room, he removed the blindfold and picked up the handcuffs. She looked at them dully. She didn't offer resistance but she didn't immediately throw herself down on the bed either. He looked at her. It was impossible to tell anything about his expression behind the mask.

When he took her arm he pushed her not toward the bed but instead to a chair by the window. There was an old-fashioned radiator under the window. He handcuffed her to it.

"I'll give you a change of scenery for a while."

"Thank you," she said. It slipped out before she could stop it.

He nodded and picked up her tray. "I'll come back to put you in bed."

She turned away and looked out the window. As she had suspected, she was on the second floor.

"Don't scream or break anything or I'll have to hurt you." He said it matter-of-factly and even as if the hurting her wouldn't be his own idea. Carol didn't look at him. When the door closed she turned to make sure he was gone.

Khai wouldn't like that, leaving her by the window. But Khai's plans and John Loftus's did not entirely coincide. Besides, Khai would never in a million years step into that room. He planned for her to be released unharmed at the end of this, and he wanted her to have no memories of Vietnamese faces.

Loftus pulled off the mask and dropped it on the tray. At the end of the hall he saw Chui watching him.

"Here, boy, take these to the kitchen," Loftus called. Chui sneered and turned away. Loftus smiled to himself.

Her fare was simple because he made it himself as well as buying the groceries. There had been no American food in the house and Khai didn't want her fed Vietnamese. Loftus prepared her meals with tenderness, almost with love. He felt the privilege of being the only one who saw her.

John Loftus had found America too complicated when he returned to it. There were too many levels of society, people wanted too many different things. In Vietnam everything had been easy. There were only us and them. Even though some of *us* were officers and not to be trusted, they were still basically us, and though some of *them* were supposedly on our side, they were still basically bugs. You could do what you wanted with them.

Now in a sense he had returned to Vietnam. He lived in a morally uncomplicated world because for him it was unpopulated. The only people he ever saw were Vietnamese, and they didn't count. What they did to each other or thought of him were matters of indifference.

The sudden appearance of the white woman in his world was jarring. Now there was one more person in the universe. He had entered into Khai's service like a man entering a monastery, seeking to put off the burden of choices. But volition had tracked him down even here. He had to decide what to do about the woman.

Bad enough that she was white, but she was a woman as well. When he first saw her, white breasts plain in the sheer white bra, then when he uncovered her pale face, he wanted her. Lust had struck him like a blow. The sensation seemed unfamiliar. It had been years since he'd had a woman without paying for her. He liked it that way. Payment was a fine thing: It made a woman your slave and distanced her at the same time. This white woman was helpless as a slave too. Khai wanted her freed after this was all over, and untouched in the meantime. The question was, what did John Loftus want? He didn't know. Rape and romance were entangled in his mind.

He would have remained loyal to Khai if Khai had stuck to their unspoken agreement, that they deal only with Vietnamese. Now all bets were off. Khai's wishes were secondary to his own.

He walked off down the hall and the stairs, oblivious of the Vietnamese he passed.

Carol sat twisting her hand, trying to make it narrow enough to slip through the handcuff. She was doing this unconsciously while staring out the window. Wherever she was, the grounds were extensive. Just below her were porch lights that cast their glow a few feet out, but beyond that the yard was dark. Fifty yards farther out was a brick wall, stretching out of her sight in both directions. It was interrupted only by an iron-barred gate.

The grounds were thick with trees. Through their tossing branches she had an occasional glimpse of downtown. She was relieved to know she was still in Houston. But the glimpses weren't enough to tell her in what direction downtown was. She didn't recognize the street beyond the gate. If she could get to it, though, she was sure she could find her way in minutes. Once she was free it wouldn't matter. If she could get out this window and down there safely she could be over the gate in seconds. No one stood in her way.

Her decision to escape if possible was automatic. She had been treated decently enough so far but there was something about the man in the mask that worried her; something in the way he so scrupulously didn't come too close or touch her unnecessarily. He conveyed a sense of dangerous restraint.

He was not one of the ones who had attacked her in the alley. He was too tall for one, too thin for the other. Those first two hadn't been so cautious about letting her see their faces. She would recognize them again if she saw them. That worried her too. They must not be concerned about her identifying them later.

Carol assumed she had been kidnapped for ransom and that her father would pay, but that didn't mean everything would go off smoothly. Most of the kidnappings one read about seemed to end with the victim dead. If she could get away without relying on the tender mercies of her captors, she would do it.

Her skin scraped against the metal of the handcuff. She almost had it. The cuff was built to hold bigger prey. She stretched the chain to its full length and yanked her hand as hard as she could.

In the next instant she had to bite down on the back of the chair to keep from screaming. She had almost dislocated her thumb.

But she was almost free. One more yank that hard, if she could stand it, should do it. She waited, breathing raggedly. Her eyes had clouded with tears.

When she looked out the window again she started to her feet, forgetting the handcuff. A man had appeared. He was standing just outside the gate, looking in. He wore a long overcoat and a stocking cap.

Carol pushed the chair out of the way so she could reach the window. Frantically she tugged it upward, but it wouldn't budge. She reached above it, found the latch, and freed it, but the window still wouldn't move. It was either stuck too tightly for her to open with one hand or nailed shut. Either way she couldn't open it to call to the man.

She looked around her but of course there was no object

within reach with which she could break the window. She would have to use her fist.

Not yet, though. The man was still too far away to hear her words if she broke the window and called to him. He would just think someone was yelling at him to go away. He would have no way of knowing the house held a captive. And the sound of breaking glass would bring the man in the mask running. "I'll have to hurt you," he had said.

She didn't care about that, but she didn't want it to be in vain.

The man at the gate was someone who lived in the streets, she saw now. Under his overcoat were layers of clothing, probably all he owned. His shopping cart stood at the curb, filled with aluminum cans and unrecognizable junk. He stood at the gate because he was eyeing the big trash dumpster that stood inside the fence.

He would respond to a promise of money, Carol thought, if she could make him understand. Would he have the capacity to remember the address, if she sent him for the police? *Come inside*, she was thinking. *Come a little closer*.

The man had the same thought. He was studying the house now instead of the dumpster, and apparently he saw no activity there. Carol had no idea how late it was. Maybe most of those inside the house were sleeping. Maybe the man in the mask was the only occupant.

That dumpster must have looked like Ali Baba's cave to a shopping-cart man like the one at the gate. He eyed it hungrily. Abruptly he decided it was worth the risk. He reached up for the top of the gate and hauled himself up and over, landing in a heap just inside. Crouched there, he peered at the house. Carol held her breath in perfect empathy with him. The dumpster stood beside the driveway, fifty feet closer to where Carol waited at the window. If he made it that far, he could hear her call. If only he wasn't frightened into running away immediately by the sound of breaking glass. The window continued to resist her efforts. She leaned almost against it, in danger of breaking it with the weight of her body, in order to pull straight up. She tugged hard, as hard as she could. Her hand was pulled out of the slight indentation of the handgrip in the wood, breaking a fingernail in the process. The window didn't budge. Carol leaned against it, her breath fogging the glass.

She gasped. The man was gone. There was no one inside the gate. All at once she felt like crying again. She pulled back from the window so she could see better. The man's shopping cart still stood in the street outside the gate. He couldn't have gone far.

She saw him then, still inside the fence after all. He had moved faster than she'd thought possible and had reached the dumpster. He was close now, as close as he would get to her. It was time to break the window and scream that she'd been kidnapped. The man was standing right in front of the dumpster now, standing on tiptoes in order to peer inside. Carol looked around the shadowy grounds, hoping no one else had spotted the man yet, hoping he'd have time to get away once he heard her call.

That's why she was the only one to see the dogs.

There were only two of them, but that was hard to tell at first, because they were black as the night. Blacker. They were almost invisible. They ran at full speed side by side, low to the ground. The dogs were Dobermans, but they didn't remind her of her own. Ham weighed ninety pounds, he was one of the biggest Dobermans she had ever seen, but he was rather stately, well fed. These dogs were probably each ten pounds shy of his weight. There was something stripped-down about them: hot rods rather than touring cars. They were jet black but not glossy. Their fur didn't shine. Only their teeth caught the light. Their teeth seemed to emerge from darkness, standing alone, unsurrounded by dog, like the Cheshire cat's grin. It was only those teeth she saw clearly, moving through darkness, propelled by deeper darkness.

The poor old street man never heard them. The dogs moved perfectly silently. They weren't there to frighten, they were there to kill. They weren't dogs to stand at the gate barking at passersby. They were dogs to prowl the far reaches of the estate and come running when they smelled warm blood.

Carol did make a sound. She screamed. It was as much a scream of fear as of warning. It carried through the closed window. The street man looked up, alarmed by that sound but not yet perceiving that the danger was his own.

That's when the dogs were on him. The first one leaped, slamming the man against the dumpster and bouncing off. The second dog already had the man's arm gripped in his teeth. The dog didn't go for a wrist or a sleeve. It clamped its jaws around the meaty part of the forearm, like a predator.

The man was already stunned from having his head bounced off the metal dumpster. But the pain revived him. He screamed. He couldn't even see what had him. It must have felt like demons. The street man tried to regain his balance, but he couldn't stand upright because of the dog pulling on his arm. He jerked the arm but managed only to pull out of his overcoat sleeve. The dog regained its grip immediately, now on bare flesh. The man staggered. The first dog reared up on its hind legs and planted its front paws against the man's chest, knocking him back again.

Carol saw a spout of blood as the second dog's teeth found the artery inside the man's elbow. She stared helplessly. The man screamed again. Men inside the house must have heard him by now, but no one came running to call off the dogs. They could have been standing on the covered porch below her, watching. Carol had a feeling they were.

The second dog never released its grip on the man's arm. It just lunged upward for a better grip as the flesh began to shred and grow slick with blood. The other dog had the man by the leg now, jerking its head back and forth to tear with its teeth. They didn't look like guard dogs subduing an intruder, they looked like jungle animals feeding. Carol's stomach was trying to come up her throat. She looked away.

When the man went down it was as good as over, because the dogs could get to his throat then. He tried to hold one off with the one good arm he had left, but the dog bit his fingers and when the man instinctively jerked his hand away, the dog lunged straight for the throat. There was another spout of blood, darker and thicker than the first. The dog was immediately covered with it. The man got his hand around the dog's own throat and tried to grip it, but by that point the dog was stronger than the man. Cords of muscle stood out on the dog's neck. The man couldn't get a grip on the slick fur. The second dog had finally released its grip on the arm and was tearing at the man's unprotected stomach and crotch.

In less than a minute after that the man lay perfectly still, his body jerking from the dogs' pulling on it. Blood no longer pumped from his wounds.

Only then did two men finally appear. They carried rifles loosely. One called a halfhearted command but the dogs ignored him, and the men let them continue to tear flesh from the body for another minute. That was their reward. One of the men was laughing.

Carol drew back, free hand at her throat. The men were Vietnamese. With their rifles they looked like soldiers. She felt completely dislocated. Where was she? The men were part of the hellish scene. The laughing man was now pointing with amusement. Carol shuddered.

She fell into the chair, sliding down in it as far as she could, until the window displayed only night sky. Clouds had rolled in to smother the moon. Carol sat there shaking as if with fever and chills. Her hand had slipped back all the way into the handcuff as if for shelter. There was no rescue from this place. Even if she could escape the house, the grounds were lethal. And God help anyone who came in looking for her.

When the man in the mask returned to transfer her to the bed, he found her apparently already sleeping. Carol slitted her eyes to look at him as he bent over her handcuffs. He gave off a strongly masculine smell of exercise and whiskey. Already contemplating her helplessness, Carol felt positively childlike when he lifted her in his arms without apparent effort. She continued to feign sleep. He walked to the bed and held her for a long moment longer before lowering her. She could feel him still standing there. It was a relief when he lifted her arm and handcuffed it to the railing. She was afraid to open her eyes even slightly. Not until she heard the *click* of the light switch and the sound of the door closing was she sure he was gone. She wrapped her free arm around her and huddled into a ball. She was on the verge of crying herself to sleep. Some time later she was startled out of unconsciousness by the scream.

It was high and loud and painful. And it was obviously a woman's. It ended abruptly. The silence was worse. What on earth was this place? How many women had they stolen? Carol lay rigid in the darkness for a long time, eyes wide and staring and sightless. No one, of course, came to explain.

It was a surprise to everyone when the woman screamed. If her captors had given a thought to her at all, they had assumed that when she awakened she would lie quietly, trying not to draw attention to herself. That would have been the wisest course. The pain that was her future could only be hastened by her creating a disturbance. So she had been gagged, but loosely so. The scream that rose from deep inside her slipped through and around the gag barely impeded.

The scream was a thing alive. The men in the room with her were bound in place by it. The woman's scream carried such terror that the men forgot for a moment that they themselves were the cause of that terror. They thought there must be a monster in the room with them.

There was the sound of running footsteps. The men realized whom they might be disturbing. One of them, Chui, finally freed himself from the spell of her scream and leaped toward the woman. His first instinct was to choke her. That cut off the scream, after which he pressed a pillow over her face, hard, trying to bury her in the bed.

"Don't kill her."

Chui looked up and saw Khai standing at his elbow. Chui cringed. He was the one who had acted, who had improved the situation, but now by his very involvement he looked somehow responsible for the scream. He eased the pressure on the pillow over the woman's face and waited for a blow to descend. None came. When Chui looked up again Khai was no longer looking at him or at the woman. He was looking back over his shoulder at the doorway to the hall.

In the doorway stood a white-haired man, as motionless as if he'd grown there. The man stood straight, hands at his sides. His eyes were sharp. He was obviously an old man, but his face was relatively unlined. The years had sculpted rather than eroded his face. There was no excess in it. His cheekbones were prominent, his cheeks tight. The old man's character was plainly visible in his features: craftiness, command, and an inescapable sternness. It was also obvious from his features that he was Khai's father.

His appearance turned those who saw him to stone. To annoy Khai was insanity, but it was best not even to be seen by the old man. He lived in the house among them but like a wraith, seldom leaving his room, his wants attended by invisible servants. The old man seemed placid enough these days in exile, but it was well known that in the old days in Saigon bad things happened to those who displeased Ngoc Van Khai, things that proved invariably, though seldom quickly, fatal. What might displease him could not always be predicted; the part of wisdom was to stay out of his sight altogether.

The woman stirred and moaned. Chui applied more pressure and the moan ceased. Chui wished he too could become invisible, but he was the cork in the genie's bottle; if he faded into the background, the scream would be set loose again.

Khai's jaw had set. He continued to stare at the old man. If the others in the room could have seen Khai free of the patina of fear he inspired, they would have seen that he looked like a boy caught at some mischief. He didn't speak. He wouldn't offer explanation in front of his own men.

The old man didn't speak either. After a long, long moment he turned away. Slowly he passed down the hall that had emptied before him.

"Quiet her," Khai said tersely. "Now." And he hurried after his father. As he passed the door behind which the American woman was held he shot a glance at it. There was silence. Loftus was nowhere in sight.

Khai caught up to his father at the top of the stairs. They started down together. At the first landing a man came pounding up into view. He skidded to a stop, his eyes growing wide at the sight of father and son together, and he turned and ran out of sight again.

"What stupid games are you playing with the woman in my own house?" the old man asked abruptly. "Even a dog knows better than to shit where he eats."

"A mistake," Khai said. "One of the men brought her here. He'll regret it."

They spoke English, a habit acquired in Vietnam. Many of their men in the house spoke no English. Of those who did, none was as fluent as Khai and his father. When the two men spoke rapid English, tinged with the slang of the GIs from whom they'd learned it, they were incomprehensible to those around them.

"He should've already cut his own throat in fear of your anger."

"I'll take care of it," Khai said shortly.

The old man made a sound like "Hmmph," a sound of both disbelief and annoyance. Khai stopped walking, glaring at him. His father immediately added, "See you do," and strolled on.

The old man knew him so well. He knew when he made the annoyed sound Khai would stop walking with him, so he added the contemptuous sentence as a sign that he had dismissed his son rather than that Khai had stopped by his own choice. Ngoc's step was almost spry as he walked on down the hall. Khai stared after him, one fist clenched tight.

*   *   *

Khai sat alone in his study listening to Mozart, the Divertimentos, occasionally following a passage through the air with his hand. Palace music, composed for an emperor. A cup of tea had grown cold on his desk as he listened, trying to clear his mind.

He knew what his father would say if he knew that things were much worse than what he had seen. If he knew that Khai was involved with Americans now. The lure, though, had been irresistible: to rule them as he had once served them. Khai thought himself intimately knowledgeable in the ways of Americans because he had grown up being a lackey and pimp for the GIs. His father had already been a wealthy man by then, but they couldn't stop scrambling for more. Khai had harbored a secret contempt for the Americans because they never knew his true status. They treated him like just another street hustler. He'd never gotten to act the young master until he came to America. But such a pose was a mere puppet show for children unless he could wield power over Americans as well.

His cheeks still burned from the encounter with his father. The old man's scorn had branded him. Khai was perhaps a legend in the making: a legend of an emperor in exile, cast out of his own narrow corner of the world only to find a greater conquest within his grasp. But the old man was a legend already. Within the boundaries of his world he had accomplished everything it was possible to accomplish. Everyone in Saigon knew him. Even the Americans when they came had to learn to deal with Ngoc Van Khai. He was more powerful than a provincial governor. He was, in a way, the shadow government of Saigon itself. His black market was more efficient and more prosperous than the official government.

The final page of the elder Khai's legend was that when the fall finally came, when no one emerged from South Vietnam unmarked, he did. He had not only escaped, he had escaped still a rich man. He was an exile, but he lived as well as he ever had. Now he was like a collapsed star, vastly shrunk in size but with its gravity intact. The old man never left his house—outside was a foreign land he did not acknowledge—but within the house the grip of his power was absolute.

The father's secret was that in making his last, boldest move—his escape from Vietnam—he had used up all his daring. He had none left. Having lost the security he knew, he cared for nothing now except what little security he had left. He wanted no trouble. It was Khai who had been bold enough to reach outside the house, to make the family name feared once again. The thought of prison if it all failed now had hardly crossed Khai's mind. The old man's contempt was the punishment he feared.

No one would have dared cross Ngoc Van Khai in his prime. Khai must enjoy the same respect. He must inspire the same fear. The Vietnamese pawnbroker had learned that. The Americans would learn it now.

The Mozart had stopped. The music in his head had turned Wagnerian. Khai rose and went out. So soft was his tread it caused no ripples across the surface of his abandoned tea.

CHAPTER 7

Carol
in Memory

HIS house seemed so alien now. Everything seemed insubstantial, like the hastily assembled set to a bad community theater play. All cast-off, mismatched furniture and knickknacks no one would have in a home. How could she ever have lived there? He expected to touch the wall and feel it ripple—canvas nailed to a framework of two-by-fours.

And when the sun went down it seemed that the house sat all alone on a prairie where the wind whistled by unchecked for a hundred miles. Daniel made another drink and felt sorry for himself.

Carol.

It felt as if they had sent him to a motel room somewhere and told him to wait for a call. But the phone didn't ring. What did they want from him? He hadn't heard back from his mysterious caller. He wanted instructions, a plan. They could have told him to catch a plane for Borneo and he would have done it.

Carol.

She was becoming mythical to him. He hadn't quite given up the idea that she had arranged this herself, gotten a friend to call him and keep him from making an uproar while she eased away, back into her own world.

At least she was all right now. He didn't have to worry about that anymore. If it had been a random Saturday night rape or robbery, they would have discarded Carol by now, and no one would have called him. If she'd been kidnapped, as it appeared, they would take care of her as long as she was important to them.

Unless she'd been snatched by some sadist, or a group of them, with long-term lusts. Periodically Daniel would be attacked by images of Carol crying, naked, beyond exhaustion and humiliation but still alive, still in pain, surrounded by indistinct but priapic figures of men. He would shut his eyes then open them again quickly, staring at some homey, familiar object, humming to drown out his thoughts. He would have to get up and walk until the images receded. Let her be dead, he thought once. If she's not safe at least let her not be in pain.

Today he had called her office to say she was sick. They hadn't contradicted him. So she wasn't, at least, going about her normal life. It wasn't only his own life that had fallen off track. He was frightened both for Carol and that he had done something wrong. Should he have told the cop about the phone call? Did the cop already know?

He made another drink. How long would this go on? He'd had to drink himself to sleep the past two nights. Without it he just lay there, the darkness an endless movie screen of horrible images. Last night he'd let Ham inside to sleep on the floor by his bed. Another warm creature to make the house seem more real. But he'd forgotten the dog was there and when he got up in the middle of the night he stumbled over him, scaring the hell out of both of them.

He heard the wind sliding by the windows like some stealthy beast. He didn't have the stereo or TV on, of course. That would interfere with his listening. Daniel longed for the sound of footsteps along his sidewalk, a furtive knock on the door. Gunfire would have been satisfactory. At least if he was attacked he would know he hadn't been bypassed. He could do something then, something other than drink and pace and hum to drown out the images.

By midnight time had stopped its jerky stops and starts and smoothed out into a powerful nightflow that swept him past one o'clock and toward oblivion. He could sleep now. He stumbled down the hall, liquor making the house feel almost whole again.

Daniel dreamed, but it was more than a dream, it was a memory of a scene that had actually happened about two years earlier, reproduced with perfect clarity and precision. At some level of consciousness, though, he knew he was only dreaming; tears streamed down his face as he slept.

"I'm sorry. Maybe I shouldn't have sprung them all on you at once."

He was sitting behind the wheel of his car parked in front of her parents' house, sulking. Carol had opened the passenger door and leaned in to apologize. He kept staring ahead for several seconds.

"I shouldn't have been so abrupt," he finally said.

He had just been introduced to her old friends en masse. Sometimes a newcomer meets a group and is absorbed into it so fluidly it seems the group had felt his absence even before they knew of his existence. All of them, newcomer and old group, suddenly feel themselves complete, old friends waiting to happen.

This had not been one of those occasions.

Carol slid into the car and closed the door. He had waited a full minute to see if she'd follow him out. The car was running but he hadn't put it in gear. It was poised at the top of the circular driveway, and the cobblestones seemed to itch to be rid of it. Tires this worn had never sat on this driveway before.

She said, "They don't really intend to be mean. It's just that they feel awkward too so they have this—*manner* they fall back on."

He considered that. "I guess I do too."

She nodded. "You act like an asshole."

"Hey! Is this your apology?"

"You know what I mean. You start acting more bumpkinish than you really are."

Did she really know him that well, so soon after they'd met? "Thanks for the vote of confidence," he said. "How do you know, maybe I really am."

She smiled at him and moved a little closer. "Maybe you are. But you also start acting superior, like under the cloddishness you have some secret."

He looked at her. His arm was extended along the back of the car seat toward her. "I do," he said.

She had a knowing smile, as if she shouldn't ask the question but couldn't help it. "And what's your secret?"

"That the best woman there loves me."

He said it lightly enough that they could laugh their way past it, but he wanted the bantering to end then, and it did. Lying in the bed alone, Daniel was crying like a five-year-old with a run-over puppy. In the dream-memory Carol came into his arms. "I do," she said.

As he held her he looked past her at the imposing brick front of her parents' house that rose up two stories with an angled dollop on top that could have been another half story or just architectural filigree. White columns made the house look even more imperial. That had been another mistake of Carol's, having him go here to River Oaks, the richest neighborhood in town. Houston was Daniel's city but he felt like a tourist here, gawking at the houses. But her parents were out of town, she'd said, and their house seemed like the best place to have the party introducing him to her friends. When he'd gotten there it had turned out her parents weren't just out of town, they were in Europe, where they went annually. That had somehow made it worse. He'd gone immediately into his tough-kid-from-the-gutter routine. He was entitled to it, he'd grown up in a neighborhood where these pansies would have locked their car doors as they drove through, but from his stance one would have thought he'd just battled his way out of Hell's Kitchen. It was true her friends had treated him a bit as if he'd come into the room pulling off work gloves and tracking manure on the carpet, but he'd asked for it.

Who cared about them, anyway? He wasn't engaged to them. He kissed Carol. She responded. They broke apart after a while and sat there as if they were driving down the highway. "The butler can clean up without your supervising, can't he?" Daniel asked.

Carol put her hand on his leg. "Let me just go in and say good-bye."

"Good. All the jerks'll swoon with envy."

"You overestimate my allure," she said, almost demurely.

No, he didn't. He'd seen men looking at her at the party. He wondered how many ex-boyfriends she had there. As she walked away, back toward that damned beautiful house, he was overcome by his familiar fear, that once she got inside with her old friends the joke would be over. He'd sit here like a dope waiting to see her again but never would. She turned to wave at him and he smiled back, but guardedly. When the door slammed behind her he was sure he'd never see her again.

That sound of the door slamming was the only thing in the dream that was real, that was contemporary. His subconscious mind had found the memory and assembled the dream in a split second in order to explain that sound and keep him dreaming. It was the sound of his own front door slamming back against the wall.

The noise woke Daniel anyway. Wind filled the house like men rushing down the hall toward him. He lay and waited. When nothing happened he got up and walked boldly down the hall to the living room. Moonlight made the room ghostly. The front door stood open. He walked to it and looked out. Wind howled down the street. There were no lights in the houses. His car and Carol's stood in the driveway, cold as iron.

He not only had forgotten to lock the door, he hadn't even closed it fast. When the wind changed direction the door had blown open. Wind was the only caller. Daniel stood in the doorway and looked at his empty yard. No wife, no attackers. No comfort of any kind. The dream covered him in tatters. He remembered the way he'd felt then, and he thought he knew the way Carol had felt, the day he'd met her snotty friends and she had come away with him. They had been in love then. He remembered the triumph of that feeling.

Damn it, they were *still* in love. Daniel was holding the front door, gripping it so hard his fingers tingled. He had been in a daze ever since Carol had vanished, but the daze burned off now, there in the dark doorway. He thought of Carol. If it was this bad for him, how much worse must it be for her? Her kidnappers had made a fool of him, thinking they could keep him quiet forever with one phone call. And he had been hampered by ignorance, by not knowing whether Carol had vanished willingly or been taken. But now he knew, and he was going to get her back. No matter what he had to do—whether he had to be charming or devious or pay money or kill someone— he was going to get her back.

"Khai may be evil," Thien responded to his father, "but he is here. He is a fact. If the sun was evil, does that mean its rays would not fall on us?"

"To join him is not the answer. To become one of his—"

"That is the only way he can be dealt with. If I—"

"No! He can be lived with, like a season of bad weather. He does not dominate our lives."

They were seated over dinner at the kitchen table. Thien's mother and sister kept their eyes lowered, as if by not seeing they could be not present.

"He will not pass like bad weather," Thien said. "Can we beat him?" He paused slightly longer than one does for a rhetorical question, but then answered it himself. "No. Then we must deal with him."

"Not this way. Not by offering up my son like a sacrifice." At first the voice of Thien's father had been authoritative. Gradually it had shifted to persuasive. "You have prospects. You can leave here, go to university. You can become someone who never has to worry about such petty tyrants as Tranh Van Khai."

"Leave here forever, and leave all of you behind to suffer under him? Besides, there are always Khais, everywhere."

"Father. Before one can prosper one must survive. The best way to survive this neighborhood is to be one of them."

"You are too smart," said his father.

"If I am smart I can rise so much the faster. I can become his right hand. And I can protect all of you."

Thien's father rose. For a moment he looked more like the army officer he had been than the clerk he was. "What makes you think we would accept help from one of his?" he said, and put down his napkin and walked out.

Thien squeezed his mother's hand. "It will not be a question of accepting," he said quietly. "When I am in position help will come like the rays of the sun."

He went out, closing the door softly, defying his father as unobtrusively as possible. It was past dusk. He walked the streets boldly, as if he owned them already. He wanted to call attention to himself.

The neighborhood of the pawnshops was empty. On week nights the restaurants closed early. There might still be dishwashers inside, but customers had long since departed. In Linh's pawnshop a light still burned. What was the old man doing—collecting fingers, trying to reassemble a wife? Linh was the foolish opposite extreme from Thien's father. He had thought Khai could be defeated through mere defiance. But defiance without power was suicidal babbling. Linh had discovered that. Now he wanted to go back to being a sheep like all the rest of them, but it was too late.

Daniel Greer's pawnshop was dark. The American's situation was puzzling. Last night Thien had taken a bus to Daniel's home address and through careful spying had discovered that though there were two cars in the driveway, there was no wife in the house. Where was she? Both pawnbrokers were missing

their wives. It made sense that Khai was behind both disappear-
ances. But what did he want from Daniel Greer?

Thien was standing on the corner, leaning back against the
brick wall, watching the American pawnshop as if it would open
to reveal its secrets. He stood too long in the dark. An arm
snaked around the corner from behind him. Before he saw it the
arm's hand was around his neck, and Thien was yanked around
the corner.

There was another one there. They threw him up against
the wall, the back of his head cracking hard against the bricks.
Tears sprang to the corners of his eyes.

Khai's two men laughed when they saw who it was. "Past
your bedtime," one of them said.

"Lost in the street, little boy?" said the other.

"What are you doing here?" Thien asked. They looked at
each other, wide-eyed at his audacity.

"Making a delivery," one of them said, showing a small
wrapped package. Thien stared at it.

"Making a delivery where?" he asked.

"You don't know?" said the shorter Saigon cowboy, the
rougher one, the one who had held his neck. "Doesn't everyone
in the neighborhood know?"

Linh's then. For a moment Thien had thought it was a
package for Daniel.

"Take me back with you," Thien said. "I must talk to Khai."

"Khai?" They laughed at him again. "Children do not work
for Khai," said the taller one. "Khai eats children for breakfast."

"I don't care about his perversions," Thien said, startling all
three of them. "I want to offer my help. I can help him."

They were amused. "How?" the taller one asked.

He didn't know. His tongue raced faster than his mind.
"Tang's men. Won't they strike back any time now? I can
infiltrate them. I can find out—"

"Tang." He had amused them again. "Tang is a sick old dog
in the gutter. Soon he will be washed into the sewer."

If this wasn't an empty boast then it was news. Thien didn't take time to absorb it. "The American pawnbroker, then. Khai wants something from him. I can get it. I can find out—"

Now he was boring them. "What could Khai want from the American?" the shorter one asked. The taller one was already turning away.

"Come," he said to his partner. "We must get back."

"I'll come too," Thien said, falling in step behind them.

Casually, without even looking back, the shorter one back-handed him across the face. Then the man must have thought the satisfaction was worth doing the job properly. He turned and drove his fist deep into the pit of Thien's stomach. The boy bent over, gagging. Khai's man pushed him aside, tripping him. Thien's head hit the wall again and he fell to the sidewalk.

"Come," said the taller one again, so the other left off, grinning. "Good-bye for now, little brother." He spat.

Thien heard their footsteps pattering away. He couldn't see, he couldn't breathe. By the time he could the two men were long gone. Thien lay on the sidewalk looking up at the starless sky. The pain had turned to warmth. The sky was the face of Khai's thug.

"When I am your master," Thien said aloud, "you will owe me both your balls. And I shall have them."

One memory kept recurring to Daniel. When he had asked the faceless voice on the telephone how much money they wanted for Carol's return, the man had almost chuckled. "You don't have enough," he had said. That phrase kept running through his mind. "You don't have enough." "You don't have enough." He tried to squeeze every drop of inflection out of the memory. You don't have enough money.

But he knew who did have enough.

"No, I wouldn't care to have a seat," he said to the receptionist, and walked around her desk.

Behind him she was saying "Sir? Sir!"—her voice changing from puzzled to hostile in the space of two words.

He opened the heavy oaken door with the brass nameplate and saw Raymond Hecate reaching for his phone. The phone was buzzing frantically.

"That's your receptionist telling you a wild-eyed intruder is bursting in."

Hecate looked at him absolutely blankly. Then he picked up the phone and said, "No, that's all right. I know."

Then he came around the desk, all hearty joviality. "No sense scaring the help," he said, extending his hand. "How are you doing, Danny? Have a seat, have a seat. What brings you downtown?"

Daniel extracted his hand from the larger man's grip. "Carol," he said simply.

Hecate looked blank again. But Daniel had known him just long enough to realize that Raymond Hecate's blank looks didn't mean no one was home. They meant Hecate had drawn back, mind racing through his options. Mentally he was a sprinter rather than a marathon man. He tended to find his first acceptable option and stop.

Daniel decided to help him along. "They haven't contacted me again so I figure they must have talked to you."

"Who's 'they'?" Hecate asked. He had retreated behind his desk. Daniel was sitting in front of it.

"If I knew that I'd have gone to the police by now," he said.

Hecate looked relieved, but he probably didn't realize it. He thought he was the master of his face, not realizing how often it turned transparent.

Daniel had been watching for that look of relief. Now he knew he was right.

"Do you know where she is?" he asked.

Hecate wasn't giving up anything yet. He touched his tongue to his upper lip and said, "You mean she's left you?"

"Hope springs eternal, right, Ray? No, I mean somebody took her. Somebody who called and told me to sit tight while they dealt with you."

That was a lie but he was trusting Hecate wouldn't know it. He was right. Hecate didn't look relieved or blank again. He returned to bluff heartiness.

"Then why don't you just do that, son?" He came out from behind the desk and put his hand on Daniel's shoulder, drawing him up from the chair. This was certainly the first time Raymond Hecate had ever called him son. Daniel didn't thrill to the sound. "This really doesn't even involve you, you know. I'm sorry it's had to worry you, but it'll all be over soon and Carol'll be back safe and—"

Daniel shrugged off Hecate's hand and involuntarily glanced down at the top of his shoulder to see if it had left a stain. "You don't understand. I *am* involved. Even if they don't want anything from me. She's my wife."

Hecate was disconcerted. Having some pissant raise his voice to him when he was being charming was probably the most startling thing that had happened to him since the turn of the decade. "Now look, Dan. I know you're upset. But there's just nothing you can do about this. You'd be gettin' in way over your head."

Daniel was staring at him icily. "Like I did when I married her, right? But you've already tried to undo that and she wouldn't have it."

"I never—"

Daniel rode over him. "Maybe I'm not one of those preppie dinks you would have picked for her. One of those dull rich boys she had too much life and too much nerve to settle for. If you weren't one of 'em yourself you'd've seen that."

"You better watch your mouth, boy. I ain't so old or worn out that I—" Hecate's face had reddened right up to the roots of his hair.

"Listen." Daniel leaned close into his face. He could feel the man's breath coming hot and faster. "I worked my way *up* to pawnbroker. In the neighborhood I come from that was like minor royalty. It was like bank president. I can always go back to what I was. You and whoever has her better remember that."

Hecate pushed him away. Just like kids on a schoolyard. If

there'd been anybody in the room observant enough to see
Daniel's eyes narrow and his hands curl, he would have thought
that Hecate had made a bad mistake. But Hecate himself was too
headstrong. He didn't notice anything but his own rage.

"You little wormy piece of shit! Do you think you have any
place in this? You think you could do *any*thing for her? This isn't
pawn tickets. This is about *power*. And you don't figure in it."

This was the breaking point. It was going to be tough to
smile at each other across the Christmas turkey after this. Daniel
was exhilarated. His nerves sang the way they had in those
moments just before someone threw a punch.

"One way or another I will," he said.

Hecate's anger was still mounting. "You've already done
enough," he shouted. "If she'd stuck to her own kind—" He
abandoned that tack and stepped forward and poked a finger
toward Daniel's chest. "If *you* had the sense to get out of a losing
proposition, she'd still be right here."

Daniel waited. Hecate bit off whatever else he was going to
say. He turned away and went back behind his desk. Daniel was
sorry to see him back off.

"You have to let me help," he said. "I don't have your
money, but—"

"This isn't about money," Hecate said. He sounded weary
all of a sudden. Rage was more exhausting than a fast game of
racquetball. His heart was beating him. "And there's nothing
you can do. Can you just take my word for that? They told you
to stay out of it. Now I'm telling you too. If you fuck it up you're
only going to hurt her."

Daniel stared at him, but Hecate wouldn't even look back.
He wasn't going to get anything more here. He turned on his
heel.

That roused Hecate. "You hear me, boy?" he called after his
son-in-law. "Stay out of it."

Daniel rode down in the elevator feeling himself pulse.
Other people got on and off but they seemed like robots, lacking
body heat. The cool wind felt good when he passed through the
lobby doors.

He had been cut out of this scheme by both sides. But they were wrong. They would have to deal with him.

He hadn't expected Hecate to tell him anything outright but he had hoped that if he got him mad Hecate would let something slip. And he had. At least Daniel hoped so, because it was the only thing he had to go on.

If Carol had stayed with her own kind, Hecate had said. Daniel had taken that to mean his marriage. If Carol had stuck with her own kind and Daniel didn't own the pawnshop she'd be safe now. Because what did Daniel and his business expose her to?

The Vietnamese.

Not the pawnshop itself but the neighborhood. And who ruled the neighborhood? Who would be ruthless enough to do this?

He had to find Tranh Van Khai. Daniel strode down the sidewalk to his car. He had a purpose. He might have to hurt someone to get to Khai, but that didn't matter. He didn't really care if he made a mistake.

CHAPTER 8

In the Garage

THE house still felt forlorn. Worse than that, it was fragile. Daniel wasn't sure why he went back there after his visit to Raymond Hecate's office that morning. It was as if he wanted to pick up Carol's scent again. He sat in the quiet living room and felt cold, hard thoughts. The immobility was good for him. It made things come clear.

It was Khai, of course. Carol wouldn't have gone this way unless she had no choice. Khai was the one who left people no choice.

He knew what he had to do now but he needed a retreat. He might need a fallback position. This house was certainly no fortress. Wondering what he could do to fortify it, Daniel wandered into the kitchen and looked out the window. Ham was sleeping in the sun. He roused himself as soon as Daniel's hand touched the doorknob. When Daniel stepped out the dog was all over him. Daniel rubbed his ears. Ham went bounding away joyfully. Rudolph, the furry white dog in the house behind Daniel's, was standing at the fence barking and Ham stopped in front of him, only the fence separating them. Ham and Rudolph had reached an accommodation long ago, but for the moment they forgot that. They pranced back and forth on stiff legs barking and growling at each other.

Their barking set off other dogs in the neighborhood. This was a suburban subdivision, where the crime most pervasively on people's minds was burglary. Everyone had a dog. There were dogs in the yards on either side of Daniel's too. They ran back and forth beside their own fences, barking and growling. Daniel stood watching them. He surveyed the domain of his backyard and thought about what equipment and tools he had in the garage.

After a few minutes he set to work.

She realized the house was swarming with Vietnamese. In two more visits by the window she had seen nothing else, including a blade-thin man who seemed to be their leader. Carol had seen him only once but the impression had been strong, both on her and on the lounging men on the porch who stood straight and silent when he passed.

She didn't know how many she had seen because few were distinctive enough in appearance for her to tell them apart from her second-floor perspective. They made her skin crawl. Seeing them made her think she had been transported far away, out of her world into someplace alien.

At first her new knowledge made her more fearful of the masked man who brought her meals. But she had seen his arms, she had studied his hands. He was white. The only other besides her in the whole house, as far as she had seen. He hadn't said much to her, but he went out of his way to give her as much freedom of movement as possible. He always lingered longer than necessary, waiting to see if she had other requests. He kept reassuring her that she would be all right.

She realized now why he had to blindfold her to lead her to the bathroom. They didn't want her to see that her captors were

Vietnamese. That meant he was defying them by letting her sit near the window. She made sure to keep her head down so she wouldn't betray him. She wondered what would happen to him if they knew.

Carol had begun to entertain the theory that the man in the mask was a captive himself. Of course he had more freedom than she, but perhaps not much more. She hadn't seen him pass through the front gate. Maybe his presence there was as unwilling as her own.

Her world had narrowed down to that room, the view from that window. It had been days now. Her hope of rescue was beginning to dwindle. But at the same time her hope that she had an ally here inside the house was growing.

She looked forward to his visits.

This was taking too long, Loftus thought. He stood in the hall outside the bathroom door listening to her shower water fall. The droplets were trickling down her skin. Thin streams would course across her torso, sliding and turning. Her head was thrown back in pleasure at the contact. Her hands moved down her body, soap making them slick. She stroked herself with the only pleasure she knew these days.

Loftus had pulled off the mask but even without it he was sweating. He had thought about drilling a hole through the bathroom wall, but it was unnecessary: his imagination supplied all the details. His hand was on the doorknob. He thought, as he did every time, about opening it sooner than she expected. He pictured her startled look, her frozen pose.

But it wasn't good enough. That was a twelve-year-old's thrill. Loftus was contemplating much more. This is taking too goddamn long, he thought again. What do they expect, leaving me alone with her for days? The consequences were going to be on Khai's head. And if it ruined Khai's plans, who gave a shit? Loftus was ready to bolt this gook nest anyway. If she cooperated he might take her along. If not . . .

She knocked when she was ready. Steam moistened his skin when he opened the door. Hers was damp as well. Her hair was wet but combed, hanging straight to her shoulders. She stood straight and passive, the blindfold already in place. He took her arm and steered her out. She laid one hand on his. A door in the hallway opened and Loftus glared at the Vietnamese, who drew back.

He would put her on the bed, probably, for now. He liked her handcuffed to the bed, but he also liked to release her so he could see her move. He wished she had something sexier than those jeans and blouse. She must be tired of the dirty clothes by now. Maybe he could suggest she give them to him to wash. She could stay naked under the covers until his return. Maybe he would suggest that right now. And maybe he wouldn't leave her room for a while.

Carol felt again that sense of vulnerability as he guided her, sightless, down the hall. She stayed close to him. When she heard the door close behind them she sighed with relief. Like being home again. She waited for him to tell her she could move. Gratefully she raised her hands to the back of her neck.

When she took off the blindfold she gasped. He had removed his mask.

"Have you heard of a man named Tranh Van Khai?" Daniel said musingly, almost to himself.

Concentration kept Thien's head from jerking at the sound of the name. He turned slowly. "Of course," he said. "Everyone has."

That confirmed what Daniel suspected but had recently been denied to his face. He had just completed a short tour of the block around the pawnshop. Some of the merchants recognized him, but their faces went blank again when he asked his question. The Vietnamese waiter who had originally told Daniel about Khai had vanished, and no one else would even admit to having heard of the gang leader.

"Where does he live?" Daniel asked Thien casually, as if they were only exchanging neighborhood gossip.

"No one knows," Thien said solemnly.

"What?" Daniel looked closely at the boy. He had thought everyone else was lying to him, but he didn't expect it from Thien. There was a glaze over the boy's features. If he was lying he was lying, there was nothing Daniel could do about it. But Thien's next words convinced him, after Daniel said, "He doesn't give parties, people don't go to his house for—for . . ."

"No one knows," Thien repeated. "He does not entertain. He has messengers for anything else. People do not go to his home. Or if they do they do not return." Thien looked across the street at Linh's pawnshop. It was dark that afternoon.

They both fell silent. Thien was the first to notice the length of the silence. He looked at Daniel, who was lost in thought.

After long minutes Daniel returned to the world. He realized what he was staring at through the plate-glass window of the shop. The two Saigon cowboys were back at their post across the street. The two who had accompanied him on his trip around the block without ever drawing closer and without ever turning away. Earlier he had noticed the restaurateur to whom he was speaking glance past him and shake his head all the more emphatically. The cowboys leaned against the wall now, knife-edged, casually confident of their dangerousness.

Of course someone knew where Khai lived. And someone would tell him.

"He is going to the police."

The cowboys whirled, startled. Thien had come up behind them. One immediately pinned him to the wall. "You want to die?"

"He is going to the police," Thien repeated calmly, and

indicated with his head. "The American. He has decided Khai has his wife and he can't find her himself, so he is going to go to the police and let them find Khai's house."

"Is he on the phone?" the taller man hissed, turning to survey the shop.

"He won't telephone," Thien said. The shorter man had loosened his grip, and Thien pulled away. "They put him off on the telephone before. He is going to go to the station and find the police detective he knows is working on the disappearance. The pawnbroker wants to go with him when he looks for Khai."

Khai's men talked to each other in low, hurried tones. They were not original thinkers, but luckily their instructions covered this eventuality. The taller one noticed Thien listening. He pushed the boy.

"Go away."

"Remember I told you," Thien said. "Without me you wouldn't have known." He paused a moment longer. "You will need a car."

"Think we need your guidance?" the shorter one shouted, starting toward him.

The other pulled him back. "Get the car," he said.

Thien's smile disappeared as soon as he turned his back on them. He hurried away.

It was the first of December. Christmas decorations were up downtown, green wreaths in a city that stayed mostly green through the winter anyway. The tinsel was drab in the daylight. To Daniel it looked like failed American voodoo, a pitiful attempt to ward off the current recession. Shoppers didn't come downtown anymore.

Traffic was heavy, though. That was a constant. The Saigon cowboys in their metallic blue compact Ford had fallen three cars behind Daniel's brown Toyota, but they still had him in sight. Daniel turned onto Franklin and headed for the freeway. Behind him the Vietnamese didn't make the light. They turned anyway, through a blare of horns. Daniel's window was down. The air was crisp and a wind was beginning to stir. He heard the tinkle of bells and flags snapping on their staffs. His scalp was tingling. He turned again. This time he was the one running the red light, in front of a wave of cars. The Vietnamese had to stop for that. One of them was leaning out his window, keeping Daniel's car in sight. He didn't care about that, he just wanted distance between them. He needed time to complete his preparations, begun this morning. He was headed home, and he assumed the Vietnamese knew where he lived. He was counting on it. He was counting on their continuing to follow him even after it was clear he wasn't going to the police station.

He beat them to his house, but he didn't know by how long. He parked in his own driveway and leaped out. The afternoon was still sunny but the wind was stronger now. A cold front was blowing in; leaves hung suspended in the air, caught in the conflicting currents. Daniel raced inside his house, slamming the door behind him but not locking it.

He plunged through the house. Table legs and bookshelves clutched at him. The air seemed to be thickening, as in a nightmare where forward motion becomes impossible. He had brought home the gun from the shop but he didn't want to use it. Gunfire wasn't part of his plans. Neither was anyone getting killed. That was what hobbled him. He didn't want to kill the Saigon cowboys. He didn't know their intentions.

His keys were still in his hand. He ran into the kitchen and unlocked the deadbolt on the back door. When he opened it Ham was standing there curiously. He had sensed the motion in the house and was quivering with eagerness to be part of whatever happened. Daniel ran toward the back fence with him. The dogs in the surrounding yards watched them curiously.

A minute later Daniel was back inside his house. It was quiet except for the sounds of his heart and breath. He felt the quiet extend throughout the neighborhood on this weekday afternoon. He felt like the last survivor of a silent holocaust. Children were in school, husbands and wives at work. Here and there along the block might be a sick adult home alone or a mother with very young children, but not in the houses near him, he knew.

He was startled by a knock at the door. That was the last thing he was expecting. The door exploding off its hinges he was prepared for, but this polite tapping made him jump.

He would be a fool to approach it.

But he did, hand stealing into his jacket pocket. If the door burst open now—

He crept up to it and peeked through the peephole. An exasperated sound escaped him and he yanked the door open.

"Thien! How the hell did you get here?"

"By the bus," he said calmly.

That was barely possible. Daniel had stayed around the shop long enough for the boy to get well away before he had left, dragging the cowboys in his wake. Then he had veered and slalomed through downtown, leading them in circles before running away from them. If Thien had been lucky in his connections, there had been time for him to take a bus here. But he wouldn't have put it past the boy to have hidden in the back floorboard of his car.

He stood on the porch with his hands folded in front of him, looking at him placidly, as if he had paid a formal call and were waiting to be invited in. Daniel looked at his unlined face. But there was something no longer childlike about Thien. He could have been a little old man wearing a child mask.

"You must be crazy," Daniel said. "Don't you know you could get killed?"

"Then we are both crazy," Thien said.

My God, the kid thought it was an adventure.

"Go home," Daniel said, taking Thien's shoulder and trying to turn him around. The boy resisted without unfolding his hands. There was surprising strength in his thin body. "Get out of here—"

"You may need a translator."

"I won't! I just need you out of here! When those two get here—"

A metallic blue compact Ford pulled to a stop at the curb.

"Shit," Daniel said. Only then did Thien turn. He looked at the two young Vietnamese emerging from the car. Even that left him unstartled. Daniel's fingers were gripping his shoulder convulsively but he didn't flinch.

"Get inside!"

Daniel pulled the boy in and turned him toward the back of the house. Daniel was still in the doorway. Turning his head so the Saigon cowboys could hear him, he shouted, "Call the police!"

That was roughly the phrase he had planned to use to set his scheme in motion, and it worked as he had planned. The two young men had hesitated, but at the threat of police they started running toward him. The scheme was working brilliantly, except that he hadn't planned on having Thien in the middle of it. The boy was pattering softly toward the back door, looking back at him. The two Vietnamese thugs were young and strong and quick. Before Daniel could even turn they were halfway across the front yard toward him. Guns had appeared in their hands.

Daniel ran through the house. Thien was short and vulnerable and in his way. Behind them, the front door stood open.

As Daniel went out the back door with Thien he heard the Vietnamese come storming in the front. They were running flat-out now, they had lost all caution. Daniel stood on the edge of the backyard, looking around frantically for a hiding place, but as he knew—as he had planned—there was none. There were two trees in his backyard, but they were pines, two or three times as tall as the house. They were unclimbable, the lowest branches high over his head.

The overhang of the roof was much closer. With only a word or two Daniel linked his hands together and Thien stepped into them. Thien's hands clutched at the edge and Daniel practically threw him up onto the roof.

"Climb over the top," he said. "Jump down on the other

side." He had no time for further instructions. He was still standing next to the open back door himself.

A moment later the two Vietnamese came running through that door. One skidded to a stop but the other kept coming, toward Daniel who stood alone in the middle of the yard. The one who had stopped looked around suspiciously, but the other could see there was nothing to impede him. The American wasn't even holding a gun. He was just standing there, looking frantic. Dogs barked in the surrounding yards, jumping up against the fences, but there was no dog in this yard.

The grass in the backyard was overgrown. The running Vietnamese stepped on a pinecone underfoot and lost his balance momentarily as it slithered out from under him, but then he ran on.

He wasn't ten feet from Daniel when he pitched forward and slammed headfirst into the ground.

Daniel had no occasion to grin at how perfectly that had worked. That was one of the two traps he had arranged this morning when he realized others might come to the house after him. In the shin-high grass of the backyard he had strung a water hose, anchoring it with the tree trunks and croquet stakes. Hidden by the grass, he had counted on it tripping up anyone who ran too eagerly.

But only one of the men had gone for it. The other was still back near the door, his gun pointed in Daniel's direction. The man was nodding slightly, congratulating himself on his foresight. He began walking slowly toward Daniel. And the other one was already up on his hands and knees, recovering from his fall. He hadn't lost his gun either.

Daniel had lost hope that his other trap would work. He had counted on the men being disoriented when he sprang it, and preferably both of them being on the ground. The second man looked too grim and purposeful to be deterred by what Daniel had left. But he had nothing else. He yanked hard on the wire he held in his hand.

There were dogs barking in the yards on either side and the yard behind Daniel's. One of those dogs was Hamilton Burger.

Daniel had lifted him over the fence into the yard behind theirs, where Rudolph, the furry white dog, lived. Ham and Rudolph were both standing with their front paws up on that fence now, barking furiously. Ham was a big, fierce-looking dog, but against the guns Daniel had known the Vietnamese would be carrying he would have been no protection alone. But—

Daniel yanked on the wire and the fences fell down.

That's how it looked to the two Vietnamese. Actually only one section fell out of each of the fences separating Daniel's yard from the others. But those sections were enough. The dogs who had been barking ferociously and jumping against the fences suddenly found no obstruction between them and the intruders. They came racing toward the men from three directions, scrambling for traction, growling low in their throats.

This plan didn't work as well as Daniel had hoped either, and again it was due to that one damned cautious Vietnamese. The other one, the eager one, had regained his feet but did just what Daniel wanted. His eyes grew wide and fearful at the sight of the charging dogs. He started backing up as fast as he could, and he tripped over another section of the hose. He went down harder, and this time he stayed down. There was a dismal thud as the back of his head hit the ground.

The other one stood his ground. He was still close enough to the house that he knew he could reach the door if he had to retreat. The charging dogs weren't as fearsome a sight to him as Daniel had hoped. One of the dogs, a big black Lab who had apparently seen a handgun before, refused to leave his own yard at all, even with a gaping hole in the fence confronting him. He stood there whining and indecisive.

Rudolph came bounding gleefully forward, but he stopped at the body of the fallen Vietnamese and nuzzled it curiously. That left only Ham and the dog next door still advancing on the other cowboy, and the dog next door was only a twenty-pound terrier, yapping fiercely but hardly life-threateningly. The standing Vietnamese ignored it and leveled his gun at Ham.

"NO!" Daniel screamed. He fumbled frantically at his

pocket for his own gun. The Vietnamese glanced casually toward him but still had plenty of time to fire, and did.

The sound of the gunshot was not terribly loud, but it was unfamiliar. A sharp metallic *crack* ending with a solid beefy *thump*. Daniel screamed again. He ran forward and fell victim to his own trap. He tripped over the hose and went down, his gun's muzzle jamming into the soft ground.

The bullet had gone into the ground, missing Ham, but it stopped him short nonetheless. He was a smart animal, he knew something dangerous had just happened. And though he was big and had a ferocious growl, he was no trained attack dog. At the sound of the shot he backed away, puzzled and whimpering. So did the terrier.

The Vietnamese smiled and wasted no more attention on them. He advanced slowly on Daniel, watching carefully where he placed his feet, and leveled his gun again. It was a real cowboy's gun, a revolver. He cocked the hammer back. Daniel could only stare. His own gun was a useless lump of metal, mud clogging its barrel.

There was a sudden noise in the air like a buzzing bee. The Vietnamese put a hand to his cheek just as if a bee had stung him. That's what it had felt like. He glared at Daniel, thinking the American had sprung one last trap, but Daniel looked as puzzled as he. Hope hadn't appeared on his face either. He was still waiting to die.

There was another pain, this time on the back of the cowboy's neck. There was a thump, gentle as a love pat, but it carried another sting. He turned curiously.

Daniel saw it before he did. Thien was still on the roof, throwing pinecones. The roof was always littered with them this time of year. They fell in bunches from the trees.

Pinecones are light and airy, but studded with pinpricks of wood. Stepping on one was painful. Being hit by one was worse.

The Saigon cowboy turned and caught Thien's next pine-cone full on the nose, blinding him for a second. But only a second. The pain was only a nuisance, nothing disabling. He could see again before Thien had time to rearm himself. The boy was scrambling along the edge of the roof like a monkey, but he had no shelter, and he was little more than ten feet from the cowboy. He was an easy target. The man shouted something at him in Vietnamese, but when Thien ignored the order he raised his gun.

This time the thump on the man's back was much heavier. It hit between his shoulder blades and made his chest arch forward and his hands fly up. His shot went harmlessly into the air.

Daniel had thrown the .45 automatic. As a firearm it was no longer any use at all, but as a projectile it was a fine size and weight for hurling. Daniel was back on his feet and barreling forward when the gun struck. The Vietnamese was turning but Daniel got there first, throwing himself into the man's legs.

It would have been an illegal block, but it was a great tackle. The man went down in a heap. Daniel was on his feet again at once. He was exhilarated, blood racing through his limbs. The threat of death had brought him alive. Ham was bounding toward the fray again too, now that his master was directly threatened.

But the damned Vietnamese had never dropped his gun. Even while falling back he had only clutched it tighter. He was on his back now but he still had it. Daniel was standing over him but the dog was coming faster. The cowboy was deciding which to shoot first when the bundle came down on his head. At first Daniel thought Thien had thrown his clothes at him from the roof just above. But no, it was Thien himself, hurtling through the air. He landed with a thud on the man's head and almost at once let out a howl himself.

Daniel snatched the gun from the Vietnamese's nerveless fingers and picked Thien up. His howl had subsided. He was rubbing his arm fiercely.

"Hit my funny bone." He moaned.

He had thumped it, it turned out, on the bridge of the cowboy's nose. The man was out cold. For an instant Daniel felt like laughing hysterically, but the feeling died out before the laugh could rise in his throat. There was still ugly work to be done.

He gathered up the guns and went to repair the fences. He didn't want neighbors coming by to make inquiries.

He tried to send Thien away but the boy wouldn't go. When it became clear that Daniel's only option was to push him out the front door and let him stand there knocking while he worked, Daniel let him stay, which turned out well.

Not only did the cowboys not speak English, they wouldn't talk at all.

Daniel set up shop in the garage. The two men lay on the cold cement floor with their feet tied and their hands tied behind their backs, but their mouths ungagged.

"Tell them to scream if they like," Daniel said to Thien. "No one will hear them. No one would help them if they did hear."

He had no way of knowing if Thien was translating correctly. The boy's piping teenage voice didn't have the right threatening tone in any event. The men looked completely unmoved by whatever Thien imparted to them.

The garage was dim. There was one light at the far end, over the washing machine, rather than directly overhead. There were openwork beams above. An aluminum ladder hung on one wall. There was a workbench in the corner, and the hammers and saws hanging on pegs above it gave the place the vague but appropriate look of a torture chamber. Daniel needed a fire of glowing coals with a branding iron heating in it. He already felt a little absurd. He tried to keep his mind on Carol.

"All I want is Khai's address. They'll tell it to me sooner or later, so they might as well do it now while they're undamaged."

He saw a flicker in the eyes of the man who had almost shot him. Khai's name had done that. Otherwise his expression stayed flat.

The other one, the one who had gone down on the back of his head, still looked dazed. He didn't appear to be paying attention at all. Daniel stood over him until the man looked up, then he dropped to his knees on the man's chest. The cowboy's eyes brightened.

Thien translated, more than one sentence. Daniel held the man's eyes as the boy spoke. This one wasn't so good at the neutral expression. His eyes widened.

"Understand?" Daniel said again. No reaction. He slapped the man's face twice, forehand and backhand.

"Understand?"

The man nodded. The back of his head thumped the cement floor lightly.

Daniel was getting mad. That was lucky. It would make things easier.

"Just the address," he said, speaking so intently he thought the cowboy could understand. Thien spoke quietly in the background. The man turned to look at him and Daniel slapped him again. "Just the address," he repeated. The man nodded again but didn't speak until Daniel raised his hand, clenched into a fist.

"He says he doesn't know it," Thien said quietly.

Daniel stood up. His face was suddenly hot. He kicked the man in the side. It wasn't a hard kick, just an attention-getter, but the man groaned and rolled onto his side. Daniel used his foot to roll him back onto his back, put his foot into the man's stomach, and leaned a little weight on it. "Try again," he said.

The man gasped, tried to speak, and started choking instead. Daniel eased up on the pressure. He kept his foot in place, though. When the man began to get his breath back, Daniel leaned down again.

"Of course you know. And you know you'll tell me."

The man's eyes were pleading. "He says Khai would kill him," Thien said.

"What can he do to you worse than what I will?" That was the wrong question, though. When Thien translated it it caused the man's attention to wander. Daniel drew it back with another kick, but the man looked less fearful now. Of Daniel.

Daniel kicked him again, leaving him gasping. Behind his

back, the other Saigon cowboy was speaking to Thien. Daniel
left the one he was working on.

"What did this one say?"

"Nothing," said Thien, but there was a touch of color in his
cheeks. He was sitting on an overturned bucket in a corner of
the garage. The boy glared at the taller of the cowboys, who was
staring daggers back at him. Daniel stood between them.

"You are in no position to threaten anyone," Daniel said.
Thien's voice translated. It seemed he added something of his
own.

Daniel continued: "The smarter one of you will tell me what
I want to know, because that's the one who'll live."

The man just stared up at him; not cockily, not calculating;
just waiting to endure. Daniel was starting to feel frustrated.

He let the man watch him while he walked slowly to the
workbench and selected a screwdriver from several mounted on
pegs on the wall. The one he finally chose had a straight edge
and a heavy yellow plastic handle. He walked back to the taller
Vietnamese, holding the screwdriver by the blade and thumping
the handle into his other palm.

He knelt, holding it like a short sword now, the blade close
to the man's eyes. The blood that had erupted from the man's
nose when Thien landed on him had dried on his upper lip now
into an ugly brown mess. It made the man's face look even less
flexible. He didn't flinch away from the screwdriver's blade.
Slowly Daniel lowered the tip until it touched the man's cheek.
He trailed it slowly along the skin until he reached an ear. Still
the man didn't jerk his head away.

I would be wetting my pants at this point, Daniel thought.
The anger had seeped out of him. He felt disgusted with
himself.

He put the tip of the screwdriver's blade into the man's ear.
The man closed his eyes. Daniel pushed the blade a little
deeper.

"How long before I hit something that can't be repaired?"
he asked, and Thien translated. Daniel's voice had softened.
Thien's was the same quiet tone it had been from the beginning.

When the screwdriver met resistance Daniel just held it there. He couldn't bring himself to push it farther. He tried again to think of Carol, but that was too theoretical to justify this. He thought he could bring himself to kill them if he saw them hurting her, but this was too dirty.

He pulled the screwdriver out, reversed it, and thumped the man's forehead with the handle. The cowboy's eyes opened.

"Think about this," Daniel said. The man's eyes remained locked with his. Thien was translating, but the man watched Daniel as if he could understand English. Intelligence gleamed in the man's eyes, which made Daniel hopeful.

"There are two of you here. One of you will tell me where Khai lives." There was that same flicker at the mention of the name. Daniel talked on. "When you do, I'll let you go. You can go wherever you want. Out of the state. Out of the country. Khai will never find you. The other one, the one who doesn't tell me—I'll take him with me when I go to Khai's. Tied up in my car, like he came along to give me directions. Whatever happens to me after that, Khai will have him. Understand?" He looked over at the first Vietnamese, who had rolled on his side and was listening. "If you talk, you're free. If you don't talk, Khai will think you did."

He stood up. He hoped he was keeping his face stony, but inside he was melting. Take this deal, he begged silently. It makes sense.

The two men looked at each other. The shorter one, the one who had gone down on the back of his head earlier, spoke quietly and jerked his head at Thien. The other answered shortly. Daniel stepped between them. "It's a race now," he said. "This offer is only good for one of you. The other one gets fucked."

This was supposed to be a torture session, he thought, and instead I'm bargaining with them. He was still disgusted with himself. He couldn't win.

The taller cowboy licked his lips, but that was as close as either of them came to speech. *What the hell has this Khai done to them?* Daniel wondered.

The shorter one had an ugly expression. He was talking to Thien. Daniel looked at the boy for the first time. He had been sitting so quietly in the corner that Daniel had begun to think of him as a disembodied voice. He saw Thien listening to the cowboy, running his hands uncomfortably along the tops of his thighs.

Abruptly Daniel was mad again. He was furious.

"All right, God damn it! I'm just gonna kill this one. Then I'll talk to you!"

His words were aimed at the taller man, the one who seemed to be in charge. Daniel couldn't even hear if Thien translated. Blood roared in his ears. He hauled the other cowboy to his feet and drove his fist into his stomach. The man doubled over, almost falling on his face with his feet hobbled and his hands tied behind his back, but Daniel hauled him upright again and smashed his fist against the side of his face. This time Daniel let him fall to the concrete floor. He took two short steps and kicked him hard in the stomach. The man's mouth was open, he was probably making some sound, but Daniel couldn't hear. He pulled the little bastard half off the ground by his shirt front and punched him again.

Outside the wind had risen. The cold front was rushing upon them like a monster. The sky would have darkened by now and the air turned heavy. There was a dim crack of thunder far in the distance.

Daniel bent over the man he was beating. This was the man who had been dazed by the fall on his head, but he looked alert now.

"You're dead," Daniel told him. "You're just going to be an example for him."

There was no responsive murmur of translation. He looked around and saw that Thien was gone. He didn't blame him. He didn't need him now anyway. The two Vietnamese knew what he wanted. They could write the address on the concrete floor in dust or blood. He suspected that at least one of them understood English anyway.

"Understand?" he screamed at the fearful man below him. "It's too late for you!"

He punched him in the side of the face again and the cowboy's head slapped satisfyingly against the cold concrete. *Scream*, Daniel thought. *Do me the favor of screaming*.

He rolled the Vietnamese over onto his face and grabbed his bound hands. They were white and limp, but the man gasped when Daniel grabbed them. Daniel pulled the hands up toward the man's shoulder blades. There was a faint tearing sound that could have been clothing. A moment later the sound was lost as the man did scream. Daniel lifted him by his arms, bouncing the man's forehead on the concrete. He went on screaming, high-pitched, miserable. Outside the wind roared like an angry giant coming to the rescue of its child. Daniel was grinning fiercely. He grabbed two of the man's fingers and twisted them around each other. The scream changed pitch and took on a sobbing quality. It was perfect. He couldn't have hired an actor to make more fearful sounds. Daniel glanced at the taller Vietnamese out of the corner of his eye.

The man was watching him with academic interest. His eyes were open but not wide. He didn't flinch. No sweat stained his face.

Daniel abruptly ran out of steam. He didn't change expression but he suddenly felt hollow. He was a bad actor in a play he knew was lousy.

He turned the cowboy over onto his back. The man was still sobbing but now that sounded fake too. "The address!" Daniel screamed into his face. The man stared at him stupidly.

Daniel turned him back over and clawed and jerked at the ropes, untying his hands. The rope parted. The man's hands moved limply. Daniel stood up, kicked the man back over onto his back, and strode back to his workbench. He picked up a hacksaw. The teeth looked tiny and vicious. There were rust stains on the blade.

Daniel went back and stood over the cowboy, one foot on each side of the man's waist. The cowboy was rubbing his hands together. He looked up at the saw and past it to Daniel's face. He froze. Even his eyes didn't move. They looked like brown marbles in his head.

"Khai's address," Daniel said softly. "Last chance."

There was no response. The man looked up at him absolutely idiotic with fright, but it was as if Daniel hadn't even spoken. They were not communicating, and that wasn't simply a matter of Daniel's having lost his translator. They might have been from different planets.

Daniel reached down and grabbed one of the man's hands. It was moving feebly but the man offered little resistance. His arms were probably numb from the rope. Daniel gripped the arm between his knees and pulled one finger free of the rest. The index finger.

"One finger at a time," he said. "Until you talk or bleed to death."

He held the index finger as tightly as he could with his left hand. He was anticipating the resistance, but the man still almost jerked free when Daniel touched the saw blade to the base of the finger. But Daniel held on. He stared down into the man's eyes as if trying to hypnotize him. Again he brought the blade into contact with the finger. This time the man's whole arm stiffened, but he couldn't pull free. His mouth was wide open but he wasn't screaming, at least not in a tone Daniel could hear. The man's head flopped back and forth in frantic negation. Daniel gritted his teeth and sawed.

One of them screamed but he didn't know which. Maybe both. The wind was too wild outside for the sound to carry, but it filled the garage.

Daniel tried to think of Carol, but that only made it worse. It was as if he had joined in the conspiracy of torture that included her as a victim as well. They would retaliate against her for whatever he did. Besides, no matter what was happening to Carol, she would be horrified if she could witness this scene. She might never touch him again.

When he struck bone he quit. He couldn't make himself go on. The blade wasn't even a quarter of an inch into the finger, but it took all the strength Daniel had left to pull it free. Blood and gristle clung to it. Daniel dropped the saw on the man's chest. Blood was flowing freely, but the damage was minimal. The man had stopped screaming and was whimpering instead. He sucked on the finger like an injured child.

In the cool of the garage Daniel felt tears on his cheeks. He couldn't bring himself to look at the other Vietnamese. He knew he'd still be watching him with that look of detached curiosity. He knew the man would watch without changing that expression while Daniel sawed off every one of his partner's fingers and fed them to him. Empathy was a concept neither of the Vietnamese could grasp. Damage to one was only a TV show to the other. As for the one Daniel had been torturing, he knew for a certainty the man would never tell him anything. He was terrified of what Daniel might do to him, but he didn't even seem to understand how to stop it. Khai had an unshakable grip on him so fundamental death wouldn't unlock it. Daniel could saw him to pieces and he would die with that same puzzled, fearful expression on his face. But without opening his mouth.

I'm sorry, Carol. At the thought of her, rage stirred in him again. He would go back to work on the men. He'd kill them if he must. But the feeling of hopelessness had emptied him.

He finally looked at the second man, the relatively undamaged one. Time to work on him. He had an intelligent look Daniel hoped would mean heightened self-interest. It was a tiny hope.

Daniel looked at the man, who was still lying on his back, humped upward because he was lying on his bound arms. The man's eyes glittered. For the first time his expression had changed. As Daniel watched the man's tongue peeked from his mouth like a worm fearful of birds, and wet his lips.

The man didn't even notice Daniel. He was staring into the corner, where Thien had returned to his post on the overturned bucket. Daniel hadn't heard him leave and he hadn't heard him come back in. Thien was sitting there not looking at anyone, concentrating on what he held in his hands. In one was a butcher knife he must have gotten from the kitchen. In the other was a croquet stick, one of the stakes Daniel had used to anchor the garden-hose trap in the backyard. Black dirt still clung to the stake where Thien had pulled it from the ground. The croquet stick was brightly painted with bands the colors of the croquet balls, orange, black, green, yellow. One end of it was a blunt point that Thien had sharpened with the knife. The fresh wood exposed by the sharpening gleamed palely in contrast to the rest of the dirty stake. Thien was working on the other end now, sharpening it to a point as well. It was this sharpening process the second Vietnamese was watching with such interest. Thien didn't return his stare. He turned the stick over in his small hands—a solid length of wood a foot and a half in length and maybe three-fourths of an inch in diameter, now with a gleaming skewer on each end—and began sharpening the other end again. Both ends of the stick looked wickedly sharp.

Thien glanced up at the Vietnamese watching him and said something that caused the cowboy to draw his legs up a little. Daniel had no idea what the boy had said, but he felt a tightening in the pit of his own stomach in response.

"Thien? I thought you'd gone. What are you doing?"

The boy didn't look at him. Neither did his audience. The other Vietnamese, Daniel's victim, was craning his neck to look around Daniel's legs and see what Thien was doing. His half-severed finger was forgotten. His expression looked almost hopeful, as if Thien had something he wanted. He was half in shock, his responses inappropriate.

"We will need more rope," Thien said.

Daniel stood staring at him. Thien's voice was flat and not at all childlike. His voice had deepened slightly, but that wasn't what made it adult. It was the hardness and the clipped words, the unwillingness to waste speech. It was the way a dying man would speak if he had something important to say.

He looked up at Daniel, who hurried to find rope. Thien's eyes were old as well.

"First tie that one's hands behind him again," he said when Daniel had the rope. "Tight. We have to lift him by them."

Daniel didn't know what that meant, but he obeyed. The cowboy offered no resistance to having his hands retied. His

finger had almost stopped bleeding. When Daniel pulled the
rope tight a large blister of blood oozed sluggishly out.

Thien was still sharpening the stake, slowly. The pieces of
wood he was whittling off the point now were no bigger than
splinters. The point held the fascinated stares of the two
Vietnamese until Thien spoke again, when their eyes moved to
his face. He spoke in Vietnamese but Daniel nonetheless
strained to hear. Thien lifted his eyes but he was staring into
space at a point between the two Saigon cowboys. His attention
seemed to be fixed on something else. He seemed to be in a
trance state.

The man below Daniel started shaking his head again.
Thien's stare suddenly shifted to the other's face. Daniel had
been wrong about the trance state. Thien's eyes had a grip. The
taller Vietnamese licked his lips again. His forehead was oily.
Thien spat one last syllable at him and he flinched.

He lifted the stake and with the butcher knife clipped off
the very tip. The stake still came to a point, but a duller one.
The unhurt Vietnamese started saying something. Thien ignored him. He spoke over the supine cowboy's voice. It was a
moment before Daniel realized Thien was speaking English.
The boy explained what they were going to do. Daniel glanced
upward at the open rafters of the garage, wondering if they
would support a man's weight. That was the only question in his
mind. He didn't question Thien's instructions.

The garage door shook in a gust of wind. No one paid it any
attention. Daniel set about following Thien's directions, which
took only a matter of two minutes. He threw one end of the rope
in his hands up over a beam. The image was very Western. It
lacked only a noose on the end of the rope.

The taller Vietnamese began speaking. Daniel glanced at
him, but the man was obviously talking to Thien. Though he
spoke Vietnamese he kept his voice low. Thien was not looking
at him. He was studying the points on his croquet stake. The
man's voice grew in confidence. Daniel glanced at Thien. Color
was growing in the boy's cheeks.

Daniel returned his attention to the man whose hands he

had just retied behind his back. He pulled the man's bound feet up behind him as well and tied them to his hands, so the cowboy was bent like a bow. The man started babbling when Daniel tied the knots, but Daniel knew it was just pleading, it wasn't the information they wanted. Daniel felt almost cheerful. No, that wasn't it. He didn't feel anything. He was just an employee, a man going about a task that had little to do with him. He tied the end of the rope hanging over the beam to the rope binding the man's hands and feet, working with emotionless efficiency.

The other man was still speaking. His tone was angry now. He was lecturing Thien like a parent. Thien was standing over him holding the sharpened stake. The cowboy's voice faltered and stopped as the point of the stake touched his nose. Thien suddenly moved with blinding speed, pulling the stick back and swinging it down like a golf club. He swatted the side of the man's face once, leaving a red line from his ear to his chin. Thien's face worked furiously as he barked at the man in Vietnamese. It was the first emotion the boy had shown. The man on the ground kept his eyes closed and his face turned away from him. He didn't speak again.

The other cowboy gasped when Daniel hauled on the rope. The beam overhead creaked. It worked like a pulley, but with more drag on the line. The prisoner skidded across the floor until he was directly under the beam, then Daniel put his back into it and the Vietnamese rose off the ground. He went up backward, face down toward the ground. Words spilled out of him. Daniel put the rope over his shoulder and walked away one slow step at a time, lifting the Vietnamese higher. The man couldn't have weighed more than a hundred and fifty pounds, he wasn't that much of a burden. Daniel stopped and turned back. The man was about four feet off the ground, still babbling. There was a louder *crack* from the beam above.

A piece of two-by-four jutted out of the garage wall next to where Daniel stood. He had nailed it there to hold coiled garden hoses, but it was empty now. Daniel wrapped the rope around it a couple of turns and it held. The Vietnamese dangled like a piñata. Daniel bent at the waist to look him in the face and grinned.

"You know, I don't even care if this works or not. The fun is in the doing."

Thien had picked up the other man's feet and was trying to pull him. The cowboy was kicking at him. Thien dropped the feet, picked up the stake, and held its point against the man's throat. He pushed it until the man gagged. When Thien picked up his feet again the man didn't resist.

Daniel didn't offer the boy any help. It was Thien's show. Thien dragged the Vietnamese along the floor until the man was beneath his partner. Daniel almost laughed as the picture made him think of preparations for some elaborate sex act. The two Vietnamese were face to face for a moment three or four feet apart, but the dangling one was spinning slightly and they fell out of alignment. The one on the ground was still lying on his bound arms, so he was bowed slightly upward, as if offering his stomach for sacrifice. The one above was bowed downward. They were mirror images.

Thien leaned over the one on the ground and pulled open his jacket and shirt. Buttons popped and rolled on the concrete. The man's stomach was very bare. He looked pot-bellied, like a child. Thien had dragged him through a small patch of oil, which had somehow released its smell. The air smelled oily and sweaty, like an auto repair shop. There were bits of grass in the man's disordered hair.

Thien held up the stake, close to both men's faces, but he didn't seem to notice that. He was examining both points. He found the one he had dulled slightly and held it against the belly of the man on the ground, an inch above his navel. Soon he would have two. The man tried to squirm out from under the point, but he couldn't move without pressing it harder into his stomach. Thien held it there, gripping the stake with his fist like a child about to choose which side got first bats in a baseball game.

"Now," he said.

Daniel loosened the rope from its turns around the two-by-four and slowly let it play out through his fists. The dangling Vietnamese came slowly down. His shirt was hanging open too, its wings parted like curtains so that as he came down they hid the stake from Daniel's view. Now the scene looked like a magic trick: the Vanishing Stake. Daniel put more pressure on the rope and lowered the Vietnamese even more slowly. He could still see the point pressing into the stomach of the man on the ground. Thien was kneeling, holding it in place, looking up to position the stake against the other man's stomach as well.

The man on the ground suddenly groaned, and Daniel saw the point press harder into his stomach. The dangling Vietnamese had come down on the other end. The other point. The dangling one screamed. The pressure was only enough to hold the stake in place between the men, not yet enough to puncture. Thien took his hand away and the stake stayed in place. He nodded in satisfaction, as if he were trying a science experiment at home and it was working as well as it had in the classroom.

The one on the ground turned his head and said something impassioned to Thien. The boy smiled.

"He says he can't tell us anything if he's dead."

Daniel smiled too. He was no longer the one doing the bargaining.

"One will die first. The other will have time to talk," Thien said. He didn't bother to translate the remark into Vietnamese. He too must have suspected the cowboys understood English. Or maybe he had already said it to them in Vietnamese.

Thien's and Daniel's smiles had been brief and fierce, like flinches. They hadn't seen how much the expressions made them look like wolves. There was no amusement. The man on the floor groaned again.

"Lower," Thien said.

Both men started babbling. Thien didn't bother to translate, so they weren't saying anything important. Daniel spread his legs wider for balance and let the rope in his hands inch upward. The babbling turned to gasps, then screams. Neither man was hurt yet. Their screams were too healthy. They were trying to suck in their stomachs. Daniel had seen that, Thien as well. But there wasn't much more slack. The point of the stake was pressing deeply into the stomach of the man on the ground, making no puncture yet but a deep, deep dimple. There wouldn't be much more give to his skin.

"Wait," Thien said, and Daniel tightened his grip on the rope.

The boy bent and examined the stake again. He looked like a baby engineer inspecting a drilling shaft. Maybe that image was suggested by what he did next. He put a hand on the leg of the dangling man and pushed. He started spinning, slowly. His scream soared in pitch.

When his head came around Thien grabbed it, stopping his spin. His small hands on the cowboy's cheeks, he held the man in place, staring into his eyes. Thien spoke earnestly to him. The man was beyond reach, though. His eyes were crazed. Thien set him spinning again.

"Lower," he said again.

Daniel barely let the line play out this time, but it was enough. There was a small but distinct *pop*, a sound he would remember. The dangling man abruptly stopped screaming. He sucked in air futilely. The man on the ground was staring pop-eyed up at him. The dangling man had stopped spinning, embedded in air almost face to face with his partner. He was choking now, his face darkening severely. A spasm went through him. Daniel felt it through the rope.

The dangling man made one more horrible, gurgling sound and vomited blood. It spattered on the concrete and the face of the man below. And the dangling man went completely slack. No more struggling, no more sounds. He was just dead weight.

"Lower," Thien said again.

The man on the ground gasped out two syllables. Daniel held the rope steady. That man had the duller point pressing into his own stomach, but it was pressing deep. It must have been very close to puncturing pressure too. When he drew in breath to speak his face contorted. His eyes were open wide, the only light in his blood-drenched face. He said a sentence to

Thien. Daniel could tell what he was saying: Get him off me and I'll talk. Thien shook his head.

The light in the boy's eyes had gone flat again. He showed not a trace of excitement. Daniel was sweating. The rope was growing slippery in his fingers. The smell of oil and blood in the garage made his nostrils flare. He glanced up and saw his lawn mower in one corner of the garage. It looked like a completely alien piece of equipment, maybe even a living creature.

Thien hadn't spoken. He wasn't negotiating. Perfectly still, he looked somehow as if he were flying through space, set on a course no one could stop. The man on the ground looked up at Daniel, appealing. Daniel just stared back.

"Lower," Thien said.

The man on the ground spoke in an utterly defeated voice, almost no breath supporting his words. Two lines of sweat or tears had parted the bloodstains on his cheeks. After he spoke he turned his face away.

"Lower," Thien said to Daniel, urgency straining his voice.

Daniel held fast to the rope. "He just told you, didn't he? Khai's address?" He had heard the street name in English.

There was a long pause. "Yes," Thien said.

Daniel lifted one foot and set it against the dangling man's side. He kicked him aside, letting the rope slide as he did. The two Vietnamese twisted and pulled apart. As the dangling man fell to the ground, the stake pulled out of him and fell on the concrete floor. The two lay there motionless, the sounds of their breathing very quiet.

"Tell me," Daniel said to Thien.

"We can't leave them here alive. They'll warn him."

"Tell me the address," Daniel said more loudly.

"You'll need me," Thien said in the same low voice, looking at the two men on the floor.

"Not for this."

The wind howled outside. The cold front was seeping under the garage door, robbing the room of its heat. The sweat had already dried on Daniel's face.

"Six-twelve Shamrock," Thien said abruptly.

Daniel knew the street. Montrose. It was such a varied area the address could be a mansion or a shack.

He was already in motion. His gun was still in his jacket pocket. He slipped the jacket on as he ran for the door.

"Call the police," he called back. "They won't go anywhere. Call the police to come get them. But don't tell them where I went. You don't know anything. You just arrived and found them. Understand?"

He raised the garage door overhead, emitting the peculiar yellow light of a darkening winter day into the garage. The scene he looked back on was bizarre to him. He had already put aside the emotions that had made it seem reasonable. He was thinking about Carol again. His mind was racing ahead.

"Understand?" he said again.

Thien nodded.

He slammed the garage door down and ran for his car. He had told Thien to call the police, but it didn't even occur to him to try to enlist their help for what he was about to do. He had the gun and he knew where his wife was. His initial squeamishness over the torture of the two Vietnamese had disappeared like a childhood memory he hadn't thought of in years. He knew he could do anything he had to do now.

His car's engine roared into life, barely louder than the wind. Rain hadn't started yet but it was coming. He backed out into the street in a screeching curve and went racing away.

Back inside the garage, Thien stood still. Daniel's instructions about the police had passed over him like a breeze.

The two cowboys were conscious. They had fallen with their heads close together. He heard one of them murmuring to the other something about dogs. Thien thought they must be talking about the dogs that had come at them in Daniel's backyard.

Their voices stopped when he stepped between them. They turned to look up at him. Thien looked like a giant standing over them. The light was returning to his eyes.

"Have I impressed you?" he asked softly.

The taller one spoke angrily, gesturing with his head and his bound hands. Thien knelt suddenly and gripped the white hands. The chatter ceased.

"We are not done yet," Thien said.

CHAPTER 9

Khai

KHAI sat alone in his study, waiting for too much. He was waiting to hear that his rival had been arrested. He was waiting for the regular report from his men who were watching the American pawnbroker. There were no indications that his plan had gone awry, but there were no indications it was proceeding either. The beauty of the plan was that once it was set in motion, it required no tinkering: no more contact with the parties, no chance to reveal his own fine hand at work. But the beauty of the plan was making him impatient as well. He wanted a sign. He wanted to take a personal hand. He was tempted to go up and have a look at the American woman himself, just for reassurance value. That she was in his hands was the only tangible sign of his genius. He wondered fleetingly if he should kill her now, dispose of her body. Then there would be no sign at all of his involvement, yet the plan would proceed apace.

His mind drifted. He allowed himself to feel contentment. But his restless thoughts lit on the other rankling note in his life:

his father's scorn. Khai thought, not for the first time, how much sweeter life would be if the old man were dead.

But before that happened Khai wanted his father to live to see his son control a greater empire than the old man had ever dreamed existed. It would happen. Khai would make sure of it.

His hands were clenched again. Calm, he thought, and consciously relaxed. Anyone watching would have thought him the picture of serenity.

Daniel drove slowly past the front gate of 612 Shamrock. The address had been chiseled into the brick fence beside the gate. The numbers were fading now, sinking back into the stone from which they had so grandiosely emerged. The big house seemed to be fading too, back into its shelter of trees and lawns, as if the past had too firm a grip on it to let it emerge fully into the present day.

Montrose was an enclave of elegance gone brittle with age only two or three miles from downtown, almost in the shadow of the tallest towers, but it tenaciously clung to its own identity. That identity was linked to a day when Houston was a much smaller and more identifiably Southern city. Here and there in the streets of Montrose was a wrought-iron-festooned, magnolia-bowered cottage that would have looked at home in New Orleans' garden district. The streets of Montrose were narrow and tree-laden: not the pines of Daniel's neighborhood, but more spacious and sheltering oaks and elms. In some places their branches spread all the way across a street. The trees might have been designed to hide the inhabitants from watchers in those downtown towers.

Some of the homes under those trees had been kept up for years, some had been restored, and a few had taken a long slide toward ruin, turning into stopovers for rats and transients, traps for children. Khai's mansion hadn't turned into one of those, but it looked as if it might have been barely rescued from such a fate.

It must have been elegant in its day, but its day was fifty years past. Daniel stared at it from the street and wondered if the Saigon cowboy had lied to him, just plucked an address at random. Then as he watched, the front door of the mansion, fifty yards inside the fence, opened and a Vietnamese man emerged onto the wide verandah. He was a young man wearing matching khaki pants and jacket that made him look like a soldier. He carried a rifle.

Daniel drove on, following the curve of the tall brick fence. He had the right place. He hadn't seen a guard at the front gate, but that had been no butler coming out the front door with a rifle. There was no sense, then, going in the front way. He had to slip inside unobserved and capture Khai himself. Then he would force them to bring Carol to him. That was as elaborate a plan as he had made. All it called for was stealth and luck and a willingness to shoot people who got in his way. He could do that. The rage he'd felt in his garage when balked by the Vietnamese hadn't ebbed away. It had solidified into a determination to do whatever he had to do. And the torture in which he'd participated had made more vivid for him what they might have done to Carol—might be doing to her now. He was no longer humming to distract himself from the images. They played like a horrible drive-in movie across Khai's house and fence.

He drove halfway around the fence and parked. He was glad the grounds were so extensive; it would make it easier for him to sneak up on the place. When he stepped out of the car, the .45 dragged down the right-hand pocket of his jacket. He had cleaned mud out of the gun hastily at stoplights along the way. On the street he took time to break it open and peer through the barrel at a streetlight.

Night had fallen during the short drive from his house, a night lurid with storm. Thunderclouds had closed around the city like curtains. Rain was almost on them. The wind carried it. He felt a patina of moisture on his face as soon as he was out in it.

The brick fence was tall, but its top was within his grasp

when he leaped. He pulled himself up and crouched for a moment atop the fence. In spring he couldn't have seen the house from there but this was December, the trees were bare, and the house was visible through their tossing branches. Daniel realized how big the mansion was, how many men its rooms could hold. For a moment he thought he should call the police instead, that Detective Rybek. But police would be no good. They'd need a warrant to get in. Police would only alert the people inside to kill Carol and dispose of her body.

The loudest crack of thunder yet split the air. Daniel looked back over his shoulder. One of the downtown towers seemed to be falling. But it was only an illusion caused by the swaying trees. Daniel turned back, dropped to the soft ground inside the fence, and the towers were abruptly lost to his view.

The Dobermans were standing near the kitchen door of the mansion, staring intently. They had been lounging there for an hour, but now they were pacing and quivering. It was past their feeding time. They had been forgotten. The dogs didn't know time, they only knew hunger. When their food was late they had no faith that they would ever be fed again. If they had been ordinary dogs they would have been whining for attention, but their training had been powerful and cruel. They remained silent.

One of the dogs suddenly turned away from the door. Its ears stiffened into even sharper points. The storm wind had been carrying a rich array of smells, but now one stood out clearly. The dog bared its teeth.

The other Doberman turned too, nostrils flaring at the scent of an unknown man. It smelled like fear and, more than that, like food. The smell converted the animal's hunger to fury.

The dogs went loping away into the grounds of the estate, black as the wild night, almost invisible except for their gleaming teeth that rent the air like lightning flashes.

* * *

Daniel scurried from tree to tree, staying hidden behind their trunks, but after a few minutes of that he felt melodramatic. There was no one around to catch a glimpse of him. The stormy night was cover enough, and it had also apparently driven any guards inside. He wasn't going to have any trouble until he reached the house itself. He stopped trying to sneak up on the place like a commando and instead just ran, watching the ground, concentrating on not tripping or twisting his ankle. He felt curiously sure of himself.

The dogs ran silently. They never barked or growled. That had been beaten out of them when they were puppies. Their job wasn't to threaten, it was to kill. Under normal conditions they were quiet enough, but tonight under this roaring wind their steps were as soft as the patter of raindrops. A rabbit wouldn't have heard them coming.

The lead dog was two or three steps ahead of the second one, a matter of less than five yards. They were trained to work in tandem, but that didn't mean simultaneously. One always attacked slightly ahead of the other, his attack startling the prey and throwing it off balance, the second dog then attacking without impediment, drawing the first blood. The order of attack wasn't a matter of training, it was a matter of desire. The dogs competed.

Now the lead dog put on even more speed and drew farther ahead. Suddenly he had caught a whiff of something other than prey. He smelled blood. There was already blood on the intruder. And blood meant food.

The dog caught sight of the prey. The man was a few yards ahead, running slowly and clumsily, his back to the Doberman. The man obviously smelled nothing and heard nothing. In another moment the lead dog would be on his back, bearing him to the ground and getting the man's neck in the grip of its teeth.

And then the dog smelled something else, something it had rarely smelled this close. It smelled another dog. More than that: another Doberman. The smell was on the man but not of him. For an instant the dog smelled only this other dog, a challenger on the lead dog's own territory. Such a challenge demanded response, and the dog made it. Years of training gave way before millennia of instinct. A few short yards from the intruder's back, already bunching its muscles to leap, the dog growled.

Daniel heard the growl, piercing the wind, rising as if from the ground itself. His response was primitive. The hairs on the back of his neck stood up. His spine stiffened. The low growl sounded not only inhuman but like no beast he had ever heard. He expected a reptilian claw to fall on his back; the earth had opened to emit a monster.

The gun was back in his pocket. He hadn't wanted to hurt himself with it as he ran.

He whirled, too late. The dog was already in the air, muscles straining to reach him. Daniel couldn't even see what it was before the animal was upon him. He saw only teeth and black fur. Daniel screamed.

The Doberman's front paws struck his chest and scrabbled for traction. The teeth came for his throat.

The force of the dog's pounce saved him temporarily. Daniel went straight over backward. He grabbed for that fur as he went down, got one hand around the dog's own throat, and fell back. Instinctively he curled up into a ball. That brought his legs up under the dog's body. As Daniel's back hit the ground he kicked. The dog hadn't managed to get a grip on his throat, or anywhere else. Daniel fell out from under it and the dog kept flying, from its own momentum and the force of Daniel's kick. Daniel landed flat on his back and the dog went flying over him.

The sky broke open. Rain fell in a solid wave. Daniel's hair was immediately plastered to his forehead, falling into his eyes. The ground turned to mud and slick eels of grass.

Daniel spun onto his stomach, trying both to rise and to see the dog coming back at him through the rain. His hand slid along the side of his jacket but for a moment he couldn't find the pocket.

The second dog landed on him with the full force of its eighty pounds, all muscle and claws. It felt like a sack of hardware had been dropped on Daniel's back. His face was pushed back down into the ground. This dog wasn't off balance, and Daniel had no leverage to throw it off. The second dog's job was to sink its teeth into flesh. It did. Its jaws clamped down on the back of his exposed neck. Daniel tried to scream and got a mouthful of mud.

Blood squirted into the dog's mouth, driving it crazy. It widened its jaws for a better grip.

Daniel rolled over, smashing his elbow against the side of the dog's head. Daniel was crazed too. He had forgotten about the gun in his pocket. He kicked at the dog, driving it back. But it was quivering, waiting for an opening. Daniel was still on his back. He couldn't rise without the dog getting him again.

And behind him he heard the growl again. The first dog coming back.

Daniel suddenly stiffened his body and rolled again, spinning over and over along the slick ground. The second dog kept up with him easily, but couldn't find an opening to attack. The first dog, coming back on the fly, missed him completely and went skidding in the mud.

Daniel curled up tighter, rolling like a ball. The second dog kept lunging at him, biting and clawing but not finding another good hold with its teeth. It was patiently harrying him, waiting for the ball to come to a stop.

But Daniel was groping for something as well. He came out of the spin on his knees, facing the dog, on its own level. The Doberman lunged joyfully for his throat, thin and exposed and already wet with blood.

But now Daniel had the gun in his hand. His hand was flung out to the side. There was no room to aim. Instead Daniel swung it like a racquet, into the dog's head as it charged. He felt its teeth on his fingers as he slammed the heavy pistol against its muzzle.

The dog fell aside, stunned and maddened. It shook its head and lunged again.

But the moment had given Daniel the time he needed to aim. He fired straight down the dog's throat.

The dog yelped as its head was flung back. It didn't even realize it was hurt. It gathered its legs for another leap and Daniel fired again. The dog was knocked off its feet onto its side. Daniel advanced on it.

And remembered the first Doberman. Where was it? The rain was still falling in sheets. It had drenched Daniel already. It covered noise as well. He never heard the other dog coming. As he turned lightning flared. Coming out of the light was the black Doberman, already in the air, eyes red. Daniel threw up his hands in front of his face. When the dog hit him the pistol went flying.

What Daniel did was purely instinctive. He would never have done it intentionally. Those teeth were the most horrifying sight he'd ever seen. They were only inches from his face. Instinct made him save his throat. He did it by sacrificing his arm.

He jammed his left elbow down the dog's throat, straight into those horrible teeth. They raked his arm, burning. Daniel screamed again, a sound lost in the wind.

He fell to the ground with the dog atop him. The dog's teeth were grinding, ripping into the flesh of his arm. Daniel's mind vanished. If he had been thinking he would have tried to pull his arm free, but instead he drove it deeper down the dog's throat. Blood flowed on the already mud-slicked arm. The Doberman was growling again, furious, ripping at the meat.

The dog widened its jaws for more leverage and Daniel pushed his elbow deeper into that maw. The dog's growling abruptly choked off. It tried to yelp and couldn't. It had no air.

The dog tried to scramble back, to free itself from the blockage in its throat. Its paws couldn't find a purchase on the mud or Daniel's drenched body. Daniel rose with it, keeping the pressure on its windpipe. The dog's sides heaved.

After a long moment they broke apart. The dog jerked its

head back and its teeth gouged deeper cuts as Daniel's arm pulled free. The pain was blinding.

For a moment the dog just stood there, grateful to breathe again. It planted its legs wide and gasped in air.

Daniel had regained his feet. He stepped forward and kicked as hard as he had ever kicked in his life. His foot went between the dog's front legs and hammered into its chest. There was hatred and terror in the kick. Daniel felt bones break in the dog's rib cage.

The dog fell onto its side. Daniel kicked it again. He was insane. There was no relation between this creature and his own lovable Doberman at home. This one was a monster that had tried to kill him. Daniel tried to kick again, lost his footing, and fell. Being on the ground horrified him. He felt both dogs atop him again. He rolled over and covered his face. As his rage subsided, the pain in his arm rose to the forefront of his mind again. He pushed the elbow down into the mud as if it were a poultice. Rain fell steadily. Mud rose up to bury him alive.

Carol watched the storm grow to a tidal wave in the sky then begin to slacken. She was thinking about John, the man who brought her food. The first time she'd seen him without the mask it had scared her to death. She thought it meant he, like the first two who'd kidnapped her, was no longer concerned that she'd ever have the chance to identify him. But he'd made no threatening moves. He had talked softly to her. He told her his name. And now, two days later, life went on as before. He was the only person she ever saw face to face. He looked more and more unwilling. Her hope that he would help her had turned to expectation. Sometimes when he entered her room he looked furtive, like a secret lover at a rendezvous. She thought he'd been searching the house, checking the guards, looking for a way out for both of them. Carol was certain that someday soon he would enter her room and tell her he'd found a way out. When he did, she would go with him.

She leaned against the window, trying to see the ground. Tonight might have been a good time to try to escape, while the storm masked sounds and kept everyone inside. But the chance was probably gone already. The storm had tapered off to a light rain. She looked down to see if any guards had emerged from the house. Carol started. Her mind played tricks on her after her days in captivity. There were two men on the grounds below. They were two stories down in dim light but her imagination made her think she recognized one of them.

As she tried to peer down, the clouds parted briefly and moonlight illuminated the grounds.

She *did* recognize them. She filled her lungs. There was joy and terror in her voice as she screamed her husband's name.

Behind her, the door opened. She looked back and saw John Loftus in the doorway. He was wearing the mask again.

The hour felt very late but the storm was remote as Khai sat alone in his study. It moved on the fringes of his mind, a herd of dream-cattle over the horizon. Khai was listening for the phone. Within the sphere of his house impatience made his senses acute. He thought he could hear the lines humming.

Footsteps pattered up to his door and there was the usual pause before the knock came timidly. Khai spoke a syllable and the man poked his head in.

"Chui sent two others to check on the men who went to the pawnshop," he said before Khai could ask. "He expects to hear from them any minute. If they—"

"I will take the call," Khai said. "Any call."

The man choked back the rest of his explanation and bobbed his head. He looked disconcerted, no doubt thinking how startled the men would be when they called in and were answered by Khai himself.

"Give instructions."

The messenger didn't pause for interpretation. "Oh yes," he

said. "Quickly at once." He almost closed the door on his nose in his haste to depart.

Khai's senses dulled down to placid normal. He didn't hear the man's departing footsteps. He thought he heard something else, as if the messenger had stumbled and fallen, but the slight attention he paid only brought back his smile. Fear was homage. Khai sat waiting, engulfed in good feeling. Now when he heard from his men in the field joy would be complete.

His study door opened again, with no bidding from Khai. A most surprising event. No one but his father would do such a thing, and he expected no visit from his father. Perhaps the fool messenger hadn't shut it all the way and the wind seeping through the house had opened the door.

The apparition stepped through the open door. It was as if it brought the storm inside the room. Khai felt the cold wind in his blood.

It was a man, but so covered with mud he might have risen from a grave. There was blood on the man's face and clothes as well, adding to the appearance of living death. But ghosts don't carry guns, and this one did. The .45 automatic was the cleanest-looking thing about the man.

"Tranh Van Khai," said the apparition.

Daniel was no longer afraid. The dogs seemed to have torn that out of him. Even the storm had calmed after the dogs were dead. The rain wasn't heavy enough to wash the mud off him as he made his way to the house. He encountered no more opposition, which surprised him. It wasn't that they were all sleeping. The house blazed with light. Daniel made little attempt at furtiveness. He marched up to the front door of the mansion and after only a moment's cautious pause opened it. Still he saw no one.

As he walked slowly up the hallway he saw a young Vietnamese man hurry across the room ahead of him, going so fast and purposefully he didn't even glance in Daniel's direction.

Daniel followed and saw the room the man entered. From his manner it was clear the man was going to report to his leader. Daniel waited and struck the man down almost casually after he emerged again. Then he opened the door and had found the man he was looking for. It was so easy now.

"I've come for her," he said.

Khai just sat there like a statue. He obviously had no clue to his response. Daniel moved toward him, raising the gun slightly. He wasn't going to say it again without striking first.

Light dawned on Khai's features. "Daniel Greer," he said wonderingly. For a moment he had thought it was John Loftus. He couldn't think what other American would be there in his sanctuary.

There was some admiration in his voice. "I sent men—" he began.

"Yes," Daniel said shortly.

He had stopped advancing. The men regarded each other appraisingly. They had been so much in each other's thoughts the last days that it seemed they had met more than once, but that wasn't so. Each hardly remembered what the other looked like. They had become figures in their mutual imagination. It took a long moment for reality to assert itself in that narrow room.

Daniel was the first to speak again. He sounded tired but not impatient. "Just tell someone to bring her to me. Outside the house."

Khai didn't respond until Daniel stepped forward again, and then the Vietnamese only shrugged and stood. "I can't do that," he said thoughtfully. His mind was obviously racing. His fingers fidgeted on the desk.

"You will," Daniel said.

Khai shook his head. "And then what? Police here in this house?" The idea was obviously unthinkable to him.

Daniel hadn't even thought that far ahead. "Just bring her to me," he repeated.

Khai was beginning to shake his head again when Daniel stepped forward and slapped him, left-handed. It was as if he faced the Saigon cowboys in his garage again, but this time he had no qualms, no hesitation. The slap was hard enough to rock Khai aside. He staggered and regained his balance.

"You don't understand," Daniel said, his voice steady. "It's not your choice anymore. I'll kill you and everyone else in this house to get her. I don't care about police. Just bring me my wife."

Khai's eyes were bright with more than pain. "We'll see what we can do," he said softly.

Daniel grabbed his arm and steered him out of the study. The fallen messenger was just rising to his feet with a groan. Khai looked at him thoughtfully, marking the man's identity for later.

Daniel prodded the messenger with his foot and the man looked up with sudden fright.

"Send him," Daniel said.

Khai nodded acquiescence and spoke to the man in Vietnamese.

"English," Daniel said sharply.

"He doesn't understand English." Khai finished speaking and the messenger, eyes still alive with panic, nodded and hurried away.

"Tell him to bring her outside," Daniel said, and Khai shouted after the man.

They were alone again, but Daniel could feel the house vibrating with Khai's men. He waved the gun toward the front door and Khai obediently preceded him. They went out onto the front porch. There was no outside light on, which suited Daniel's purposes. He didn't want to be a target. He took Khai down into the yard below the porch and several feet out into the darkness, then turned so that they faced the house. Daniel stood close behind Khai. Light rain caressed them, beginning to soften the mud on Daniel's face.

"When they bring her, what?" Khai asked.

"We go away. That simple. We take you a little way just to be sure we're safe."

"'A little way,'" Khai began with amusement. "Just as far
as—"

"*Daniel!*"

He jerked as if he'd been shot. Looking up, following the
scream, he saw Carol spotlighted in a window high above.

"Carol," he said softly, stepping away from Khai, forgetting
him. Then he shouted her name and waved. He forgot everything else. She was alive.

Carol waved joyously, forgetting about the man behind her.
When she first looked down into the rain-streaked grounds of
the estate she had been sure her imagination was coddling her.
But Daniel was real, she was certain of it. Her heart swelled.
For a moment everything seemed safe and normal again. She
could take one giant step and be with him, home. Then fear
returned more strongly than ever. Daniel looked so small from
this height, and he was alone. The other man on the lawn was
the sharp-featured Vietnamese. There were no police. And the
house was full of men. She shouted Daniel's name again, this
time a cry of warning.

Daniel stood transfixed. It was cruel to let him see her. It
made him realize how far away she still was. The plan no longer
seemed simple. On the same floor as Carol he saw a man hurry
by a window, then return to it and stare out toward him. The
man went running away. Daniel turned to stand closer to Khai,
suddenly realizing that the Vietnamese leader was no longer in
front of him. He whirled and saw Khai six feet away, casually
straightening up.

"Drop it," Daniel said, leveling the gun at him.

Khai looked politely puzzled, then shrugged and opened
his hand, dropping the fist-size rock. Daniel stepped close and
slapped him again, backhanded. Khai's eyes were suddenly
bright but he didn't forget the gun.

"I'll kill you," Daniel said. His rage was almost overpower-
ing now that he had seen Carol. He longed to run through the
house shooting and smashing until he reached her.

Behind him he heard the front door of the house open.
Hastily he jerked Khai around in front of him and held the gun

to Khai's temple. A young Vietnamese had appeared on the porch—whether the messenger or another Daniel couldn't tell. They all looked like soldiers in their khaki uniforms. This one carried a rifle and was running. "Stop him," Daniel said softly. Khai barked out an order and the man skidded to a stop.

"Tell him to put down the rifle."

Khai called to his man and the soldier turned and ran back into the house. The door stayed open and Daniel had the impression the man hadn't gone far.

He stood close behind Khai with his left forearm around Khai's throat. That was the arm the dog had torn up. It was throbbing and he felt a fresh flow of blood trickling. He kept the gun in his right hand pressed against Khai's temple. "Tell him to come back. Tell him to bring her down here."

Khai called something in Vietnamese but there was no response. Somewhere along that darkened front porch Daniel heard a window being raised. He turned Khai in that direction. His eyes raked the front of the house. More Vietnamese were standing at the windows on the floors above. In Carol's window a man had appeared beside her. The man had a hideous face Daniel didn't recognize as a mask. The man grabbed Carol's arm and bent to raise the window. They swayed in the opening.

"*No!*" Daniel screamed. He pulled Khai toward the house. "Tell him to bring her to us."

Khai's voice was utterly serene. "He will not," he said.

While Daniel had looked upward to Carol, Khai's eyes had found another window, and Daniel had had the worst piece of luck he could have had, without even knowing it. Khai saw his father standing calmly at his bedroom window, looking down at his hostage son.

The sight drained all indecision from Khai. He was no longer afraid because he no longer had any choice. He would literally rather die than have his father see him back down.

Daniel had no idea what accounted for Khai's sudden serenity, but he sensed the change. He turned Khai to face him, their faces inches apart. "Are you insane? I *will* kill you."

"I know," Khai said. "And then my men will kill you. And her."

"But all you have to do is let us go."

Khai appeared to consider that. Daniel's puzzlement ebbed slightly as the man raised his face toward the upper window.

But what he shouted at the top of his voice was "Throw her down!"

"No!" Daniel screamed again. He stepped away from Khai, toward the window, and a shot rang out. Daniel fell to the ground, dragging Khai down with him. In the mud they struggled briefly until Daniel jerked the gun upward, striking Khai's chin. Khai fell back but Daniel hugged him close. There were no more shots.

"They won't risk you getting killed," Daniel whispered fiercely.

Khai shook his head. He was groggy but still calm. "But neither will they obey my orders if the orders are foolish," he said.

"We'll see about that." Daniel stood and hauled Khai up. Again he held the gun to Khai's head, as obviously as he could. They were observed by a few men Daniel could see and many more, he was certain, he could not see. "Tell them to bring her. Tell them in English. Somebody will understand."

Khai shrugged again. He raised his voice only slightly in the direction of the open front door. "Bring the white woman down here to us."

They waited. There was no sound of movement. Daniel looked up at the high window, higher than an ordinary second story. Carol and her captor weren't struggling. He held her close to the open window. The man had a gun too. Carol had one hand outstretched. Daniel was too far away to see her clearly but he imagined the puzzled look in her eyes.

He waited what seemed forever and nothing happened. "You see?" Khai finally said. "They do not follow me blindly. They know letting the woman go will land them all in American prison, or worse. Even for their beloved leader they will not risk that."

His calm, sardonic tone was maddening. Daniel tried to think. He was within sight of her and everything was unraveling. The lure of irrationality was strong. If not for Carol standing up there, he would have just shot Khai and died with him.

"You're lying. They'll do what you say but you told them something else in Vietnamese. That's what they're obeying."

Khai wondered if his father could see his easy smile as the gun was pressed hard against his head. "Even if that were so," he said, "what difference would it make? *I* will not let her go."

"You?" Daniel began in amazement. "But you have no—"

"It would not be safe. I fear your police even more than my men do. I would rather have you shoot me now than fall into their hands."

Daniel sensed his sincerity. In the face of Khai's calm, Daniel's own thoughts jumbled like a kaleidoscope. He started talking, paused, started again.

"I won't go to the police. You don't understand, I just want her back. I don't care about any of the rest of you."

Even he wasn't sure he meant that. Khai barely acknowledged that he had spoken.

"All right then, let's go inside. If they won't bring her down we'll go up to her."

"Yes, let us do that," Khai said agreeably. It was easy to see why. Daniel looked up at the old mansion and imagined its many hallways and doors, the many corners and as many men he would have to pass to make his way up to the second floor. He wouldn't survive to find the stairs. Even if by some miracle he did, would they casually leave Carol in place, waiting for him to come rescue her?

"Yes," Khai said, reading his thoughts. "By the time we got there she would be down here, broken on the hard ground. They wouldn't want to be distracted with her while they set about trying to kill you. And then you would lose your cool and kill me and my men would hurl you down to join your wife in eternity."

"All your scenarios seem to end that way," Daniel said. And

Khai's logic was irrefutable. Daniel was beginning to believe their three deaths were both imminent and unavoidable.

"There is one that does not," said Khai. Daniel made no response, but the Vietnamese continued. "That is for you to walk away." Daniel snorted derisively. Khai hurried on. "You said you don't care about turning me over to the police. Was that a lie? If all you want is the return of your wife, this is the only way that may be accomplished. You simply leave. I wait a few days to see if you're not bullshitting about the police. If we remain undisturbed, I become convinced of your sincerity and release your wife unharmed."

"You must think I have been driven insane. Leave her with you?" Daniel shifted Khai slightly as he thought he saw a rifle barrel protruding through the open front door of the mansion. Khai let himself be positioned without resistance.

"Will I hurt her, knowing you are free and can bring the police down on me at any moment? I tell you, they scare me to death."

Daniel didn't answer. It was unthinkable, it simply could not happen—that he would walk away now, leaving her here. And yet, as he did think it he felt death recede, from all of them.

"Have I asked you for anything?" Khai said quietly. "For one thin dime? I didn't snatch her for fun. Ask her, she hasn't been touched. There are plans that have nothing to do with you, Daniel Greer. In a day's time, two, it will be over anyway. I was already planning to release her."

"Sure."

"It's true. Would I kill her with you still alive in the world, knowing? More important—her father?"

They had made a deal. Khai and Raymond Hecate. Daniel had already thought it. Now he was sure. The fact that Khai even knew her father was a powerful man was confirmation enough for him.

"Picture me in an American slammer," Khai said. His voice was low, unhearable a few feet away. "Can you believe I fear that? I do not want to die." He paused. "Do you? Does she?"

"Have them bring her down here," Daniel said, his same litany, but his tone was weary now. "So I can explain to her."

"That, no. I can't allow you to get that close to her."

"It's that or die," Daniel said with renewed heat. "I have to at least talk to her."

Khai smiled, unseen by Daniel. He spoke in Vietnamese, aiming his voice at the house. This time they heard running footsteps recede in response. They waited, Daniel looking up. The man holding Carol suddenly turned, listened, then disappeared from view, along with Carol. Daniel waited less patiently, picturing her inside that house, filled with these men. Khai seemed to be standing utterly at ease.

The darkness no longer seemed so protective. The house itself was dark on the ground floor. There was no telling what it hid. Daniel felt very visible. His elbow throbbed.

There was a stir by the front door and he could suddenly see Carol's face. She was very pale, a ghost in the dimness. Unthinkingly he lunged toward her, but stopped when he saw the gun against her throat. Only her face was visible. Someone hidden by the door jamb was holding her fast. Carol looked tattered and drained and beautiful. Obviously no one had explained anything to her. She thought she was about to be released. The joy on her face broke his heart. He had to clear his throat to speak.

"Have they hurt you?"

"No," she said.

"At all? Anything? If they—"

"No, Daniel. I'm fine. What's it all about?"

"You see?" Khai said softly. "She has gone completely unmolested."

"I don't know," Daniel answered her question. "But it'll be over in a day or two."

"Day or two?" Puzzlement had replaced her happy expression. "Daniel? Aren't you—?"

"You have to stay that much longer." He had to look away. "Carol, there's nothing I can do. It's—"

"But you have him."

"But they have you. They won't trade. They're too afraid I'll bring the police. But if we wait they'll let you go."

He continued to explain. Her face had fallen, but as he talked she nodded once, then again. She was trying to be brave, but he could see tears. Daniel was crying too, silently. He wanted to kill Khai and run toward her, firing wildly into the darkness. But he would only be killing her.

"I'll call you on the phone," Daniel said suddenly. "Whenever I like, and if they don't let you speak to me at once I'll be down on this house with a thousand cops."

"Whenever you like," Khai agreed, accepting this addendum to their bargain.

"This'll be over in a couple of days."

"Yes," she said. "Daniel?"

She wouldn't say more, there in front of their enemies, but he knew what she was thinking, and said so.

As he watched, her face disappeared, pulled back into the darkness of the house. "Carol?" he called, and her disembodied voice came back.

"I'm all right." He thought he heard a sob as well.

To Khai he said harshly, "You're coming with me," and began walking rapidly backward.

"What do you mean?" Khai sounded perturbed for the first time since he had seen his father in the window.

"They hold her and I'll hold you. In a few days we can make the exchange."

Khai dug in his heels. "Oh, no. No trade. If you take me away they'll assume I'm dead. Someone else will take my place—someone you have no deal with." Daniel was still trying to pull him. "Daniel Greer! They will kill your wife!"

Daniel stopped pulling. "Believe me, I know," Khai went on. "You and I understand each other, but no one else in that house will understand. They will be afraid. They will kill her and flee unless I am here to control them."

Daniel had no energy left. His hands had fallen to his sides. In the strangeness of that foreign stronghold, Khai with his occasional Americanisms of speech seemed like an ally. Daniel gave in to his reasoning.

"See that you do control them then," he said. His voice gained heat as he continued. "My bargain is with you. If you break it, I will find you wherever you are and kill you. You know that?"

"I will not break it," Khai said. It was almost pathetic to see how easily the pawnbroker believed him.

They were at the front gate. It wasn't locked. Daniel pulled it open, leaving Khai inside. "Remember," he said, and Khai nodded. Daniel turned and ran, feeling like nothing but a traitor as he left her behind.

CHAPTER 10

Windows

"PUT her on." With his other hand, the one not holding the phone, Daniel drummed on the countertop. The pain in that arm had dulled to a slow throbbing pulse. Daniel hardly felt it. He looked out his shop window and saw people passing in the street. It took him a moment to realize they were all Vietnamese. He couldn't spot Khai's men immediately. The watchers were being more cautious, not standing in one spot and staring. Foot traffic seemed heavier than usual. He wondered what day of the week it was.

When Daniel returned home after leaving Khai's house his phone had been ringing. They had let him speak to Carol then, and given him Khai's number so he could call back.

"Daniel?"

"Are you all right?" He spoke hastily, as if they might be cut off. This was the third time he had called that day and the shortest delay yet in bringing her to the phone. Khai had kept his word so far.

"I'm fine. They treat me— They haven't hurt me at all."

"Did you have lunch?"

"Yes." Carol almost laughed, but she didn't elaborate for Daniel. Lunch had been Chef Boyardee Spaghetti-Os.

"If there's anything you need make them bring it to you. Clean clothes . . ."

"They gave me some. I feel fine now. Daniel—"

"I'll keep calling you, don't worry."

"Just so I know *you*'re all right."

"I know. Don't worry. They don't want anything from me."

He could picture Carol nodding as she said, "I hope not."

"Yes," he said, and a little space of silence grew. Outside, the bulk of the pedestrian traffic had shifted to his side of the street. A small crowd of strolling Vietnamese passed close to his window. He pictured a similar crowd near Carol, hands reaching, afraid to harm her but curious. He hated them. There was a small sound from the office behind him. Mice.

To say something private over the phone would have been distasteful to them both under these circumstances. Silence was the most intimacy they could share.

"I assume they're listening on the extension," Daniel said. Carol made no response, as good as an affirmation.

"You'll be out of there soon, I promise."

"I know. I'm not afraid, Daniel, I'm really not. Except for you."

"I'm being very careful." Among the strollers outside were a pair of young Vietnamese men walking together. One of them glanced inside the pawnshop, and they paused as if they might come in. Daniel's hand left the countertop. One of the young men pointed at a radio in the window, the other shook his head, and they walked on.

"I know. But you need a partner when you sleep."

"I have Hamilton Burger." Daniel smiled. He knew she was smiling too. Let the damned Vietnamese figure out that code name.

"Khai wants to talk to you."

"All right."

"Daniel," she said, and there was another long moment of commingling silences.

"Don't worry, Carol," he concluded it lamely.

She was gone. It seemed to him that the receiver in his hand even changed weight and temperature ever so slightly when Khai came on the line. The soft sound from within Daniel's office repeated itself. He turned to look at the open doorway but saw nothing.

"She's being treated very well," Khai said. Daniel thought of sarcastic replies but didn't voice any of them.

"How much longer?" he asked.

"Two days. No more than three."

"I called off the police. I told them she'd never been missing at all. Once I get her back it would be too much trouble for me to report it all again."

"We have to work out a system so that you get her back and I get—reassurance."

"If she's not safe you won't—"

"Yes, yes. We both understand the threats. No need to repeat them every time we talk."

Daniel waited. Khai cleared his throat.

"My two men who were following you before you came here have not returned."

Daniel didn't answer. They waited in an almost companionable silence.

"I don't believe they are in custody of the police either," Khai finally said. When there was still no response he added, "Which is fine," and dropped the subject for good. A minute later they both hung up.

The truth was, Daniel had forgotten about the Saigon cowboys. Last night he had gone home from Khai's mansion to an empty house and hadn't even thought about the three he'd left there. He was preoccupied with his guilt over leaving Carol behind and futile planning to get her out. He returned to that futility now. An hour later he was thinking about calling the mansion again when he saw Thien among the pedestrians outside. Daniel couldn't tell if the boy was being followed. If he was being watched he appeared unconscious of it. Thien didn't look back over his shoulder as he crossed the street and opened the pawnshop door.

"You are not disliked in this neighborhood," he said without preliminaries. "They think it's curious that you've stayed on after all the other American merchants have abandoned the area."

"*I'm* the curiosity. I see. And I just don't have anything they want to buy, is that it?"

"They're still afraid of making a mistake. Across the street they know they can bargain with the pawnbroker. They don't know if you run this shop like the shops they know or like Walgreen's. Walgreen's won't haggle. It offends them. They suspect that Walgreen's will haggle with white people but thinks Vietnamese are stupid enough to pay the asking price without question."

"I see," Daniel said again.

"I'm talking, of course, about the immigrants. Americans like me, we know the difference."

He was sure the boy was making a joke but his face gave no hint of it. If anything, Thien looked more serious than usual this afternoon. Now that he was inside the shop, Daniel saw that he did watch the street outside. Daniel looked out and saw another young Vietnamese, wearing a red nylon jacket, but he wasn't lounging against a storefront obviously watching as the Saigon cowboys had done.

"I'll tell you what," Daniel said. "Why don't you buy something here and then tell everyone what a great bargain you got after dickering with me over the price?"

"You may have a good idea."

As Thien walked slowly around the shelves Daniel said, "I talked to Khai a little while ago." Thien had his back to him. He didn't turn. "He tells me that his two men we talked to in my garage didn't come back to him."

The boy didn't appear to have heard him. "I suppose they just ran away," Daniel added.

"I suppose."

"You didn't call the police to take them like I told you to do."

Thien turned at that. "I thought the police would ask more questions than you could persuasively answer."

He was damned right about that. Daniel looked at Thien's sincere little face. He didn't think he could ask more questions than the Vietnamese boy could persuasively answer. He decided not to pursue it. He hadn't told Thien what had happened after he'd left him in the garage. The boy hadn't asked. They casually shared certain knowledge, such as that Carol was still missing and Daniel was in contact with Khai, but they didn't discuss it. It was not that Daniel discounted Thien's value as an ally, nor that he thought the boy's loyalty was torn between Vietnamese and American. But Daniel wanted no partners. Not police, not civilians. He didn't know yet what he might have to do to free Carol.

Thien continued to move around the shelves and counters, but he wasn't looking at the merchandise. Daniel liked having him there. The boy assured him he was still alive in the world. Outside the world seemed to go on completely oblivious of him.

"You should go home," he said. "Your family must need you."

"Khai's gangsters are not so contemptuous of you now," Thien said, not in reply. "They duck around corners now, look."

Daniel looked but saw no one.

"You know they haven't made their collections this week? It's a curiosity in the neighborhood. Are they so busy with you they forgot? Forgot money?" he added for emphasis.

Daniel wondered, as he often had, how Thien knew about such things. It occurred to him that Thien's own father was a merchant of some kind.

He was looking out the window and this time he did see a young Vietnamese man slip around the corner across the street, glance at Daniel's shop, and stroll too casually away.

Thien was watching too. Before Daniel could speak the boy said, "I guess I had better go home. I have a spelling test tomorrow."

He was moving already toward the door. They seemed to have shared a conversation, but in fact they had hardly spoken. And Thien had never looked at him the whole time he'd been in the shop. It was as if he'd been there waiting for a time or a signal.

"Adios," the boy said as he went out the door. Daniel didn't laugh. He continued to stare out at the street but his eyes glazed after a while. His hand was on the phone. The street scene was like one of those old beer signs where the same canoe passes the same island again and again, moving but unchanging. A little while later his attention was caught by Thien's reappearance. He was coming out of the pawnshop across the street. He remembered that Linh's wife was missing too. Linh had been waiting for word of her as long as Daniel had. But more patiently? He was still open for business. Vietnamese customers came and went.

Daniel picked up the phone. It was answered on the second ring with a Vietnamese word. "Let me talk to her," he said.

Khai made a phone call of his own. Loftus and Chui both tried to talk him out of it. The whole point, they said, was that everything would operate clocklike now without any intervention from them, without their exposing themselves further. Khai was amused to see that his two lieutenants found it distasteful to be on the same side of the argument.

"What we need to worry about is this pawnbroker," Loftus said. "Even if things go smooth he's going to fuck us up."

"That is what I am taking care of," Khai said.

"But you don't have to do it. Let me—"

"Yes, let him—" Chui began. "That's what he's good for, to have an American here—"

Khai waved them both out of his study. The truth was he was simply tired of inaction. He wanted to take a hand.

"Mr. Hecate," he said a minute later, after having claimed to be someone else. "I thought we had an agreement."

There was a pause. But Hecate seemed to have been expecting a call of this nature. "Who are you?"

"I am someone who does not have much time. I simply called to ask, do we still have an agreement or should I make other arrangements?"

"Look," Hecate said, plunging into that stream of bullying that always flowed close to the surface of his personality, "you just hold your horses. What you asked for isn't as easy as going to the bank and making a withdrawal, you know. I'm getting there."

"If it was easy anyone could do it," Khai said. "But I came to you. I thought you had the ability."

"You'd better worry about your own ass. If anything happens to her—"

"I have had this tiresome conversation already," Khai interrupted. "Which reminds me of the other purpose of my call. Part of our agreement was that you would keep others from interfering. I'm afraid you—"

"What others? I haven't—"

"Your son-in-law is becoming a nuisance. He is a tiny cog but a troublesome one, because he doesn't know what's going on. You must rein him in."

There was a longer pause. Hecate's voice when it came was quieter. The anger had descended again into the undertone. It made him sound sullen. "He won't listen to me. Believe me, if I talked to him it would only make things worse."

"Then you must do something else about him." Khai's voice was clipped. Clearly he sounded like a man who was discovering that he was talking to the wrong person.

There was a longer pause. Hecate said, "You talk like this is *my* problem."

This time the pause was from Khai's end. "I see," he finally said.

"What d'ya want, my blessing? I don't give a shit about him. I only care about—"

"I will remember that," Khai said, and hung up.

* * *

If he thought that would upset Raymond Hecate, he didn't know his man. Hecate put the receiver down with a trace of satisfaction. This could work out swell, he thought. Carol back, a new ally, and no more pawnbroker son-in-law. Worse things could happen. Carol would be upset at the senseless tragedy but she'd get over it. Daddy would see to that.

He lumbered out of his office to put in a personal appearance at police headquarters. Maybe that would speed things up.

One of the other detectives asked Rybek, "You don't have enough unsolved cases, you have to keep working on a solved one?"

Rybek answered, "You have so much shit to spare, you have to give me some?" Someone laughed but most of them paid no attention. Rybek's growl was familiar background, like the buzz of the fluorescent lights. He went on talking as if someone had expressed interest.

"Her husband says she's back but nobody else's seen her. What does that say to you?"

"They're having a long reunion."

"He's back in his shop but she's not back at work. Nobody answers the phone at the house. And there's blood on the floor of his garage."

"You must know a real easy judge if you got a warrant to find that out."

"Wind blew the door open while I was standing there," Rybek said. He was looking distastefully at the mounds of paperwork on his desk. If he was stupid enough to write down half the things he had to do to bust cases, some other idiot would be sitting at that desk by morning. And it really made a huge difference to the world, didn't it?

Not that anybody was still listening, but he said aloud,

"Better make a couple of calls first just in case. If she's really back then somebody else's seen her, right?

"Right?"

Now here was one for a scrapbook. A sight he'd never expected to see: Jennifer Hardesty walking into his pawnshop. For a moment it didn't even look strange; he simply thought he must be somewhere else. But the bell that tinkled as the door opened was his shop bell, and Jennifer had to veer around his display counter as she strode toward him. She ignored the surroundings. Daniel rose automatically to his feet. Jennifer marched right up to him, so close he could see tiny flecks of mascara clinging to her eyelashes. He didn't offer a greeting. Neither of them pretended her appearance there was a commonplace.

"Where's Carol?" Jennifer said. "She hasn't been to work this week and her parents haven't seen her."

"Not here" was all he got out.

"If she'd just left you I'm the first one she would've called."

"Not nec—"

"You bastard, I tried to tell her. I told her—"

"You told her *what*? That if she married me she'd get murdered? What?"

Jennifer didn't flinch back. Her eyes narrowed. "If you've hurt her," she said, "you don't have to worry about prison. I'll see you dead."

Daniel hadn't stepped back either, so they were almost nose to nose now. "Jennifer," he said, "you are the least of my worries."

His voice was very flat but it conveyed something to her. She stepped back and studied his face. "What's happened?" she finally asked.

"I can't tell you."

"Did she take a trip? Maybe she just wanted to be alone."

"Yes, she went away."

Jennifer was wearing a bright blue, padded ski jacket that

made her look bulky, but it wasn't snapped shut. When she put her fists on her hips the jacket pulled open in front to reveal the thermal undershirt she wore underneath. He could see the points of her nipples pressing against the fabric. Her cheeks were glowing from the wind outside. She passed a hand through her hair, leaving it spikier than before. "What happened between you?" Jennifer asked. "Was it a bad fight?" But she was pretending now. She knew it was worse than that. "A *cop* called me," she said wonderingly.

He nodded without surprise, as if he'd arranged for the call himself. Jennifer continued to study his face. "Where is she?" she asked, no longer angry. He shook his head.

Jennifer's anger was a defense. With it gone she looked scared. She also seemed aware of where she was for the first time. She looked out the window at Little Vietnam, the Asian faces, the jagged characters of their writing. She and Daniel could have been the only white people in a foreign country. Jennifer wrapped her arms around herself. "Why do you stay in this spooky place?" she asked.

Daniel didn't answer. They were both looking out the window. Daniel saw two or three Vietnamese glancing curiously toward the shop. It was Jennifer they were watching. Daniel was an oddity in the neighborhood, but a familiar oddity. The short-haired white woman in the bright blue jacket was a curiosity. Jennifer was aware of their furtive glances. She turned away, almost shivering.

"Have you hired a detective?"

He shook his head.

"You must need money." Briskly she opened the purse hanging from her shoulder and took out a checkbook and pen. She sounded authoritative again. "I'll give you a thousand, you call me when you need more."

"I don't need any, Jennifer."

She hadn't started writing yet but her pen was poised. She was staring at him almost angrily. "She's my friend."

Daniel spoke gently. He was grateful for the offer. "It wouldn't help," he said.

Jennifer was faltering again, the frightened look creeping back. "It's no weakness to take my money. Money can do a lot. Hire guards, buy people back . . ." Daniel just shook his head. "What *can* help then?" she asked.

"Go home, Jennifer. Go have a good lunch somewhere." His tone wasn't sarcastic.

She capped her gold pen and looked out the window again. Her voice grew stronger but it was like reheated leftovers. "If it's you who did it I *will* get you."

He nodded agreement. "She'll want to call you when she gets back," he said. They looked out the window together for a long silent moment. "I'll walk you back to your car," he finally said.

Jennifer shook her head. "Think I'll do some shopping while I'm here. I'm running pitifully low on rattan." She still had her checkbook in her hand. "They're not so damn foreign. I see an American Express sign across the street." She snapped her jacket closed. "I'm telling you, money helps," she said in parting. But she didn't renew her offer.

They kept up the routine, but the Vietnamese knew their cover had been blown when Daniel came calling. It was no longer essential to keep themselves hidden from Carol. When Loftus took her down the hall now he left off the blindfold, and sometimes there were men in the hall, watching. That's what she hated. Now that they could let her see them it meant they could also see her. She was a kind of ghost, visible but insubstantial. They couldn't touch her. But she could feel herself fading into solidity. Their hands clenched in her presence. Their eyes were sharp as hooks. She wanted to cover herself.

She was like a princess in a fairy tale, but with malevolent servants. They couldn't hurt her but their desires were clear. They were held back by a fragile spell that was dissipating. Carol could feel her protection ebbing away. When the phone rang the men would look guilty, as if they'd been caught at something dirty.

They weren't yellow. That was another false stereotype. They were brown, some of them dark as Mexicans. Nor were they all short. Carol was five feet six. Half the Vietnamese were at least that tall. Khai was only a few inches taller than Carol, but so thin that from a distance he looked like a very tall man.

She didn't see much of Khai. She might have found it reassuring to have him talk to her, but he avoided her like a pet that would have to be destroyed soon. She saw him occasionally at the end of a corridor, disappearing to another floor. Only once he came into her room and stared at her for long minutes, without speaking. His gaze was clinical. Carol knew he wasn't thinking about her. He was thinking about Daniel. He was wondering what a man would do for a woman like her. Under his stare she pressed herself taller. She remained as silent as he. She refused to beg. No attachment formed, not a glimmer of human contact.

Some of the other men obviously studied her. Loftus was no longer the only one to enter her room. Sometimes they brought food; sometimes they came to take her to the phone. Their expressions ranged from sly to angry to thoughtful. There was not much difference among the expressions. At first Carol glared back at them, but after a while she just tried to ignore them. She was grateful for at least the pseudoprivacy of her room. She had a view of one glass skyscraper through the bare tree branches. It was beginning to look like a dream spire, something that existed only in her memory. She couldn't remember if she'd ever been inside that particular building.

Sometimes a Vietnamese escorted her to and from the bathroom. There was no lock on the door and if she took too long they would rattle the handle. Once as she stepped out of the shower the door opened and a rat-faced man stuck his head inside. Carol froze. She was half covered by a towel, but he stared at her as if he could see through it. There was a cold wind through the open door that tightened her flesh. The rat-faced man stepped inside. Carol took a deep breath and before she could scream he stepped back out, leaving the door ajar. Carol lunged across the room and slammed it. The sound echoed through the old mansion as if it were empty.

John Loftus had somewhere found other clothes for her. Her primary outfit was a green warmup suit, because it was soft and warmer than anything else he had given her. It had been made for a smaller woman, or perhaps a man. The elastic bands on the bottoms of the pants legs rode up her calves; the jacket fit tightly across her bust. That's what she was wearing as the rat-faced man escorted her back from the bathroom. They were walking side by side. He wasn't looking at her. When they reached her room and she turned aside to open the door he ran his hand across her ass, quickly but not furtively; the contact was firm. Carol gasped and jumped aside. He was already walking away. That was as far as he went that time. But she felt her protective spell slip another notch. He was testing its limits.

The ringing telephone was her lifeline. Its sound meant imaginary release. She could picture the outside world now only when she heard Daniel's voice. She always asked where he was calling from, and she saw him there. She could almost see herself beside him. If too many hours passed between calls her world narrowed down to the old mansion. She thought herself forgotten, or Daniel dead. Khai after all was planning something. That much was clear. Daniel was her anchor in the real world, and they were doing their best to erase him.

But she didn't cry when he called. She tried to sound cheerful for him. Saying his name was as close as she came to crying out. "Daniel"—and he understood. "I'm still here," he would say. That was what she wanted to hear. That meant more than his assurance that she would be released soon. In the silences between their sentences she could hear murderers creeping toward him.

"They haven't hurt me," she said. She didn't mention the rat-faced man's stare or his touch. "I'm fine," she lied. But when they said good-bye and the line went dead she closed her eyes tightly, trying to hold on to the contact. A hand touched her arm and the outside world dissolved again.

* * *

She and John Loftus had exchanged few words, but she thought their looks significant. He was usually scowling, not at her, she thought, but at the thought of her domination by the Vietnamese. When he looked directly at her his expression softened. "Don't let 'em worry you," he muttered once. She nodded.

The old Vietnamese woman who had been captured at the same time as Carol was still alive in the house as well. For a few days she seemed to have been forgotten. Now that they were allowed to see Carol but not to touch her, some of the men had turned their attention to the other captive woman instead. Khai apparently gave her no thought; the men were free to do what they liked. Sometimes they left the door of the woman's room open so that if Carol passed in the hall she could look in and see them. The rat-faced man leered at Carol as he stood over the Vietnamese woman, daring Carol to intervene. She hesitated between going in and rushing back to her own room with her hands over her ears. The rat-faced man, still grinning, bent and pulled his pants down. Carol fled.

The first night after Daniel's visit she sat huddled in her chair looking out the window at the grounds of the estate. She was staring at the spot where she'd seen Daniel holding Khai. Daniel had come that far and gotten away safely. If she could reach the same spot . . .

But she remembered the dogs. It was almost the same spot where she had seen them attack the tramp with killing fury. The dogs had been somewhere else when Daniel came, maybe penned up for some reason—maybe *inside* the house, being fed. She had no idea where they were now. She couldn't see them, but neither had the tramp until they were on him.

Her captor seemed to have sensed her fear of the dogs. He had been neglectful about handcuffing her today.

Carol's gaze traveled to the porch below her to the right.

She saw the glow of a cigarette. Gradually she could make out the shape of a lounging man. Was he just taking a break outside or was he posted there? She was stupid. Of course they'd have guards.

There was bright moonlight. It made her own room very dark by contrast. When the door opened and closed again she couldn't see who had come in. She turned and stared, but the blackness was too thick. At the same time she realized she was spotlighted in the moon-brightened window. She moved aside, toward the bed.

"What do you want? The phone?"

She could hear breathing, across the room. Then it stopped, and she couldn't tell where he was.

"I'll kill you," she said. In that moment she thought she could do it. Hook his eyes with her nails, bring her knee up into his crotch—

But he was behind her, not in front. When his arms closed around her it was so tightly she lost her breath. Her hands were useless claws at her sides. She could feel him pressed against her the full length of her back and legs. A scream stuck in her throat. She bent forward at the waist, trying to break away. Her face came down on the bed and he pressed her down into it. One hand on her neck, with the other he reached inside her warmup jacket.

His grip on her neck had slackened. She twisted aside, fell on her back, and swung her legs up, kicking him in the side of the head. He wasn't hurt badly enough though. He grabbed her legs and held them there, high over her head. She could feel him again, now pressing his legs against the backs of hers.

She put her hands down on the bed for leverage and pulled her legs as hard as she could to the side. He stumbled and fell to the side, into the moonbeam from the window.

"Damn it," she said. "What the hell do you think you're doing?"

They stayed immobile, she and John Loftus, looking at each other wildly. The nostrils of his long nose were flared, drawing in oxygen. The effort sucked in his cheeks as well, making his features gaunt as an old man's. In the moonlight the tendons stood out on his arms. Carol had lowered her legs. They were pointed toward him as she still lay back on the bed, panting as well. He looked panicked, on the verge of lunging at her again. But the moment stretched and he grew calmer.

"I was just trying to keep you from screaming," he finally said.

Carol nodded. The fact of his touch seemed not so terrible now that she knew who it was. "I thought you were one of them," she said.

He kept his voice low. "I can't come around all the time like before. Some of 'em're suspicious. They already think I might—" He shrugged. She nodded again. He looked away, out the window. "Is there anything I can get you?" he asked the night.

"Just away." Carol remained on the bed, leaning back on her hands. She kept her voice as low as his. The room seemed not so dark now. The old house creaked around them. There were still men moving about.

Loftus looked as if he hadn't heard her, but after a long pause he said quietly, "I'm working on it." Carol leaned forward eagerly but he held up a hand and stopped her question.

Instead, after another moment of silence, she asked, "How can you work for them?"

Loftus was still looking out the window. The expression that crossed his face made her wish she hadn't asked. His rage made her afraid to be in the same room with him. But the expression fled in the moment it took for him to turn to her. "It's just a job," he said. "There were no problems until they—"

The scream pierced them both. It was a woman's scream, shocking in its strength. It stopped as abruptly as it had started, but its echo lay between them. Loftus and Carol looked into each other's eyes. The scream had obliterated speech. But they looked at each other for a long time before he turned and walked quickly from the room. Carol lay there frightened but also in a measure relieved. Just having had a conversation in English with someone in the house made her feel less hopeless.

* * *

Loftus pulled the door shut behind him and strode down the hall. He was furious with himself. He had gone into her room still not knowing exactly what he wanted and that had been his undoing. When he had touched her in the dark he had suddenly known what he'd come for, but then he'd fallen into the moonlight and she'd seen him, and her white-bitch voice had stopped him dead like a boy caught at dirty tricks by his mommy. He'd found himself playing up to her, acting the stalwart hero.

He threw open the door of the other bedroom, freezing the actors inside into a tableau. The Vietnamese woman was naked on the bed. A Vietnamese man knelt at her head, holding rags pressed into her mouth. She was on her back. A long red welt crossed the disgusting flesh of her belly. The rat-faced man stood over her with a strap in his hand. His arm was pulled back. Loftus snatched it from his hand. "You little shit," he said fiercely.

There had been one satisfying moment in the bitch's room. When the scream had interrupted them. In that instant she had lost her imperiousness and looked at him with pure little-girl terror. Loftus promised himself that he would see that look again.

The Vietnamese woman was looking up at him not gratefully but warily. She was an insightful woman. Loftus slashed at her with the strap. She squirmed over onto her stomach, exposing her back and buttocks to him. A mistake. But when she began to scream the Vietnamese men hurriedly stopped Loftus's arm. He knocked them away and slammed out of the room.

Chui was glad when they got near the pawnshop because he wanted his passenger out of the car. Being confined in that small a space with Nguyen made him sweat. He should have let Nguyen drive. It would have given him something to do instead of just twitch with eagerness, until Chui thought he'd turn and start cutting *him*, just out of frustration.

Nguyen had joined Khai's gang because it gave him more opportunities to hurt people. That was Chui's theory. Nguyen seemed to have no ambition to assume command. In fact, he couldn't even be used to intimidate clients, because he didn't have the restraint to let an encounter end with fear alone. But when someone needed to be hurt, Nguyen shone. When Khai had decided that Daniel Greer was to die, Nguyen's name had sprung naturally to his tongue.

Chui stopped at the curb a block away. They might have been able to take him at his home, but if anything had gone wrong in that lily-white neighborhood Chui and Nguyen would have stood out like gargoyles. Here no one would see anything. Even as the car glided to a halt the few pedestrians hurried away from it. Police would find it a matter of great frustration to question these witnesses.

"You have already broken through?" Chui asked.

Nguyen nodded. His hand was on the door handle. He had stopped twitching. His eyes shone.

"There will only be a few moments," Chui said. Nguyen turned and looked at him. "All right, all right," he said. "Just remember, wait until I am outside."

Nguyen was gone without acknowledgment. Chui breathed. He watched his partner hurry up the street and disappear into a shop. Nguyen was short, barely five five, weighed a hundred and twenty pounds, and was thin and tough as wire. His chest, Chui had seen once, was cross-hatched with tiny scars that spoke of intricate suffering. Was that when Nguyen had fallen in love with pain? Or when he'd decided the whole world must suffer in kind? Chui didn't know or care. He was just glad to have him out of the car. He waited. It was almost 6 P.M. Closing time. There were only a few moments during which it could be done. This was the time.

Why not just walk in and shoot him, make it look like a robbery? That had been Chui's first idea; he had sent men past and even into the shop, posing as customers. They had seen the pawnbroker's hands go under the counter when anyone even came close to the door. One of them had heard a distinct *click* once he was inside the shop and momentarily turned his back on the proprietor. The man had turned very, very slowly and kept his hands in sight as he walked out.

The only time Greer appeared vulnerable was when he crossed the shop to lock the door at closing time. But there was no spot just outside the door where they could both watch him and remain unseen. He wouldn't approach the door unarmed if someone was standing outside it. And as soon as he did lock the door, he activated the burglar alarm. Chui didn't want police interrupting his work.

Nguyen had come up with the plan. He had promised he could get inside. He had done some reconnoitering and discovered that he could get into the pawnshop's office from the shop next door, after a little work the merchant gladly permitted. He had come out above the ceiling tiles. At six he would lift one of the tiles aside and slip down. When Daniel Greer stood up from his stool and crossed to the door, Nguyen would be behind him. His job was just to keep the American from activating the burglar alarm until Chui drove up to do the shooting.

Chui feared he would do more.

Daniel heard the rustling in the walls. Rats. He needed to set out poison. Probably he wouldn't get around to it today.

His hand was on the phone. But it had only been forty-five minutes since his last call. He would wait a little longer. Until after he'd closed up the shop. He tried to picture the layout of Khai's mansion. Where was Carol, where was the phone? Who took her to it? How many others were nearby? He couldn't risk asking her questions.

The street was dead. Had been all day. There hadn't been much point in opening the shop, but he had to be somewhere and it might as well be there. He thought he might learn something if he stayed available. Silly thought. Nobody was going to tell him anything. Even Thien hadn't shown up. But somehow he felt closer to Carol there as well, looking out at the street from which she'd disappeared.

The gun was close at hand. He didn't even see it anymore. He knew it would be there when he set his hand down. But now he stepped away from it so that he could look sideways out the window, to see no one was hiding near the front door.

Ten till six. He could afford to close early. He didn't want to be disturbed when he made his call.

Leaving the gun behind, he stepped out from the counter and walked toward the door.

Chui was startled. He was parked across the street and down half a block, from where he could see the door of the pawnshop and its plate-glass window. He saw the pawnbroker crossing behind the window, heading toward the door. He was early, very early. Chui hoped Nguyen had had time to get in.

He put the car in gear.

He needn't have worried about Nguyen. He was there in the doorway of the office when Daniel rose from the stool. As Daniel passed his position Nguyen stepped out, shadowing him silently.

In Nguyen's hand was a weapon the sight of which had made Chui wince. It was a chopstick such as could be found in any Oriental restaurant, but the innovation that had lately appeared in the ghetto made it as vicious a weapon as a man could carry. The trick was to slice off the small end diagonally, leaving a keen point, so fine it had an almost unmatched penetrating power. The stick was smoother than a knife and did more damage than an ice pick. Nguyen had once stabbed a man with one under the ribs and the stick had shimmered slightly going in, wriggling like an otter sliding into water. Going into softer matter, though, the flexible stick wasn't impeded at all. It could be thrust through an eye into the brain faster than a blink. Nguyen raised it like a sword as he fell into step behind his victim. It didn't matter if Greer heard him now. As soon as he turned the stick was going in his eye. That wouldn't kill him, Nguyen hoped, but it would incapacitate him. He could take his time then.

Daniel heard something but didn't pay attention. His thoughts were already with Carol.

The louder noise, though, he couldn't ignore. Outside in the street a car had squealed its tires. He glanced out the window and saw it pulling away from the opposite curb, coming toward him.

It was dark out there, still bright in the shop. The plate-glass window had gradually become a mirror. When Daniel looked into it directly he saw not the car, not the street outside, but himself and his weird shadow. The shadow lunged.

Nguyen had expected him to turn, but he never did. The thrust of the chopstick went not into yielding eyeball but into hard skull. Daniel screamed with the pain, but it wasn't incapacitating. He fell forward to escape, fell against a counter. He saw Nguyen from the corner of his eye. The eye he was about to lose. Nguyen had come around him and thrust again. Daniel jerked aside just enough to save his eye. The chopstick's point seared along the side of his head, opening a path of blood.

Daniel lashed out blindly, a lucky punch into Nguyen's nose. More blood. But the little assassin just grinned at him. Daniel's blow hadn't been enough to hurt him, even to drive him back.

Outside the car had pulled to the curb in front of the shop. Chui was out of it, running. He didn't like the looks of things inside, but it was salvageable. He just had to open the door and fire. They would be on their way in ten seconds.

Daniel saw him. He recognized both the man and his intent. He took a step back, knowing it would draw the assassin in. When the little man lunged again Daniel barely sidestepped the thrust. Then he was beside the Vietnamese. Putting both hands on the man's back, Daniel pushed as hard as he could. The assassin fell into a counter. Without even looking back the little man swung backward with a vicious swipe.

But Daniel hadn't closed on him. Instead he turned and ran for the door. He beat Chui to it by a step and turned the bolt. They stood there for an instant face to face, separated only by the glass. Chui's hand went into his jacket and Daniel fled.

But Chui paused. He saw the thick stripe of the burglar alarm in the glass of the door and hesitated to shatter it. For the moment he was a mere spectator.

Daniel turned. The other one was already closing on him. Daniel picked up something—what the hell was it? a lamp, a porcelain figure—from the top of a counter and swung it at him. In an instant Nguyen changed from a swordsman into a martial arts flyer. He leaped off the ground and came through Daniel's swing feet first. His kick caught Daniel in the chest and slammed him back against the plate-glass window. The back of his head hit it with a *crack*. His eyes closed.

To slits. He stood there looking groggy and watched the little man come at him with the chopstick again. There was triumph in the slowed tread, pleasure in the raising of the stick.

Daniel let it come. He stepped just to the left. The assassin's stick and then his knuckles cracked against the glass. The little man shrieked.

Daniel stepped forward so that he was to the side and just in front of his would-be killer. He raised his arm across his chest and swung his right elbow into the side of the man's head. The blow was good and solid and satisfying. Daniel tried to kick him as he went down too, but missed. Nguyen, dazed, grabbed his foot and twisted. Daniel fell to the floor.

Chui was pounding on the door. Nguyen looked down at himself in amazement. The chopstick was sticking out of his thigh.

Daniel crawled rapidly away, out of his reach. Nguyen was dimly aware that he couldn't reach him. Instead he staggered to his feet going the other direction.

"No!" Daniel screamed when he saw what he was doing, but it was too late. Tag team murder: Nguyen's scrabbling fingers found the bolt on the door and turned it. The door burst inward. Chui's gun was in his hand.

Daniel was already running. He took the one chance he had and dove through the air. Chui fired, once, twice, and again. Daniel fell over the counter.

The silence seemed very long, though it was no more than a second. Chui bent toward his partner. Then instead, still bent, he dived forward, behind the open door.

Daniel's head and shoulders had come back up above the counter. The gun was in his hand, arms extended, both hands steadying it. He fired. It was too late to hit Chui but that wasn't his target. His shot shattered the glass of the door. An alarm shrilled.

Chui's hand came from behind the door. He fired a barrage, not aiming, just sweeping the far wall. Daniel ducked down behind the counter again. In the momentary silence Chui grabbed Nguyen's collar and hauled him half upright. Nguyen fell out the open door.

Chui stood there a moment longer, waiting for the American's head to reappear. Instead only a hand did. Daniel did what Chui had done, fired blindly. But as soon as he saw the gun Chui leaped back out of the door. There was a fine array of shattering sounds but no hits. Daniel cautiously raised his head. Outside the car door slammed, the tires squealed.

The air smelled burned. Daniel lay with his cheek on the countertop, sightlessly staring.

Chui did not rush back to Khai's house to report on this fiasco. His first thought was to flee the state, maybe the country. With that in mind he called the house rather than appearing in person. He called from a pay phone, with the car running a few feet away. Nguyen sat in the passenger seat looking despondent. He hadn't said a word since they'd fled the American's shop. Chui knew without even having to formulate the thought that he was going to blame their failure on Nguyen. After all, Nguyen was supposed to be the killing machine, wasn't he, the ninja? The only question was how subtly Chui would shift the entire blame onto Nguyen's thin shoulders. He hadn't decided that until he heard Khai's voice on the phone.

"Nguyen failed," Chui said.

After a pause and a heart-stopping lack of response from Khai, he went on: "Instead of following our plan he tried to make the kill himself. But he could not. By the time I got inside it was too late. Nguyen was wounded. I've had to take him for medical treatment." He named an unlicensed Vietnamese doctor they had used for such problems before. "He's taking care of him now." It would be nice if Nguyen would scream at that point, for the sake of verisimilitude, but he just sat there in the car like a lump of meat. Which is just what he would soon be if Chui had his way.

"The pawnbroker lives," Khai said tonelessly. His deadened voice sent a chill down Chui's spine. Undoubtedly premonitory, that chill. Soon Chui's whole body would be cooling.

There was a long pause, which Khai ended with a more decisive snap to his voice. "Perhaps I was hasty anyway. It may be for the best. Come back to the house. I will soon have another task for you."

Of course I believe that, Chui thought. I *am* a five-year-old child, am I not? He licked his lips. "And Nguyen?"

"Nguyen." Khai had obviously already dismissed the assassin from his thoughts. "You say you're having the doctor tend him? Why did you bother?"

A heartening answer. Khai had accepted the explanation that Nguyen was responsible for their failure. And alas poor Nguyen would have no opportunity for rebuttal. Chui was still unpersuaded, though, that his own brightest future lay in returning to the house. Khai's next words soothed him.

"We have had news here. Concerning Tang."

Truly? thought Chui. If Khai's plan had really worked, celebration might be the order of the day. He might still be able to worm his way back into Khai's good graces. The thought was daunting, but it sounded no worse than being a hounded fugitive.

When Chui settled back into the driver's seat, Nguyen turned to look at him. It was the most curiosity the would-be ninja had displayed since they'd left the pawnshop, but his face still looked like a sick dog's.

"He has another job for us," Chui said cheerily.

As he put the car in gear he felt with his left elbow the .38 automatic in his belt, under his jacket, and he remembered with satisfaction that it was a point of pride with Nguyen never to carry a firearm.

Nguyen asked no questions. Chui began to whistle. He was thinking, Now where in this bright happy city is there a dark corner for the small yellow body beside me?

PART THREE

Raptorial

Night

CHAPTER 11

Tang

HE didn't go out like an American criminal, head down, hands covering his face, resigned to wait for his call to his lawyer. Tang fought like a schoolchild. He twisted, he clawed, he screamed for his men. It was very irritating for Rybek, who was irritated enough to begin with. He threw the fifty-year-old Vietnamese against the side of his car and managed to get the cuffs on him. He would have done more than that if not for the TV cameras.

How the hell had they known to be here? Rybek hadn't known himself until half an hour earlier. A lieutenant had walked by and dropped something on his desk.

"What's this?" Rybek growled.

"It's a warrant. I'm not surprised you don't recognize one. Go serve it."

"Why me?" Rybek had said, not touching the thing.

"Look at the name on it" was all the lieutenant said, and walked away. It wasn't even his lieutenant. Rybek barely knew the guy. He didn't like it. When he looked at the name on the arrest warrant, he liked it even less.

He knew Tang. They had never met face to face but Rybek thought he knew him well. He was a gang leader, Tranh Van Khai's chief rival for power in the Vietnamese community. Their war was responsible for the Vietnamese corpses that had littered the city for the last few weeks. Rybek had had little hope of pinning anything on him directly, or on Khai. He had just been waiting for them to decimate each other's ranks, let the smoke clear, then start making some lower-level arrests and hope against hope someone would talk. Now someone higher up had stepped in and short-circuited that plan. The warrant was for Tang's arrest for the murder of— Rybek didn't recognize the names, but he figured they were the white couple who'd been killed in the car bomb explosion. Who the hell's bright idea was this?

Once they had Tang in the car, he cowered against one of the back doors, babbling nonsense. "Be cool," Rybek's partner told him, and that calmed the Vietnamese down about as well as a cattle prod would have.

"What's his problem?" Leveur asked.

"Don't you know?" Rybek said. "He's in the hands of the Man."

"Hmmph. My *kids* ain't this scared of me."

Normally if he was conducting a murder investigation, Rybek would have taken the suspect back to Homicide and seen if he could get anything out of him. But this didn't seem to be his investigation. So he just booked the cringing gangster straight into jail and went off to find out what the hell was going on.

Raymond Hecate saw the footage of the arrest on the evening news and thought, Okay, it's over now.

Khai saw the same newscast and thought, Almost done.

* * *

Tang pressed back against the bars, then looked behind him and thought better of that. On the other side of the bars was a tank just like this one. A skinny tattooed white man stood close behind him, eyeing him through his cigarette smoke. Tang stepped away from the bars. Doing so, he brushed against a man in his own tank and flinched away. The man stared at him.

The tank he was in was designed to hold sixteen men. That night it held about twenty-five. Most of them looked listless as cattle. The sixteen bunks had been staked out and the men on them looked hot-eyed, ready to defend their hard-won territory. The others milled around or squatted on the floor. In a back corner of the cell on one of the bunks something was going on that Tang wanted to be as far away from as possible. Men's backs blocked his view. Someone whimpered.

Most of them seemed resigned to being there for a night or a month or a year. Only Tang was terrified. He was not American, and he was not insignificant trash like these. In Vietnam he knew what it meant when a gang leader was arrested. It meant his rival had gained control of the police. It meant he would not be seen again. It hadn't occurred to Tang that here another Vietnamese could gain such control. He had been a fool.

But he was not going to lie down and wait to die. He moved warily through the men in the cell, keeping his distance as best he could. Khai would have an agent there. But maybe the man was afraid to act in front of these others. He would wait until they slept. Tang had a little time. He studied the faces.

When the small gang in the back corner broke up and began drifting out, the cell grew even more crowded. Someone pressed against Tang's back. He leaped away, banging into someone else, who shoved him aside, into the bars. The noise sounded loud because the men in the cell were starting to settle down. A few were already sleeping. Soon the lights would go down.

Tang took a deep breath. He had already picked out the

biggest man in the cell. He sidled up next to him and said, "I talk to you?"

The man looked far, far down at the middle-age, pudgy Vietnamese. He didn't say anything.

Tang said, "I need help. I pay for it."

He stuck his fingers in his mouth, far back, behind his teeth. The fingers emerged holding the ring he had saved when the guards searched him. The ring was gold. Its setting glittered with small diamonds. He handed it to the big man, who took it and wiped spit off without apparent distaste. Tang let the man study the ring, hoping he knew value when he saw it.

"I rich man," Tang finally said.

The big man grinned for the first time. "You *was* a rich man, Jack." He closed his hand and the ring disappeared.

Tang looked placidly into his face. "I still rich," he said. He inclined his head. "Outside. Have much more."

"So fucking what? Know what it's worth in here? Jack shit." The big man started to turn away.

Tang put a hand on his arm. The man looked down at it—fat little fingers on the hardwood of his arm. Then he looked into Tang's face. The whites of the big man's eyes were cloudy. They seemed to be roiling even when his face was stony and unmoving.

Tang removed his hand, but without haste. He had committed himself to a course and strangely was no longer afraid.

"I need protection," he said. "You."

The big man looked down at him with something like amazement. "Screwy little gook. What makes you think you can buy me? I *take* what I want." He held up his clenched fist. It looked half as big as Tang's head.

Tang said calmly, "Outside you could not get near me if I said no. In here you already have everything I own. You protect me now, I give you more once outside."

"You talk big, little thing." But the man hesitated. He opened his fist and looked at the ring again. It was not a poor man's ring. He studied the placid little man in front of him. "What if I say no?"

Tang's eyes slid around the cell. "Then I try to hire three others to take the ring away from you."

The big man grinned broadly. "Better make it *five*, Tiny. And there ain't five in here could do it." He clenched the fist again, so hard the muscles in his arm leaped into prominence.

"That why I came to you," Tang said.

The big man kept smiling. He was easy now. The tension had dissipated. "What you offering?"

"Keep me unharmed. When we get out, three thousand dollars."

"Five."

Tang appeared to mull it over, so the man would think he had made a good negotiation. Then "Done," he said.

"All right." The grin disappeared. The big man was working now. He turned to look over the cell. There were two or three men close to them. The big man's scowl drove them back. He took Tang's arm and steered him toward the back. The bunks there were against a wall, not bars. They weren't accessible from adjoining cells. Tang began to think he had chosen wisely.

The big man chose a corner bunk. It was, of course, occupied. "Out," Tang's protector said shortly.

The man on the bunk was thin and wiry, and his eyes had the reddened look of someone coming down from something and not liking the plateau to which he had fallen. "Fuck you, pal," he said.

The big man's hand was around the other's throat before Tang even realized it was no longer holding his arm. The hand was so big the palm alone covered the whole front of the man's throat. The fingers met the thumb in back.

"You got that wrong, Jack," the big man breathed. "I ain't your pal. And you ain't fucking me."

The fire in the thin man's eyes flared and died. He sat up and Tang's protector let him go, off the bunk and away. The big man kept watching him. The thin man glared around him, picked out another bunk across the cell, and displaced its occupant after a brief skirmish. The ripple effect continued until the most easily intimidated bunk-holder trickled down to the floor. The cell grew quieter again.

"In here," the big man said. Tang stretched out on the bunk. The big man sat on the edge of it, his back to Tang. He glared around the circumference of the cell. A few eyes met his, once.

There were lower bunks and upper ones. Tang was on a lower bunk. It was like a cave, with his hireling guarding the entrance. Tang began to relax. Terror was exhausting. As he relaxed he found himself very sleepy. Tomorrow, he thought. It was the first time since his arrest he had thought about tomorrow.

A head edged cautiously over the edge of the bunk above them. "You want to keep those eyes?" the big man said, and the head withdrew. After a while the lights went out. There was movement in the darkness, but none of it nearby. The big man folded his arms but didn't close his eyes.

Behind him, he heard his charge's breathing grow deeper. A little later there was a gentle snore.

The big man watched and waited.

"What the hell does that mean?" Daniel asked. He was watching the evening news with Thien, watching Rybek arrest Tang. Thien had appeared suddenly just after the attack on Daniel, as if they had an appointment. He had turned on one of the TVs in the shop and they were watching it just as if two men hadn't just tried to kill Daniel.

"That is Khai winning," Thien said. "Tang will not be heard from again. I think it's all over now."

"What does that have to do with Carol?" Daniel asked. "What did she ever have to do with it?"

"I don't know." Thien watched the television intently.

Daniel still had the gun in his hand. He had turned off the burglar alarm and called a glass company. Thien had suggested that.

What did it mean—Khai's enemy arrested and an attempt made to kill Daniel at almost the same time? Was Khai tying off loose ends? Daniel reached for the phone. Thien had already told him wait, wait, but they had seen the newscast now and Daniel didn't know what good it did him. It was time for police.

"Police will be worse than useless," Thien said, reading his thoughts. "Call Khai instead, let him know you are still alive."

"If he tried to kill me, he may have already killed her. Or be about to." Daniel picked up the phone.

"And surely will if police come."

Daniel paused.

"The situation is the same," Thien said. "Except that now it is almost over. Whatever use Khai had for your wife, maybe he has it no longer."

Daniel hesitated. Events called for some response from him, but what? Did he go forward, back, sit tight? It wasn't about him, he knew that, or even about Carol. Somehow they had just been caught in it. He felt as if he'd stumbled out into the middle of a giant ballroom, where hard-eyed men glided by in intricate patterns while Daniel slithered and slipped and tried to stay out of their way, expecting any moment that one of them would stab him or his partner in the back. He and Carol were adrift in a predator's waltz, elegant and deadly.

He started dialing again. When the call was answered he said, "Let me talk to her. Now."

And then he would talk to Khai. As Daniel waited to see who would come to the phone, he watched Thien watching the television. All he could see was the back of the boy's head. Later he would remember that, that it was Thien who had talked him out of calling the police.

The Vietnamese was just a lump on a lower bunk when life in the cell began stirring. The men who'd slept on the floor were the first ones up, shuffling around, waiting for someone to abandon a bunk. The men looked different after a night's sleep. Some of the crazed ones looked less so. The sullen ones were more so. Those who'd been patient the night before were now restless, waiting for lawyers and family and bail bondsmen.

Those who'd been in longer than a day knew to start congregating near the front of the cell early. Breakfast was served at seven, and sometimes there were fewer trays than there were prisoners. When the metal cart came creaking down the aisle almost all the bunks were empty. Tang's was one of the few still occupied. The big man was nowhere near it.

The guard kept order while passing out the trays, but that order broke down as soon as a man got his hands on one. He might keep it only a second. Men grabbed trays, hunched over them, and tried to break out of the mob. They grew louder, fueled by the perpetual anger of jail.

Tang woke with a start. He couldn't imagine where he was. But before he could sit up, calling for his men, he remembered. He lay unmoving. His protector was gone. Tang moved ever so slowly. He was covered by a thin blanket now. It seemed to have removed his body. He couldn't feel his legs.

There was no one near him. He was quarantined like the first victim of a plague. Slowly Tang pulled back the blanket. He felt so weak.

"Breakfast in bed, Tiny. Sit up there."

The big man had suddenly reappeared in front of him, two metal trays in his hands. Tang sat up, glad to see his legs moving. His whole body felt still asleep from having slept on the thin mattress over the metal bunk.

His guardian thrust a tray into his hands and shoved him gently aside to make room for himself on the bunk. Tang looked at the food solemnly, as if he couldn't remember its purpose. Beside him the big man was wolfing down eggs and bologna.

"I am alive."

"Damn straight," the big man said. "I take a job, I do it. You owe me five big ones."

"I am alive," Tang said again. He was starting to smile. He left his tray on his lap and clapped his hand on the big shoulder beside him. He laughed loudly. The big man looked at him strangely.

"Khai failed," Tang said, to no one. "Even in here I beat him. He is dead man now. When I get out—"

His laughter stopped abruptly. He had survived one night. How many more would there be?

That worry was assuaged two hours later when a guard appeared along the corridor calling his name—mangling the pronunciation, but undoubtedly Tang's name. The guard ignored the black and white and brown men thrusting their hands through the bars, pretending to answer. "Here!" called Tang, and the guard stopped.

The big man was still at his side. Tang turned and grasped his hand, his smile restored. "This bail is wonderful thing," he said eagerly, like a new citizen. "We do not have in my country. We have rot in jail."

"We got that here too, Jack. But I be out in three more days. I know where you live. Five big ones."

"Five big ones," Tang happily agreed. "Gate will be open for you. Maybe you work for me again, eh? I have big job for someone like you."

"First the pay, then we talk continued employment," the big man said. He was smiling too. He found the eager little man amusing. Might be fun to work for him. "But first the five, right, Jack?"

"Right, Jack," Tang babbled happily. He was overjoyed. He was alive and Khai would pay. Retribution would be sweet. It would almost be worth the fearful night he had spent.

He had only this short gauntlet of sullen prisoners to run. They were all turned to look at him, envious of his good fortune.

"Back away," the guard said wearily. "Get away from the door there."

Tang hurried. There was no way to keep his face toward all of them. As he passed he turned his back. The door in the cell was just ahead of him. He looked back. His protector was back there behind the crowd, head and shoulders rising above them but still far away.

The door opened ahead of him. The guard waited patiently, looking down at his watch. Tang leaped the last few feet. He was there. The door closed behind him. Tang sighed hugely. He turned back and waved to the big man. The big man just nodded and held up one hand—five fingers. Tang nodded too. Well worth the price. He might even pay it.

The guard was already walking away. "Somebody's gone your bail," he said. "Come on, hurry up."

The cells they passed were still full. Tang seemed to be the first one being released. That was as it should be. Someone was going to catch hell that he'd had to spend even one night in this foul pit. But he had survived it. Not only Khai would be surprised. Tang's own men would see what the boss could do when thrown strictly on his own resources. The superior man always prevailed.

He had to hurry now. He must strike while it was still unexpected, while Khai thought him dead or imprisoned. Tang's thoughts raced ahead as he followed the guard down a dank corridor. The cells on each side now were empty—small, temporary holding cells. Far ahead Tang saw a gate. Beyond it were desks, linoleum instead of concrete, civilians: freedom.

The guard stopped to let Tang catch up. Tang started to pass him, walking fast now. "In here," the guard said, and pushed him. Tang stumbled off balance into one of the open holding cells.

"What?" he said angrily. "Is there more—?"

The guard didn't reply. He stepped into the cell and swung the nightstick he was holding. It caught Tang high on the side of the head. Tang fell against the wall, putting up his hands. Too late. The nightstick cracked down on his temple. Tang fell on his back. His eyes were open, staring, but he didn't move. The guard grabbed his collar with both hands and pulled him up, letting him drop on the bunk. The guard stuck the nightstick back in his belt and pulled out a homemade shiv, the kind so many prisoners in there would be carrying after only a day or two inside. A sharpened triangle of metal that had started life as a spoon or a bunk support.

The little Vietnamese was out cold but his blood still flowed. It came in a spurt when the guard drew the shiv across his throat. He worked like a butcher, dragging the bit of metal all the way across. The blood bubbled out freely, as if it had somewhere it was eager to go.

The "guard" dropped the shiv beside the corpse and hurried away. The shift was about to change. He would be lost in it. He brushed at the droplets of blood on his sleeve.

The secret was always to have more plans than anyone else knew about. That was what made everyone else into pawns, Khai thought: that each knew his own function but did not know his place in the grand design. Only Khai held the entire scheme in mind at once.

He had accomplished what he had set out to do: Kill Tang, win the war. But that had necessitated secondary schemes, so that now the conclusion was not neat. The Americans were left over: Greer, Greer's wife still in this house, her wily father.

It had been hasty of him to try to have the pawnbroker killed. He had done such a thoughtless thing only because of his distraction with his other plans. Hecate had almost suggested it and Khai had embraced the suggestion because it seemed simple. But now he doubted whether it would have worked. There would have still been the wife to deal with. He couldn't kill her or he would make a powerful enemy of her father. The only alternative would have been to release her to find that her husband had been murdered. Hecate had implied that he could control her after that, but Khai had his doubts.

He still faced the same dilemma. What Khai would have liked to do now was kill the wife and be done with all of them. But he was afraid. He had seen the power her father could wield. But how could he just let her go? She had seen him and so had her husband. He was willing to take a chance on Hecate because he had something on him: The councilman had been a party to murder and knew it. Besides, Khai sensed Raymond

Hecate's ambition, suspected they were two of a kind. They might be able to work together in the future. But over the pawnbroker and his wife he had no hold, if he let her go. It was not in Khai to give up an advantage.

And so, in what should have been his moment of triumph, he remained lost in thought over the problem of the Americans.

Chui was a sort of ghost in the mansion. A ghost waiting to happen. He had the perpetual look of a man checking his mailbox for an eviction notice. The other men avoided him. They knew the walking dead when they saw one. No one wanted to be exposed to his terminal disease.

Poor Nguyen was already a maggot motel by now, somewhere beneath the dirt of a vacant lot. That seemed to Chui not so terrible a state—to have passed on already to the next phase of nature's plan for one's flesh. It was the difficult transitional period that worried Chui. Khai was not so kind as nature.

In fact, Khai's hand had not yet fallen on him. But Chui did not delude himself that Nguyen's demise had been atonement enough for their mutual failure to kill the American. Chui's own destruction seemed perpetually imminent. Khai kept him close now, always within the mansion itself. No more outside errands for Chui. Khai was distracted now with his plan for Tang, but surely an occasional stray thought lingered on his own bungling henchman as well. It was a measure of Khai's cruel genius that he allowed Chui the faintest of hopes that he *had* been forgotten in the rush of events. Chui admired his technique even while suffering under it.

Chui tried to make plans of his own. He was confined to the mansion. Within that small world his best hope seemed to be the American woman. Her disposition remained uncertain. And it seemed to Chui that John Loftus took a greater interest in her fate than was strictly necessary to his role as go-between. He was American as well, was he not? And he could be observed slipping into her room at odd hours.

Chui's own fate remained quite the most fascinating topic in mind. But because of that damned faint hope that Khai had forced on him, Chui continued to watch for opportunity. Someone else would slip up. The woman was bad luck, and she was rubbing off on others in the house now. John Loftus seemed to Chui the best possible candidate as his stand-in in mortality.

Chui continued to watch and worry and chew his nails and, damn Khai for this, to hope.

When Loftus came into her room with breakfast, Carol said, "Something's happening."

"Something's about to," he said candidly. "But only Khai knows what it is."

"He's thought of what to do about Daniel."

Loftus could have told her that she and her husband both were only small cogs in Khai's scheme, but he thought it best to let her think she was the focus of the terror. He said nothing.

Carol was pacing the room, ignoring the tray. He didn't like her like this. She looked like she'd been up all night thinking, and now her stride was purposeful.

"Tell Khai I want to see him," she said.

He almost laughed. It was so startling. Khai would be delighted to take a few minutes out of his busy schedule to get her perspective on things.

"There's something he doesn't know," she went on.

"I doubt that."

"He doesn't know that my father is a city councilman. If I remain missing much longer—"

Loftus almost corrected her ignorance, but instead he shut up and let her talk. While she was marching back and forth like this the clothes moved on her body. There were glimpses of skin where her warmup jacket rode up above the waistband of the pants. The pants were much too tight, the way he liked them. Loftus just watched her.

She spun out some plan but he paid no attention. When she

ran down he said, "Here's what might be a better idea. *I*'ll get in touch with your father. Maybe if he knows where you are, and I'm already on the inside, we can work something out between us."

Her eyes glowed and then slid sightlessly around the room as she considered it. It appeared to Loftus that she was only thinking about methods, not questioning the basic suggestion. She trusted him.

"Yes," she said finally. "Yes. Let me give you his home number. Can you memorize it?"

He assured her he could. When he left a few minutes later she was looking at him intently. Her reliance on him was absolute. He smiled at her confidently and she smiled hesitantly back.

Plans, Loftus thought as he walked down the hall. Everybody around here's got plans.

His own plans concerned only her.

Alone in the room again, Carol thought only, *Daniel*. If only Daniel could stay safe long enough for her to save them both. Finally she had some hope that it would all come out all right. She waited for him to call. She wouldn't be able to say anything on the phone, but she thought her tone alone could convey to him her new hope.

Daylight grew stronger until it filled her room. She caught glimpses of the sun as it climbed higher behind clouds. She listened intently but couldn't hear a ringing telephone. No one came to fetch her.

Khai was almost as isolated as his prisoners. He spent hours at a time alone in his study, sitting behind the desk in trancelike concentration. Daytime turned to night while he pondered, the night of Tang's arrest. It was always dim in the room. Khai plotted murder.

He conjured intricate plans that always ended in the simplest acts of violence. Both of them must be killed. And yet that desire always foundered on the fact that the woman could not be murdered with impunity. What had made her worth taking now kept her safe.

Near sunrise of the morning Tang awakened in jail, light dawned in Khai's study as well. Khai blinked. He had been on the verge of falling asleep and his grip on the problem had loosened. The situation blossomed in his mind, his horizon broadened, and he realized that he had been too tightly focused on Daniel himself. When he allowed himself to look beyond the Americans in his path, a solution presented itself.

The problem seemed simple now, and it still ended, satisfyingly, in murder. Khai fell peacefully to sleep, smiling on his desktop.

Daniel's hand was on the phone and, like a fool, his back to the door, when the little bell tinkled its warning. He whirled, dropping toward the floor and his hand going to the shelf under the counter, but he realized how exposed he was and in that instant knew the dead certainty that this mistake was the fatal one. He thought in that moment of his wife, left unprotected.

The door closed again with a small *thunk*. Daniel's head came up above the counter.

"Dropped my pen," he said, and rose to his full height holding one.

Rybek looked no less menacing than the men Daniel had expected to see. He was wearing a heavy overcoat, but even inside its deep pockets his hands looked bulky, as if they were holding something or his fists were clenched. He stood planted just inside the door, looking as if it would disgust him to come any farther.

"Twenty-one shopping days till Christmas," he said. "You having a busy season?"

"You can see," Daniel said.

"Must not be advertising enough. People want to avoid the Galleria this time of year, they like shopping these little out-of-the-way places, if they hear about them."

"I guess I'm a little too far out of the way." Daniel sat back down on his stool, laying his hands flat on the countertop. Outside his window the street scene had subtly altered, but he hadn't been watching it closely enough before to put his finger on what was different now. He and Rybek seemed to be wallflowers at the dance, swaying to a rhythm the orchestra wasn't playing.

"Luckily you're a two-income family," Rybek said. "But I've just been to your wife's office and they haven't seen her for a few days. I know she's back okay because you told me she is, but I was wondering exactly where she is."

"She's at home."

"No. Try again."

Rybek came forward finally and pulled his hands from his pockets. They were empty. He laid them on the counter a few inches from Daniel's. Daniel realized that the detective was slightly shorter than he but this close he looked half again as broad. From the street no one would be able to see anything of Daniel but the top of his head.

"If she's not at home she must be out shopping. I don't keep her tied up." Daniel hesitated. "That was one of the things we argued about. She needs more 'space.'"

Rybek didn't roll his eyes in sympathy as Daniel had hoped. The cop seemed to be listening for something other than what he was hearing.

"Where's your little gook sweeper-upper?" he asked abruptly.

"I don't keep him tied up either. Isn't today a school day?"

"He doesn't seem much concerned about that anymore. His English teacher misses his contributions to the class."

Daniel shrugged. It was news to him that Thien had been

missing school, but not a surprise. He had seen the boy around once or twice during the days. "Maybe his parents need him around the shop. They must be doing more business than I am."

"Everybody must," Rybek said.

The silences between their sentences were growing stupidly melodramatic. Daniel fidgeted, glancing at the clock and the phone. "Anything else I can do for you?"

"Anything *else*?" Rybek raised his voice for the first time. Daniel saw that he was furious.

"I'll tell you what," the cop said. "Somebody's used me to do a dirty job for him. Maybe you could tell me who that was."

Daniel hesitated. He almost spoke a name. Instead he said, "You'd have to tell me what you're talking about first."

Rybek's hands clenched on the countertop. He drew one of them back. After a long moment he dropped it to his side.

"That's what I thought you'd say. Maybe you'll get lucky, find out something before I do. If you do, you'd best give me a call.

"And I still want to talk to your wife too, when you hear from her."

Rybek turned, self-consciously slowly, Daniel thought. He waited, knowing the detective would pause with his hand on the doorknob and look back with one last penetrating gaze and heavy-handed exit line. But the cop surprised him by going straight out the door. Must have already used up all his A material.

Daniel had forgotten reporting Carol missing. That was coming back to haunt him. He was the natural suspect. The next time Rybek returned to the shop it might be with an arrest warrant. He couldn't be here when that happened. They couldn't both be prisoners.

They were leaving him no official options. He had to go the same place Carol had gone: into the shadows.

The phone rang. Daniel wasn't even surprised by the sound. He picked it up and Khai said, "You have been talking to the police."

"No. The police has been talking to me. He's still curious

about what's happened to my wife. If she doesn't come back
soon, or if I disappear suddenly—"

"I know that," Khai said irritably. "We don't have to growl
at each other anymore.

"I have a plan."

CHAPTER 12

Khai's Genius

LATER, when Daniel really thought about it, he said to himself, *Why not?* He'd been ready to kill someone anyway. *Why the hell not?*

But when he first heard Khai's proposal, as he listened to the quiet, self-assured voice make the horrible suggestion, his reaction was conventional outraged refusal.

"You must be insane!"

"I am not," Khai said quietly, "and you know it. Don't act bourgeois. This is not a common situation and it can't be resolved in a commonplace way."

Khai's genius had never served him better nor pleased him so well. In the predawn dimness of his study his idea had seemed brilliant. Later in the light of morning, after refinement, its allure had not faded. Now as he described the plan to Daniel Greer, it still had the sweet simplicity of perfection.

"I can't release your wife because there will then be nothing to prevent your going to the police. You on the other hand could hardly—"

"We had an agreement."

"You on the other hand could hardly *fail* to go to the police, out of fear that if you didn't have me imprisoned I would strike back at you."

"There'd be no—"

"We will never trust each other unless we have to," Khai went unheedingly on. "Only if we are partners will we have to. You must do what you wanted me to do in the first place. Kill your rival."

Khai let Daniel run out his protestations without listening. He was continuing to admire the plan. Khai could actually afford to let the woman go if Greer first killed Linh. Daniel Greer would never go to the police then. Even if he told them that he'd been blackmailed into murdering Linh, the police wouldn't believe him, because the American *did* have a motive for killing the Vietnamese. His original motive: Linh was putting him out of business.

The plan also had the beauty of achieving Khai's original objectives: killing Linh as an example to the other merchants, and putting Daniel Greer under his thumb forever.

He cut off Daniel's protests. "I have found you not to be so lily-livered as you pretend. You came here with a gun, prepared to use it, I think. Use it now. When I hear that your rival is dead you can come and take your wife away."

"You're crazy," Daniel said feebly.

"It's entirely in your own hands."

Both men waited. Daniel said, "Let me talk to her."

"No. No more. After."

"You've murdered her already."

"No. Remember there is still the threat of her father. But you don't have an eternity to ponder anymore, pal. I dislike suspense. If I don't hear soon that you've accepted my partnership, I'd rather bring matters to a head another way and take my chances with the police. Understand?"

Everything having been said, they hung up without goodbyes. Daniel laid the phone gently in its cradle, as if too much force would explode it, and looked out the window of his shop.

It was midafternoon of a bright, bitter December day. The sky was clear but the sun was far and pale. When you stepped out into that street the wind went through you like a shower of needles. The Vietnamese, who never seemed adequately dressed for the cold, had abandoned the street. It almost looked like a part of Houston again, but for the alien characters of their shop signs.

Daniel's mind had been stopped dead by Khai's outrageous suggestion. Gradually it began working again. What could he do? He had a deadline now, though he didn't know exactly when it was. He should talk to Rybek. He could tell him the truth now. Could they get enough police to storm the old mansion to rescue Carol before Khai's men could kill her? If Khai was going to kill her anyway, the risk was now worthwhile.

But he still recoiled from involving police. That would be a clumsy, unsecret operation requiring too many people. And they'd need a warrant or something first. Would his word that he knew his wife was being held inside be enough to get one? Would Rybek even try, as suspicious of Daniel as the cop now seemed? Even if he did, how long would it take? Long enough for Khai to find out what was going on and get Carol away? Daniel had no idea about the legalities except what he'd seen on TV.

It would be better for him to slip in alone again, maybe informing Rybek just before he left, as a backup. But even as he began planning his attack, he knew it was hopeless. It had worked so brilliantly last time, hadn't it? And this time Khai would be expecting him. It would play right into Khai's hands. He would have them both then.

He went blank for a while. When he came to himself again he was sitting near his window staring across the street at the Vietnamese pawnshop. He wondered idly if Linh was inside. There was no traffic of customers. He tried to picture Linh inside, behind his counter, and realized he couldn't remember what the man looked like. He had a vague impression of the man's size, but he couldn't put a face to the haze. The one time they'd talked Linh had hardly paid him the courtesy of looking at him. Mostly Daniel remembered his back.

Don't be such a virgin, he thought suddenly. Who was Linh to him anyway? An obstacle. A rude competitor. Weighed in the balance against Carol's life, Linh's hadn't the moral weight of a sigh. It was only the physical act that was repugnant. If he could wish Linh off the earth in an instant, wouldn't he do it?

Daniel tried to think honestly about his motives in starting this affair. Why did he approach Khai in the first place? What kind of *influence* did he think Khai would bring to bear to persuade the Vietnamese pawnbroker to abandon a successful business and move it elsewhere? He hadn't been naive, he hadn't thought Khai was the damned *spiritual* leader of the community. He had known exactly what he was. Hadn't that been the real reason he hadn't reported the attack on him in his shop to the police—because he didn't want them to trace his tie to the gang leader? He'd been protecting himself, not Carol. Telling the police might have provided them with a clue to Carol's whereabouts, but he hadn't given them that.

All right. Then it was no longer time to think about his own safety. Only Carol's. He tried to picture her in that dark old mansion, surrounded by the bastards. Hate surged through him, lifting him to his feet. To hell with them all. He had no love for Vietnamese, Linh in particular. Carol was the only one who mattered. If the death of one Vietnamese man would free her, that was no price at all to pay.

A shadow passed behind the window across the way. He recognized the bulk, though the man remained faceless. A world behind glass, that's all it was to him. When he had first approached Khai, the Vietnamese community had seemed to him more like an ants' nest than anything else. What happened within it was mysterious and of no concern. However they dealt with each other was okay with him, as long as he got what he wanted.

Now it was time to descend into the ants' nest himself. He was still turning it over in his mind, philosophizing, but his body had already decided. He had moved behind the counter and was examining the guns there. His eyes slid across them and he settled on the .45 he'd taken to Khai's. It was a heavy gun, clumsy in his hand. He had fired it a few times out in the countryside. With one inadvertent shot he had knocked a good-size limb off a mesquite tree. The gun had stopping power, that was certain. It was a conversation-ender.

He found a clip of ammunition in another drawer and examined it at some length before loading it into the gun. His hands turned the clip over and over. After the gun was loaded, he held it for long minutes until it felt like part of his arm. There was a sensation of loss in laying it aside, on the shelf under the counter.

For the next hour he moved softly around the shop, adjusting the merchandise on the shelves, even dusting. He could not sit still. But the physical movements were mindless. He would move a VCR two inches to the right and five minutes later move it back to its original position.

The sun seemed disinclined to move. He was waiting for dusk. He almost called Khai back to tell him: "I'm just waiting for the sun to go down." No one went into or out of the pawnshop across the street. Once Linh came to the door again and opened it. The wind grabbed the door and slammed it back against the wall—silently from where Daniel watched, but it looked like quite a crash. Crazy Linh was trying to sweep dust out onto the sidewalk. The wind must have blown it back in his face. He stood there for a moment holding the broom. Linh was wearing a long white apron. He looked like a grocer, or a butcher. He stared at the empty street, though not across it at Daniel. Missing his customers. Daniel watched him coldly. Linh went back in. The sign on his door still said OPEN.

The sun slowly declined. Daniel continued to move restlessly around the shop. When his door opened he was standing with his back to it, across the shop from where he'd left the gun. He turned slowly. The air was suddenly crystalline from the cold blast that had come in from the street.

It was Thien. Daniel didn't relax. The boy stared at him. He looked very slight and Asian. He was wearing a jacket that was much too thin for the weather. His skin must have been blue beneath it, but he wasn't shivering.

"Shouldn't you be at home?"

Thien didn't answer the question, but it broke the silence. The boy walked deeper into the shop, toward the small electric heater glowing red in the middle of the floor. Daniel walked back toward his stool and the counter.

"Khai's men came collecting again today," Thien said. "They claimed the payments were late, even though they hadn't been there to pick them up until today. They charged more interest. One man didn't have it and they beat him in front of his children."

Daniel had no response. So it was back to business as usual for Khai. He must be very confident of his scheme. He was no longer distracted from the daily chores.

"Have they gone in the other pawnshop?" Thien asked.

"I haven't been watching for them." Not technically a lie, but he knew no one had gone into Linh's shop. Khai had that much delicacy, not to try to collect payment from a man he was having killed.

"Have they been here?"

"Here?" Daniel laughed mildly. "No, of course not."

Thien had been holding his hands out toward the heater on the floor. Now he turned his back on it in order to face Daniel. The Vietnamese boy put his hands behind his back, still warming them. Daniel wondered if he had a pair of gloves to give him. Thien's expression was strange, not at all unfriendly and yet remote. In a moment Daniel realized it was because the boy was reminiscing.

"Do you know why I started coming in your shop?" Thien asked.

"I thought you enjoyed my company."

"That was after," he said matter-of-factly. "What first drew me in was I saw that you were the only one who didn't pay Khai. Everyone said it was just because you were American, but I hoped there was something else, something—"

"Transferable?" Daniel suggested.

Thien nodded. "Something I could learn."

"Linh didn't pay either," Daniel pointed out. Strange to say the man's name so lightly.

"But everyone knew he'd suffer for it eventually. You they didn't even approach. That's what I wanted to learn. I thought maybe Americans had a system to protect them."

Daniel spread his hands. "Sorry, kid. No secrets."

He nodded again. "I know. And now Khai knows it too."

Thien's eyes were lowered. He was looking at the shelf under the counter. When he looked up at Daniel again his black eyes were opaque.

But of their two expressions, Daniel's was the less scrutable.

The lone young Saigon cowboy across the street was on the far side of the Vietnamese pawnshop, peeking around the corner at the American's shop. Damn job. Khai should have given them shorter shifts in this bitter cold. The wind crawled under his red windbreaker, making it billow like a sail. He clutched it tighter around him and peered across the street at the pawnbroker talking to the little Viet boy. The boy was a pest. The older Vietnamese had seen him all over the neighborhood without taking any notice of him. He wished the boy would go home now so the American could get on with what he was supposed to do. The young man had made a small bet that the American wouldn't do it. If Greer didn't, the cowboy was supposed to do them both. He put his right hand under his armpit to keep it warm, but that was a losing battle.

When his colleague came up behind him and tapped his shoulder he jumped, almost crying out, turned, and snapped in their hard-edged tongue, but then gratefully accepted the hot coffee the other had brought. They had a brief conversation to the effect only that nothing had happened. The young man gestured and his colleague peeked around the corner. He saw the boy in the shop. He seemed to be talking quickly, animatedly, with hand gestures. The American was shaking his head. He didn't seem to be paying much attention to the boy.

The two Vietnamese walked back down the block to stand in a doorway that partially sheltered them from the wind while they drank their coffee. One argued that they shouldn't move so far from their post but the other just shrugged, and they both stayed until the coffee was gone. When they returned to their surveillance, the boy was finally gone from the shop. The American was alone behind the counter, toying with something beneath it. The two Vietnamese watched him, speculating in low voices. The sun was touching the horizon. In a few minutes it would turn even colder.

Rybek drove by the Greer house. When he stopped a dog started barking but there was no response from the house. No curtain twitched, no light went on. The house was not just dark, it was obviously empty. The first time Rybek had driven by it it had looked like a home, but now, just a few days later, it looked like abandoned rental property. Trash blew through the yard. Nevertheless he went through the motions, getting out and trudging through the wind to the front door. No one answered the bell or his loud knocking. He wouldn't have been disappointed if the door had swung open when he banged on it, but it was locked and he decided it wouldn't be worth the trouble to open it. He didn't expect to find a body in the living room.

He had called her friend Jennifer again and now Jennifer said yes, Carol was away on a trip. Rybek had a gift for sensing when someone was lying to him, but he wasn't sure of the reason. He tried not to speculate about people's motives. It was too distracting, trying to fit facts to a theory. Minds were too squirmy to predict anyway. You could never tell what lay back of someone's forehead.

Rybek stood on the porch in the whistling wind and knew that the house was empty. The barking dog in back sounded petulant. Probably hungry.

He trudged back across the front yard. The wind felt wet now. Fall was the rainy season in Houston and they weren't out of it yet. The damned heater in Rybek's car wasn't working. When Rybek had complained about it the garage mechanic had said, "When d'ya ever need a heater in this town anyway?" *Today*, Rybek could have told him. He sat in the car blowing on his hands. No place to go and a lousy day to go anywhere. He'd spent too much time on this already. Six more murders had been committed in the two days he'd spent investigating this one, which no one even believed *was* a murder.

Slowly he pulled away from the empty house, heading for the pawnshop one last time.

Daniel watched the dying sun shoot its last rays straight down the street, red as neon. A moment later it was gone. The streetlights hadn't come on yet. The block looked dim and dead, like an abandoned movie set. His own shop lights were on, spotlighting him. There was dimmer light inside Linh's shop across the street. A few days ago sitting isolated and well lighted like this would have made Daniel paranoid. Now he moved around as freely as if he were at home behind curtains. He checked the clip in the .45 again and slipped the heavy gun into his overcoat pocket. He unplugged the electric heater as he passed it and snapped off the overhead lights at the front door, leaving the dying glow of the heater the only illumination.

The two Vietnamese were still around the corner, watching intently as Daniel closed the door behind him and started across the street. His head was down against the wind. The men nudged each other into watchfulness. They peered up and down the street for witnesses. The American seemed to be paying no attention, so they acted as his lookouts. It was other Americans they were concerned about. The Vietnamese merchants were *supposed* to know what was about to happen.

Greer went straight across the street and into the Vietnamese pawnshop. Khai's two men stepped out from the corner.

Through the picture window of Linh's shop they had a good view of everything.

Linh looked up when Daniel came in. The tinkling bell was shrill. Linh didn't speak, didn't even nod. He might have been dead already, sitting slumped behind the counter. His hands were resting on top of it. Daniel didn't speak either. He had thought about engaging the man in conversation first, but neither of them had anything to say. Daniel just glanced around to make sure that they were alone.

When he looked back Linh's hands were gone from the countertop. They were beneath it, scrambling for what Daniel knew lay under there, being a shopowner himself.

He shouted, something without words. Linh might have shouted too. He stood up straight, knocking his stool back, because he had found what he was looking for. His hand came out from under the counter with the gun.

Daniel leaped aside as Linh fired. Glass shattered. Daniel could still hear the singing of the path the bullet had traced past his ear. He ripped the .45 out of his pocket, tearing fabric. Linh had his own gun balanced atop the counter, holding it with both hands. His eyes glittered a few inches above the barrel.

Daniel didn't even hear the bullet hit. Bad sign. Daniel stood stock still, his arm fully extended ahead of him, and fired.

The Vietnamese went crashing back into the shelves behind him. His arms were flung out to the side, one of them still holding the gun. For a moment he was crucified against the bric-a-brac of his stock. Daniel fired twice more. He was deaf from the noise. His hand was numb but perfectly steady. It might have been someone else's hand.

The Vietnamese gurgled something inarticulate in any language as he slid down the wall. Daniel stood there like a statue, the gun still extended the full length of his arm.

Outside, Khai's men were coming closer for a better look. There was a whir of motion behind them. One of them turned to meet it and Thien flew past him. He flung open the door of the pawnshop and screamed, "What have you done?"

Daniel stood in the same spot, looking stunned. In a moment he had the presence of mind to put the gun back in his pocket, but he had no response for Thien. The boy continued to scream at him. Daniel started toward him.

The two Vietnamese outside headed for the boy too, toward the door of the shop, when one of them grabbed the other's arm. People were coming. Thien's cries were drawing a small crowd of running footsteps.

The streetlights snapped on. That was decisive. Khai's men drew back, but only after a last long look into the pawnshop. Sticking out from behind the counter were the Vietnamese pawnbroker's unmoving feet. Only one of them still wore its slipper.

There was the sound of a siren in the distance. It couldn't be coming here. Who in this crowd would have called the Houston police? But the sound was coming closer. Khai's two thugs turned and ran.

Daniel ran too, brushing past Thien in the doorway. The boy's fingers tore at him. Daniel pushed him back against the door and ran. It was December, one of the longest nights of the year, and the night had just begun. Daniel ran into it.

When Rybek arrived he found a crowd of jabbering Vietnamese, none of whom, of course, had seen anything. Greer's pawnshop across the street was as empty as his house. Rybek looked around for the only other person on this block he knew by sight, but for once he wasn't there. The detective wondered fleetingly where the boy was.

CHAPTER 13

Raptors

THIS time he went right in the front gate. It was closed but unlocked. Daniel lifted the latch and went in. He didn't look up at the windows as he crossed the lawn. On the front porch was a lounging young Vietnamese who watched him come but didn't move. He did glance at the .45 Daniel still carried. The Vietnamese didn't appear to be armed. He straightened up as Daniel came up onto the porch, but didn't move to bar Daniel's way or announce him. Daniel almost expected a nod of greeting. He was one of them now, one of Khai's men.

He walked inside, crossed the front hall unmolested, and went straight into Khai's study. Khai was behind the desk. He flinched ever so slightly at the sight of the gun but didn't appear alarmed. Daniel raised the .45. His eyes were dead, much flatter than Khai's, which still showed lively interest in the world.

He dropped the pistol on the desk. "All right. It's done."

"I know," Khai said. He looked at Daniel speculatively. He was wondering how to make the best use of him in the future.

On the other hand, it might be better to go ahead and kill both Greers now while he had them here together. Khai was still thinking, but in a lazy, happy sort of way. He had already won.

"Have a seat, why don't you, while we talk about it."

Upstairs, John Loftus stood at one of the windows and watched Greer walk in. The fool wasn't even cautious. He didn't have Khai bring the woman out to the gate. He walked right into the house like the vicar come to call.

Khai was going to let him have his wife back. Loftus was as sure of that as you could be of anything Khai had in mind. Khai wanted the American couple back in the public eye in Little Saigon, visibly under his thumb. He'd let them walk out tonight.

But the woman was no longer just Khai's *or* her husband's to give and take at will. John Loftus had some say in her future.

Loftus didn't speculate over why he felt so possessive of Carol Greer. They had been the only two white people in this house for days. It was like Noah himself had paired them up. Loftus didn't think like that, though. All he knew was that he had promised himself he'd have her, and he didn't break promises to himself.

If she wasn't willing it would have to be rape, which meant he'd have to kill her afterward, but those were the breaks. There were plenty of slants around to blame it on.

Something seemed to be going on, but no one, of course, had told Carol what it was. At dusk the rat-faced Vietnamese had slipped into the room with her. He carried a rifle and leered at her, but he'd been there for half an hour now and hadn't done anything more. But he hadn't left, either.

Outside her window the night was turmoil. Clouds roiled and churned, brewing another storm. As soon as the sun departed the night was black and isolating. She could see neither stars nor buildings. Carol was alone with the rat-faced man and she hadn't talked to Daniel all day. That was the worst part. She knew that somewhere out there Khai's planning had come to fruition. That would account for the rat-faced man's grin. Maybe they were waiting for final word that Daniel was dead. Ratface was here to make sure of being first in line when they were certain Carol was no longer of any value to them.

She sat on the bed. When she started crying she grew furious, because it made the rat-faced man's grin grow even broader. Instead she started thinking about just how many of them she could kill. Ratface would get close to her, that was certain. When he did she would get his rifle, one way or another. Then into the hallway, down toward Khai. She wasn't thinking of escape. With Daniel dead she had no home to escape to. But there was revenge.

The hall door opened. Carol's hopes fell to nothing. Reinforcements had come for the rat-faced man.

John Loftus stepped into the room. Her heart lifted at the sight of him. She hadn't gotten over that instinctive reaction. Lost in the Vietnamese nightmare as she'd been for days, Loftus looked to her like a fellow traveler from the homeland.

The rat-faced man grinned at Loftus, said something in a gruff undertone, and gestured at Carol with the rifle. His grin was a horrible thing. He didn't have enough teeth to fill it, for one thing. John Loftus stepped close to him and the rat-faced man inclined his head to receive the whispered instruction. Loftus's right hand came from behind his back, holding the leather-covered sap. He swung it from about the level of his waist, all the way across his body, and laid it just in front of Ratface's ear. That wasn't quite the right spot. It only staggered the Vietnamese, made him drop the rifle. Loftus took his time placing the second strike, to the back of the rat-faced head. The Vietnamese went straight down like a building imploding.

Carol had come catlike off the bed. She didn't even exult in the rat-faced man's fall, she just saw the chance she'd been waiting for. Her hand was on the fallen rifle.

But in the next moment, so was Loftus's foot. She struggled

to jerk the rifle out from under him, but it might as well have been welded to the floor. She leaned forward to bite his leg.

Loftus stooped and pushed her back before she could bite. "Stop," he said mildly. "I've come to get you out of here." He picked up the rifle.

She was back on her feet and laid a hand on the gun again. "They killed my husband."

Her voice was low and fierce and determined. This wasn't the way he liked her. "No, they didn't," he said in the same mild tone. "What gave you that crazy idea?"

"He hasn't called me all day. He would've called if he was alive."

Loftus shook his head. "Khai hasn't been letting him talk to you. He's been putting the pressure on."

Carol stepped back in confusion. She'd become so convinced of Daniel's death that this sudden uncertainty left her feeling hollow. "Why?" she said.

"He's out doing a favor for Khai right now. He's killing the old gook pawnbroker."

Carol shook her head, not looking at him. "Daniel would never do that." Would he? A week earlier she would have said the same thing about herself, but she'd been more than ready to kill a minute ago.

Loftus was looking at her coolly. He saw the weakness taking her. Her shoulders slumped. She was staring at the floor. Helpless.

"No?" he said. "Bad for you if he doesn't."

"What do you mean?" she asked, but that was a form of question he didn't even bother to acknowledge.

"Come on," Loftus said. "I'm getting you out of here."

She looked up at him, finally. Her eyes were hopeful as a child's. "How?"

"Looking like a prisoner," he replied. He dropped the rifle and grabbed her arm, high, just under the shoulder. He knew his grip was hard enough to leave bruises but she didn't resist. Loftus smiled to himself as he pulled her out into the corridor and she came along willingly.

* * *

"She is safe enough," Khai said. "One of my men is guarding her."

Daniel nodded. He didn't want to ruin things by being in too big a hurry now.

The house was aswarm with Vietnamese men. Carol hadn't realized how many there were. Most of them were armed too. She hung her head so she wouldn't have to look at them.

She looked so submissive now it was obvious her fierce look in the room had been a shallow pose. Loftus hurried down the hall, making her walk faster. She stumbled a little. Her feet were bare. They went down the back stairs, the ones that came out next to the kitchen—and the closet with the door into the tunnel.

John Loftus had not been the only occupant of the house to see Daniel walk in. Chui had been watching from a different window. He too thought at once of the woman. But he also thought of Loftus. He had been waiting, praying, for Loftus to do something stupid. This was his last chance. If Loftus betrayed Khai, maybe Chui's failure would be forgotten. Especially if Chui was the one who stopped him. He hurried to a spot from which he could watch the woman's room. John Loftus did not disappoint him. When he emerged with the woman Chui followed leisurely. The other fools Loftus passed in the hall assumed he was taking the woman to Khai. Only Chui knew there had been no command. He slipped down the dark back stairs behind them. He wished he had another witness to Loftus's treachery. Was there time to turn back and fetch someone?

Loftus and the woman disappeared into the closet. The woman looked a little apprehensive now.

*   *   *

Daniel was seated in front of Khai's desk. The door of the study was open behind him. He saw Khai glance up and frown slightly.

"What is it?"

"Nothing," said Khai. It was a very minor crease in his ego. One of his men had just walked by the open door without even glancing in and bobbing his head deferentially. The man had paid no attention to the study and its occupants. He had been walking toward the front door with a curious expression on his face.

Khai dismissed it. Until a minute later when another man walked by in the same direction. This one was hurrying a little.

Khai had no window in his study to see what had attracted four or five of his men to the front porch. They stood there watching the gate. A small crowd of Vietnamese had gathered there. They weren't threatening—they seemed to be mostly women and old men—but their presence was a mystery. This wasn't a Vietnamese neighborhood. Where had they come from? They were a middle-class–looking group. One man even had a camera hanging around his neck. It was as if the old mansion had been included on a tour. Khai's men stood there on the dark porch keeping an eye on the small crowd. The soldiers were unworried, smoking, leaning on the rail. They made comments about the women at the gate and laughed to each other.

"Where are we?" Carol finally asked. It was the first curiosity she'd shown since they'd left her room. Loftus heard the apprehension in her tone. It made him grip her all the harder. He had turned on only one bank of the few lights in the tunnel so that it was dim enough to look forbidding. They couldn't see more than ten feet ahead of them.

"Khai's escape hatch," Loftus said. "He was a little worried that if you got out of your room you might find your way down here. That's why he had me spend so much time with you, to see you didn't. But you never tried."

Carol shook her head. There were rustling echoes in the tunnel. She couldn't tell if they were caused by their own movements. The floor of the tunnel was dirt and she was barefoot. That made her feel like a child. Unconsciously she was walking on tiptoe, setting her feet down as lightly as she could. Imagination made the dirt move underfoot.

Loftus took her arm and pulled her deeper into the tunnel. He stopped under a light where he could see her face. He saw her glance aside into the darkness.

"This is good-bye," he said. A line from some movie he'd seen. It drew her attention back to him, her eyes on his face. She was still wearing that green warmup suit. It was tight enough to show what she had, but that wasn't good enough. Pretending to be getting another grip on her, he gave it a little tug, so some skin showed between the top of her pants and the bottom of the jacket. She didn't seem to notice.

"What do you mean?" she said.

"I mean this is the way out. I'm letting you go."

He pointed into the darkness. Her eyes followed the gesture but she didn't move.

"Are you sure?" she finally asked. "There aren't any—?" She didn't even know what to ask. Holes? Guards? Alligators?

"It's okay," Loftus said. "Want me to come all the way with you?" She was the one holding his arm now—ever so lightly but still, the touch was there. It communicated her fear. He stepped closer to her, slightly surprised she couldn't feel him already.

She started to answer but he didn't wait. "But before you go," he said, and put his arms around her. His hands went under the jacket and slid along the smooth skin of her back.

She was making a nominal protest but he smothered it with his mouth. Her hands were on his chest, pushing feebly. In a minute they would go around him. His hands went higher, pulling the jacket up in front now as well. He let her go for a second to pull his own shirt off.

"You bastard," she said. To his surprise that fierce tone was back in her voice. And that's when she tried to knee him.

He blocked it easily with his own leg, then grabbed her thigh in his hands, holding her leg up off the ground. She had to lean back against the wall of the tunnel to keep from falling. He towered over her.

"All right," he said agreeably. "That way's just as good or better." He was not at all disappointed. He let go of her leg and before she could regain her balance he stepped in close and put both hands inside the waistband of her pants, pulling them down. Then he stepped in even closer, mashing her bare butt against the wall of the tunnel. She squirmed, which was pleasant, and tried to claw at his face with her nails, which wasn't so pleasant but was part of the game. He buried his face in her shoulder to protect it.

The only trouble with it turning out to be rape instead of seduction was it meant he'd have to kill her afterward. That was a waste, but he could live with it.

Khai hadn't bothered to take Daniel's gun off his desk and put it out of sight. Its display was a display of Khai's confidence. The .45 was easily within his reach but both men ignored it.

"I'll probably be moving," Daniel was saying. "Even with Linh gone, the business isn't there for me. You can turn the whole block into—"

"Perhaps I can help," Khai said. He and Daniel looked at each other, understanding that this was not an offer of help and that it could not be refused.

This time the man who passed Khai's open door was running, so Daniel heard the patter of his steps and he too turned to look. When the man had passed, Daniel looked back inquisitively at Khai, who made a dismissive gesture.

"Nothing to concern us. The men have their little games."

The commotion outside might have been the wind of the approaching storm. It sounded like the murmur of many voices.

There was a crack of thunder and the lights flickered. In its aftermath the air felt charged with electricity. It carried the sound of voices. There was a small thump against the outside of the house, like a heavy first drop of rain. But it wasn't rain.

A shot was fired. Its sound engulfed the charged air, so there was no telling its source. Daniel and Khai sat frozen. Each glared at the other mistrustfully.

There was another shot. It came from the front porch. The sound was followed immediately by a scream from farther out in the darkness.

Khai moved, but Daniel was quicker. He snatched up the gun from the desk and ran out of the study—not toward the front porch, but still the wrong direction. He ran up the stairs. Vietnamese men were swarming down, but word had already spread among them that the American belonged to Khai now. They let him pass.

Daniel stood at the head of the stairs shouting, "Carol? *Carol!*"

The only answer was the sound of running feet, that seemed to come from all over the house.

His breath seemed the vilest touch of all. It was hot, panting, burning her neck and cheek. His mouth so close to her ear made her want to retch. A degree of numbness had taken her body where his hands touched it, but the caress of his breath continued to horrify her. She kept twisting her neck to escape it, trying to smash her forehead against his nose. But he stayed too close, mirroring her movements like an evil shadow.

She kept fighting him. Even after he ripped her pants down to her ankles so that she was hobbled. Even after he opened his own pants and she felt him against her stomach. She kept squirming and trying to knee him. Her feet were hopelessly entangled in her pants; if he had let her go she would have fallen. But he didn't let her go. He had her pressed hard against the wall of the tunnel and his hands were behind her now, clutching for a grip on her buttocks so he could lift her up.

The lights went out for an instant that seemed eternal. In that darkness he was inescapable. She was smothering under his weight.

Then the lights came back on, dimly but bright by contrast, and the horror was right there against her, his beard stubble scraping her shoulder. She had stopped struggling during that moment of darkness and he had pressed his advantage. He lifted her clear off the ground. Carol tried to keep her knees clenched but he was already between them, pushing forward. They squirmed against the tunnel wall in what might have looked like passion to an observer.

There was a brighter flash of light. Lightning, Carol thought, far in the back of her mind, but there was no lightning down there belowground. The light was followed by a whirring sound she had heard before but couldn't place.

Loftus seemed oblivious to these tiny distractions, even after the flash and the whir came again. It was the low chuckle afterward that stopped him.

"Oh my," said Chui. "These will be lovely additions to my collection."

Loftus stood dead still. His back was to Chui. He didn't know how many people were back there. Carol didn't move either. She could see over Loftus's shoulder, see that Chui was standing there alone, ten feet away. A Polaroid camera was hanging by its strap from his right wrist. In that hand he held the two pictures he had just taken. Chui looked at them admiringly. In his other hand he held a gun.

"Help me," Carol said. Her voice was low and wavering. "Help." Her voice died to a rasp. Chui glanced at her with a simper of fake sympathy. He didn't give a damn what happened to her. His eyes were gleeful.

"After Khai sees them, of course," Chui went on to Loftus. "After Khai sees what you're doing to his plans. So to speak."

Loftus unfroze. Carol felt his muscles relax slightly. She thought he was going to set her down but instead he turned, still holding her, so that now her naked back was to Chui and Loftus was facing the Vietnamese.

"Carry on if you like," Chui said lightly. "The damage is already done. I'll just take these to Khai and be right back."

Loftus stepped out of his pants. They were looser than Carol's and didn't snag on his feet. He took a step forward. Carol started struggling again, but he had her tightly, one hand under her thigh and the other across her back, clamping her against him. He took another step, carrying her easily.

"There's enough here for two," Loftus said. His voice was a growl, as if his panting breath had burned his own throat.

"Enticing sight," Chui said. "If only I had the time."

Loftus took another step and Chui dropped the camera in order to shift the gun to his right hand. He slipped the photos into his shirt pocket. "Stay back there," he said. "You don't need to come along." The lightness was gone from his tone.

"Go ahead," Loftus said. "Shoot her. See what Khai thinks of that." They lashed each other with Khai's name like a whip. Carol squirmed harder, almost falling out of Loftus's grasp. He shifted one hand to her neck and squeezed. Her breath was gone instantly. She struggled only to breathe. She sagged in Loftus's arms on the edge of unconsciousness.

Chui took a step back and his shoulder bumped the tunnel wall. He edged sideways along it. Loftus kept walking. Carol, on the verge of passing out, felt him shift her weight.

"I'll shoot your leg," Chui said. He lowered the gun barrel appropriately. Loftus didn't flinch. He lifted Carol higher in his arms as if to give Chui more of a target.

Chui wavered, afraid to take a shot and miss. This was going badly suddenly. He had only to turn and walk away, but his fear of Loftus's physical strength kept him from turning his back on the ghastly stalking figure.

"I'll be back," Chui said, and finally turned to run, but it was too late. In one last surge of power Loftus lifted Carol and hurled her. Chui could have stepped out of the way but made the mistake of putting up his hands to catch her instead. Carol's body struck him in the chest and slammed him back against the tunnel wall. They both fell to the ground, entangled in a breathless heap.

Loftus was there in an instant to separate them. He pushed Carol aside and put one hand around Chui's throat. With the other he reached for the gun, still held in Chui's hand but no threat anymore. Chui's hand twitched briefly in a tiny struggle to point the gun, but he was much, much too slow. Loftus shook the wrist and the gun fell out of Chui's grip.

Loftus pulled the rotund Vietnamese to his feet. The flesh of Chui's face squeezed up under his eyes, narrowing them to slits. Dimly he could see Loftus grinning. One lust had replaced another in Loftus's skeletal face. It looked the very face of death.

Chui's back was against the wall. He lifted one foot, planted it in Loftus's midsection, and kicked with all the strength he had left. It wasn't much, but it took Loftus by surprise. He fell back, losing his grip on the throat. Chui shook his head, struggling to breathe and to see. Loftus stood there for a moment, surveying his helpless condition, and laughed, as he had laughed while raping Carol. Killing a man barehanded gave him the same sense of power.

He stepped in and struck Chui in the stomach with his fist. Not hard, just enough to knock the air out of him again. Enough to keep his victim helpless while Loftus did the real damage with his fists and knees.

From the corner of his eye he saw Carol roll over, pull her pants up, and start limping away. It didn't concern him. She was headed deeper into the tunnel, and there was no escape there. She would find the locked gate at the end. When she came back this way they could start over again.

Carol was too breathless and frightened to feel triumph, but after she turned a corner of the tunnel and was out of sight of Loftus she felt a giddy sense of hope. She was almost free, not only of him but of the whole horrible house. Once outside it she didn't care if she'd be barefoot and alone on the nighttime streets. They'd be Houston streets. Home would be within her reach.

The tunnel lights weren't on at this end, but there was a faint glow from up ahead, leading her to hope she was getting close to the exit. She stumbled, brushing against the tunnel wall, pushed off from it, and ran harder. In her imagination she could feel something right behind her, stretching out a bony hand. It was the house itself, unwilling to let her go.

She rounded a last bend and saw the gate ahead. It was a heavy gate of iron bars, six feet across and eight feet tall, its framework anchored in concrete on the bottom and sides. For an instant Carol saw only the gate, saw freedom, and ran desperately toward it.

But in the next instant, seeing what lay just beyond that gate, she skidded to a stop and screamed. The scream was startled out of her, taking the last of her breath.

Outside the tunnel was a crowd of Vietnamese, straining against the gate, their faces pressed between the bars, their arms reaching through them. Their faces were contorted with the effort to get in, and their bodies were pressed together into one flesh. At sight of Carol they strained all the harder, groping toward her, their fingers turning to claws. A horrid murmur arose from them.

After the days Carol had spent in the house, surrounded by malevolent Vietnamese, this sea of brown faces was the worst sight she could have imagined. Her safe world had vanished. There was no home to escape to anymore. Inside the house and out, the whole world had turned Vietnamese.

She sank to the ground, trapped.

Khai followed Daniel out of his study but then swerved toward the front door. On the porch he found a small crowd of his men. A few more were out in the yard, trotting toward the fence. A storm was approaching. From the smell of the wind it was almost here. It swirled Khai's hair.

"What is the problem?" he asked in Vietnamese.

A man who was startled by his boss's sudden appearance answered, "No problem. People at the gate. They started throwing rocks. We shot and they ran away."

"You fired rifles here?" Khai asked angrily. He strained to hear anything unusual in the night but couldn't.

"Two shots only. Just to frighten."

"If police come—" Khai began, but interrupted himself. "Why would a crowd of Americans be at my gate?"

"Not Americans," said his man. "Vietnamese."

"Viet—" Khai was even more startled. He glanced back at his own house, as if to assure himself that its bulk still stood behind him. "Tang's men?" he asked.

"No. These were women. Old men."

Khai looked at his imposing front gate. There was no one there. "Where did they go?" he asked. Something was stirring in his mind but he couldn't place the anxiety yet. "They may be trying to get in somewhere else along the fence."

"That's what they're going to check," said his informant. Khai saw another of his men drifting back in toward the house, shaking his head. Others were spreading out across the yard. The fence was long, it would take time to check. He should have replaced the dogs already.

Khai's thoughts were back inside his house, on Daniel Greer. Khai was enough of a tactician to know a diversion when one was described to him. Women and old men at his gate were not the threat.

"Come with me," he said. The man picked up his rifle and obeyed, of course. In the hall they found more men running toward the front porch. Khai intercepted them and turned them around, heading back upstairs. "The American" was all he said to them, but they understood.

Daniel had tried all the rooms on the second floor without finding Carol. Each empty room increased his fear. He had been insane to trust Khai. She was dead already.

In the last bedroom he found the Vietnamese woman bound and gagged. Her eyes were open. Daniel swept his eyes around the room, saw there was no one else in it, and started to run out again, but something stopped him. Her simple aliveness. His wife was dead and here was Linh's still living. Something about that didn't make sense. He closed the door and approached her. Her eyes didn't plead with him, nor did they flinch away. She just stared, enduring.

He pulled the gag from her mouth, but when he asked her a question she answered in muttered Vietnamese. He untied her. She sat up slowly, as if very tired. She was looking at his gun. Daniel glanced at it himself. The woman didn't look afraid of the gun; she looked as if she wanted it.

"Where's my wife?" he asked again. "The other woman?"

He thought maybe the Vietnamese woman understood, but she couldn't or wouldn't respond. He almost said something to her about her husband, but refrained.

No more time to spend on her. Daniel ran back to the door and out. There was a third floor, or an attic. He knew that from having seen the outside of the house. He started back for the stairs and saw Khai appear at the head of them, with a few of his men. Daniel stopped.

"Where is she?" he shouted.

Khai's response was too soft for him to hear. The man next to Khai raised his rifle and fired.

Carol's fingers were scrabbling in the dirt, as if she could dig a new tunnel, or a hole for herself to hide in. It was a mindless action. She couldn't go forward and she couldn't go back. She wanted to run back the way she'd come, away from those clutching yellow fingers, but she knew what lay behind her. She imagined she could hear footsteps now, Loftus coming after her, and behind him the whole Vietnamese army she couldn't escape.

There was no safe place to look. She was staring down into the dirt, afraid she'd lose her mind if she looked up again at that yellow Hydra of arms reaching through the gate. She didn't look up until she heard her name.

"Please, Mrs. Greer."

She thought it must be an illusion. But when she looked up the crowd of Vietnamese had pulled back slightly. A teenage boy stood in front of them, just outside the gate. He stood straight, hands at his sides, just looking at Carol.

"Please, Mrs. Greer. We have to get in. I unlocked the gate, but there's a latch on the inside we can't reach."

Carol crawled slightly forward, eyes straining through the dimness. The Vietnamese were standing outside, and it had just started to rain. Two or three of them were almost twitching with eagerness, but the boy held them in thrall. They stood behind him, their hands withdrawn from the bars.

"You remember me, Mrs. Greer."

Strangely enough, Carol thought she did remember him, but she couldn't recall from where. It seemed that the boy was someone she had known in childhood, now turned Vietnamese along with the rest of the world. The boy appeared out of context, even in the middle of that crowd of similar appearance.

Carol still hesitated. But back down the tunnel now she *could* hear movement. She looked back but there was nothing she could see.

When she looked back at the gate a man had appeared there beside the boy. A Vietnamese man of some years but also of imposing height and bulk. His hands gripped the bars. His dark eyes held Carol's.

"My wife—" He looked toward the house. Carol saw that his hands were straining on the thick bars, as if he could pull them apart.

She knew him. It seemed years ago, but he was the pawnbroker whose shop stood across the street from Daniel's. The man whose wife still lay bound and helpless upstairs in this house.

Carol began nodding unconsciously. She crawled forward and stood. If the hands had come groping through the bars again she would have shrunk back, but the boy's discipline was tight.

The Vietnamese stood there like soldiers, though their eyes implored her to hurry. There were mostly men in the crowd, but a few women as well. The teenage boy was the youngest of the lot.

"Thien," Carol said suddenly, and the boy nodded.

When she got close to the gate she saw that there was a thick metal plate at the top of the bars. A horizontal bar that fit into a slot in that plate was holding the gate closed. It was too high above her head to reach.

She looked to Thien for instructions but the boy's eyes had cut away from her. Carol looked back over her shoulder and saw John Loftus. He had stopped against the wall of the tunnel some thirty or forty feet back. Still naked from the waist down, he seemed to glow white in the darkness. His round eyes were wide, she could see that even from this distance. He was staring at the Vietnamese, but then his eyes moved to Carol instead. He saw her hand stretched upward, and he saw the bar still in place, holding the gate closed. He saw the Vietnamese were still locked out.

He started forward.

Carol screamed. She shrank back against the hard iron bars. Wind blew the rain in, soaking her back.

"Quickly," said a voice at her shoulder, and Carol did the bravest thing she had ever done. She turned her back on Loftus.

Two Vietnamese men had taken Thien's place at the front. They were kneeling, reaching their hands through the bars, and had linked those hands inside to form a step for her. Carol put her bare foot into those linked brown hands. When they began to lift she almost fell back, but she grabbed the bars and steadied herself.

She heard Loftus's running steps behind her and knew she would feel his hands any instant. The faces of the two Vietnamese men were at her waist, straining with the effort to lift her. She lurched upward a foot or so, and the restraining bar was still a few inches from her outstretched hand.

And Loftus had her then. His arms came around her waist and he yanked her backward. She had been holding the bars only with her left hand as she groped upward with the right, and she lost that feeble grip and fell back with him. She could feel rather than hear the inarticulate growl in his throat. His chin pressed the top of her head.

She clawed at his arms and he threw her aside, into the dirt again. She saw his face, and was surprised to see fear. Loftus looked back quickly over his shoulder. But the gate still held. He had stopped her in time. He laughed. There was no restraint in him. He stood over her and laughed in triumph.

Carol had no thoughts at all. She wouldn't have planned what she did next. For a moment she was just consumed with hate. She launched herself off the ground straight at him. Loftus was completely unguarded. She threw herself against his chest and he fell back. Neither of them had any balance. Carol dropped to the ground again. She stood shakily, trying to prepare herself for his counterattack.

She looked up to see the strangest look on his face. Rage and puzzlement mingled there. Loftus was trying to lunge toward her, but he had fallen back against the bars and the bars held him like a spiderweb. Carol shared his puzzlement until she saw the arms. They had come through the bars again to encircle John Loftus—his waist, his legs, his chest.

The hands were there again, forming the step for her to reach the latch. Carol stepped into them unhesitatingly this time and they lifted her smoothly. Her hand reached the handle of the restraining bar.

Beside her Loftus exploded, kicking and straining and biting. He jerked an arm free and then a leg. The hands groped for him but failed to find a new grip.

Carol pulled on the handle with all her strength. She tried to step aside for more leverage and stepped right out of the hands holding her. One foot swung in empty space. She hung on the handle of the bar as if it were a trapeze. When she swung on it the bar moved.

John Loftus pulled free. He was growling like an animal again. Carol heard him behind her.

But by this time Linh had pulled his handgun from his

pocket. Loftus saw it. Unlike Carol, Loftus never hesitated. He turned and ran. He was a pale glimmer down the tunnel. Linh fired but Loftus ran on unscathed, already shouting for reinforcements.

Carol gave one last tug and the bar slid aside. She dropped to the ground and the gate came open with all the force of that eager mob outside. They surged past her, screaming. There were more even than she had imagined, filling the tunnel momentarily from side to side. Very few of them seemed to be armed with anything other than sticks, though. Carol watched them go rampaging up the tunnel, but that wasn't important to her anymore. What was important was that the gate was open. She could feel the wind and the rain pouring over her and they felt wonderful.

"Are you all right?"

Thien was the only one who had stopped to inquire of her, but it was obvious the boy was eager to join the crowd racing into the house. This was Thien's plan come to fruition. He was the one who had obtained the key to the secret gate, as well as knowledge of this hidden entrance itself, from the Saigon cowboy in Daniel's garage. He had given it in exchange for his life after Daniel had left Thien alone with the men in his futile attempt to rescue Carol. And it was Thien, along with Linh, who had organized the other merchants and their families into a resistance force determined to free themselves from Khai's domination or die.

"Don't worry about me," Carol said wearily. "As soon as I find Daniel—"

"He's inside."

"Inside?" Carol looked back down that dark tunnel. She shuddered.

"Looking for you," said Thien, dancing with anxiety. "I have to join them."

He ran, leaving Carol standing there alone in the soothing rain, looking back into the tunnel and shaking her head as if someone had made a horrible suggestion. Tears started in her eyes.

* * *

He couldn't stop the blood. It poured down the side of his face, blinding one eye. Daniel was surprised there could be so much blood. He could feel it pulsing in his temples, the blood racing as if eager to escape his body. He pressed one hand hard against his forehead and the flow of blood slowed, but when he took the sticky hand away it started up again.

Khai's man had missed his shot but the rifle bullet had struck the door jamb beside Daniel, knocking off a splintered chunk of wood that ricocheted into his head, giving him a deep gash over his left eye. Daniel had fled before anyone else could fire. Around the corner and up the narrow stairs he found there. It was a monkey's instinct, to seek higher ground. In this instance it had probably betrayed him. Going higher in the house further isolated him from rescue. At the top of the stairs he had found an attic door, opened it to find the attic apparently empty, but then he had stopped there in the doorway. Those narrow stairs offered his best defensible position. A rifleman had appeared in the opening at the bottom of the stairs and Daniel had fired the .45 at him. From the scream he didn't know if he'd hit the man or just scared him, but others had stayed back. Two or three bold ones had stuck their heads around the stairwell opening and Daniel had fired at them. They didn't test him anymore after that and he was glad of it. He didn't have an extra clip for the .45. He lay back against the attic door and rested. It hadn't occurred to him that there might be another way into that attic behind him.

Where was Thien? He should have been there with his merchant army by now. Clerk commandos. Maybe they had all turned out to be as cowardly as he. Daniel should have just done as Khai had ordered and murdered Linh. Instead he had let Thien talk him into this alternative, to fake the murder. The reason he had finally gone for it was that he didn't know if he really could have killed the innocent Linh, even to save Carol.

He didn't know what Thien had said to the Vietnamese pawnbroker to make him cooperate. Thien had been the go-between, selling the scheme to Linh while Daniel sat in his own shop and waited. When he'd entered Linh's shop he hadn't even been sure they had an agreement. He still remembered Linh's bullet singing past his ear.

Daniel was growing light-headed. His hands seemed to be yards away. He watched them fumble with the tail of his shirt and tear off a wide strip. He closed his eyes as the robot hands wrapped the cloth around his forehead and tied it. The blood kept flowing, but more slowly. His eyes stayed closed.

Then they jerked open and he started to his feet hard enough to make his head pound. He had remembered Carol. She must be there somewhere. If she was still alive, then Khai had sent men to bring her. That's why they weren't rushing Daniel's position at the top of the stairs. They'd bring her if they had her. Daniel's hope of saving her had trickled away. His best hope now was that they could die quickly and together. And that he could kill Khai in the process.

He *could* do that. Renewed strength flowed to his hand as he gripped the .45 and started slowly down the stairs.

It was like a party until the first of them was killed.

Thien's mob of Vietnamese were survivors of the fall of South Vietnam, many of them survivors of the last days of Saigon. They had lost everything in just such a scene of carnage as this. They had seen mobs storm through their homes smashing and looting. But this time they were the ones wreaking the carnage. The feeling was exhilarating. They burst out of the tunnel and went rampaging through the first floor of the old mansion, knocking pictures off the walls and sending shelves crashing to the floor. They met no opposition at first. Most of Khai's men were either outside or upstairs. The mob owned the house, or so they thought.

In the living room they had their first fatal encounter. One of the youngest of Khai's men was walking through, on his way to report the negative results of the search of the perimeter. He was almost to the stairs when the most eager of the mob came through the archway beside him. The young man was holding his rifle by its barrel, dragging it behind him. The forerunner of the mob was a middle-aged man armed with an aluminum baseball bat. Both of them hesitated. The young man's mind produced no thoughts at all. He had no reason to fear middle-aged Vietnamese. He saw them only in the course of collecting tribute, of laughing at their consternation when he demanded extra for himself or laid a casual hand on their daughters. He had never seen one like this before, face contorted in rage. The shopkeeper raised the bat and his voice and came at Khai's young man like fury made human.

The kid did what he'd never done before in his life: raised his rifle and fired at another human being. He did it well enough. The bullet took the middle-aged man in the chest. It knocked him down and then it killed him. The kid who had fired was no less surprised than anyone else in the room.

It cost him his life as well. The next member of the mob had a gun, not a bat. He fired it at the kid, missed, kept running forward, fired again. The kid was still stunned by the rifle's recoil and his own fatal instinct. He stood there and let himself be killed. The merchant ran right up to him and hit him in the head with the handgun, then fired it into his face as he went down. There was no glee in it. There was only fear and desperation and long-held rage.

The mob lost its festive spirit. Their eyes turned dead as glass. Linh took charge. He took up the fallen rifle and handed it to one of his merchants. Quickly he dispatched a small contingent of them to the front door, which they locked and guarded, cutting off nearly a third of Khai's men outside the house. The rest of the merchants Linh led up the stairs. They didn't run now, and they didn't loose any wild yells. They were grim as mourners.

Far up the tunnel, almost back to the hated house, Carol came across the body of her hapless rescuer. Chui looked like a wrecked doll. In death his face had lost its plumpness. John Loftus had ruined its planes with his knee. Chui's nose was indented almost flush into his face. Carol spared him a long glance. Inadvertent as the act had been, Chui had saved her life. And Loftus had killed him for it. There had been no reason. Almost from the moment Loftus began working on him, Chui had no longer been a threat. And Carol, Loftus's original target, had been getting away. Yet Loftus had taken the time to do this gravedigger's work. He had undoubtedly enjoyed it. And now he was back inside the house, inside with Daniel who had come to save her. Daniel who must still be inside searching for her. Carol left the body behind and went on. Her footsteps were trudging but resolute. When she passed through the doorway her skin turned clammy. She knew the house would never let her go again.

Daniel thought he heard sirens in the distance, but he didn't trust his hearing. There was an incessant whine in his ears, a white noise that was cutting him off from the world. He was fading away. Soon he would be a ghost, able to move at will through Khai's soldiers.

He reached the bottom of the attic stairs slowly, expecting any second to be face to face with an armed Vietnamese appearing in the doorway. None did. He reached the doorway and glanced around the corner. There were some of Khai's men, all right, but their backs were to him. Daniel stared. He had some bullets left in his gun but he didn't fire. Something made him hold off. The soldiers had forgotten him, and for the moment he wanted to keep it that way.

One had not. Khai had not forgotten Daniel. He was concentrating on him at that moment.

The second floor of the old mansion had erupted into chaos. Khai's men had been preparing for their final assault on Daniel. Khai knew what Daniel did not, that there was another staircase to the attic. Khai had sent a few men up the back stairs. The others had been positioning themselves to rush the American's position on the main stairs. That's when Linh and his merchants had arrived on the second floor. If they had come whooping and shouting—they way they'd entered the first floor—Khai would have had moments to prepare for them. But instead the merchants came silent as a funeral procession. They fell on Khai's men from behind and were already wreaking damage before the soldiers knew there was another foe in the house. Though both sides were armed, the fighting quickly became hand to hand. And it was as if someone had suddenly turned the soundtrack back on. Screams of rage and pain filled the air.

Khai was caught unprepared. He had expected his men below to guard his back. But he was no startled innocent. He saw at once what was happening, who was attacking him. He realized that Daniel Greer had been the forerunner of this army. And Khai was a man for whom personal revenge meant more than life or death.

His men had been driven back, but a hard core of them had regrouped around their leader. They were firing into the melee, sometimes hitting their own men. Hearing the noise, Khai's men from the attic came back down the back stairs and Khai ordered them into the fight.

And Khai himself slipped up those dark stairs behind the door. He was armed, and he knew where Greer was hiding.

The first floor was cloaked in an eerie silence. The mob had swept it clean, but Carol didn't know that. She could hardly force herself forward, her skin was tingling so. There was no one about. It was as if everything that had happened in the tunnel had been illusion designed to lure her back inside, and now the illusions had vanished leaving her alone in the house. She expected the hallway to begin closing in on her.

In the kitchen she found a cleaver. Gripping its handle made her slightly more confident. She hurried back down the hall and when she stepped into the living room, she could hear the noise from above. She hesitated at the sight of the two bodies, then moved faster, to the stairs and up them. Now she believed again that Daniel was there. If she just caught a glimpse of him she'd know what to do next.

Khai's men were in retreat. Some of them had been forced back the length of the hall and had fled down the back stairs. Daniel watched them go, still hidden on the attic stairs. It had finally occurred to him that that's where Carol might be, in the attic. He had searched all the rooms on the second floor already. His mind wasn't working very well. He had dropped his gun somewhere. "Carol?" he called hopefully, and opened the creaking door into the attic. Silence answered him. There was a fresh breeze on his face.

In isolated clusters the fighting continued. The mob was taking its revenge for years of forced tribute and humiliation. Sometimes the vengeance was impersonal. Middle-aged men clubbed down young men just for being in the house of the man who had dominated them. Sometimes, though, a merchant would recognize a particular one of Khai's men and lunge toward him, screaming. More often than not, the young man attacked so intimately would drop his weapon and try to flee. Few succeeded.

In some instances the revenge was most personal. When Carol reached the head of the stairs she saw Linh open a bedroom door and look inside. Carol ran to him, touched his arm, and pointed across the hall. He looked at her, took a long moment to register her presence, and nodded. He moved quickly across the hall, opened the door, and disappeared inside.

Carol had passed on by the time Linh emerged again. He had one arm around his wife, supporting her. She was walking, rather hesitantly, but with no sign of crippling injury. Linh had her disfigured hand in his and was rubbing it, turning the hand over and back again. She murmured something into his ear and put both arms around his neck. Her husband held her tightly, his eyes squeezed shut.

The fighting no longer interested him. When they moved again it was back toward the front stairs, away from the chaos. But they didn't reach the stairs. As they passed another bedroom door, it opened and the rat-faced man stood there. The woman flinched away from, hiding her face against her husband's shoulder. But that reaction passed in an instant. She turned back and lunged toward the man, her hand becoming a claw. Ratface stood there groggily, staring at Linh not as if he knew him but as if he thought he should.

Linh laid a hand on the man's chest and pushed him back into the room. His wife came with him. She was talking in a rush of Vietnamese.

Linh closed the door.

Khai heard the attic door open, heard Greer's voice calling for his wife. Khai wondered fleetingly what had happened to the woman, but it didn't matter. Nothing happening in the house below mattered now. He could recoup. This madness of merchants would pass. It was an aberration of middle-age glands, nothing more. They would be sheep again afterward. Khai's hand would fall on them more ruthlessly than ever.

Dealing with the American had made him vulnerable to this. Daniel Greer had somehow inspired them. He had made them think they were Americans too, immune from the old forces from the homeland. Khai must show them no one was immune. Greer and his wife must die as horribly as possible. He was thinking no cautioning thoughts now. Khai hoped he could somehow preserve their mutilated bodies, for display to merchants who showed the least sign of recalcitrance.

He made his way softly across the attic, holding the gun up close to his cheek. He had come up the back stairs slowly, letting his eyes adjust to the gloom. He could see like a cat by this time. The American would have no such advantage. The main attic stairs were lighted. When Greer opened that door he would be stumbling in blindness. Khai moved close to the door and waited.

It opened. "Carol?" came the American's fearful voice. He was a sharp-edged silhouette in the lighted doorway. Khai permitted himself a smile. He waited further. No blunders. Let the American come all the way in. Khai was a patient man, even in the midst of disaster.

"Carol?" Daniel called again, a little louder. He couldn't see a thing in the dark attic. He stepped inside. His hands groped forward in the darkness.

"*Daniel!*"

The scream came from behind him. He turned and saw her at the bottom of the stairs.

"Carol?" He couldn't believe she was real. After these days of absence she had become imaginary.

She said his name again and started up the stairs. He descended to meet her. He stumbled on the steps, almost fell, collected himself, and staggered into her arms. They met violently, lunging at each other as if each could find a niche in the other's body and crawl inside. But Daniel didn't want just to clutch her against him. He wanted to *see* her. He pushed her back to arm's length and stared at her. Carol stared as well. He looked like hell and she could imagine how she looked. She laughed.

At the sound the reality of her swept through him, he believed in her presence, and he did hold her tightly against his chest then. It was in that moment, when he finally held her after days of terror, that he felt least safe. Now that he actually had her back he felt more vulnerable than ever.

He was right to feel that way.

The stairs yawned empty behind him. Khai stood at the head of them. He was a man who appreciated poignance. He let the reunion moment below continue. His smile was soft and gentle. The malice was only in his eyes. He raised his gun and pointed it at the American's back. They held each other so tightly the first bullet might pass through both of them, which

would be more poignant still. Khai's finger tightened on the
trigger. His joy was even deeper than theirs, he felt sure.
Certainly it would be longer-lived.

When the demon fell on him it was like the hand of God,
falling from heaven to smash him flat. Khai was thrown forward
by the blow. He had a glimpse of the lovers below turning
startled faces toward him, then his own face hit a stairstep and
he saw no more. The weight was still on his back, driving him
even lower.

Daniel looked up, frightened out of his wits, but Khai was
already falling by that time. Daniel scrambled down the stairs to
get out of his way, pulling Carol. Khai came sliding down toward
them.

Thien was on his back. He held Khai's ears and rode him
down the stairs like a sled. Thien was shouting something, but it
was in Vietnamese. Daniel and Carol had no idea what he was
saying.

Khai landed in a heap at the bottom of the stairs. Daniel and
Carol had managed to scramble out of the way. Thien had never
lost his grip. He sat astride the tyrant's back, still screaming.
And somehow in his wild ride down the stairs Thien had
managed to snatch up Khai's pistol as it clattered along beside
him. He leaned down and stuck the barrel of it into Khai's ear.
The gun was a thin-barreled Luger, it went right inside the ear.
The pain roused Khai. Daniel saw the gang leader's eyes open.
Thien held Khai's hair in his left hand and jammed the gun into
his ear again. The boy was bending over, telling him something.
But his right hand was white on the grip of the gun. In another
moment he would squeeze the trigger.

"Thien!" Daniel shouted. He stepped toward the boy and
Thien looked up, wild-eyed. Daniel stopped. Thien's face was
frightening. He didn't look the least bit familiar.

Daniel shook his head. "You can't kill him."

Thien grinned like a demon. "*You* couldn't. But watch."

"No!" Daniel shouted.

Thien hesitated for another second. He looked more like
the boy Daniel had known. Life had returned to Khai's eyes.

They pleaded with Daniel to intervene. Daniel bent over both the fallen figures and spoke into Thien's ear, loudly enough for both of them to hear.

"He fears prison more than death" was what he said. From the look that came into Khai's face he still believed that was true.

Thien was unconvinced. "My father," he said softly. "If this one ever returns . . ."

"Think of him in prison," Daniel said. "A little scared gook who thought he could be king. There are Vietnam vets in there. You know what they'll do to someone like him?"

Thien's face was his own again, the face Daniel remembered. The boy looked thoughtful. He spoke as if to himself. "You hear, warlord?" he said softly. "And after what happens to you in there, who will follow you again?"

Khai struggled briefly. Thien casually lifted the man's head and banged it against the stair. Khai subsided, dazed. Thien leaned down and spoke words for only him.

"When you emerge," he said, "I will be grown."

Loftus was free. He was the only one who'd escaped. That was as it should be. He was the only one with brains. Even Khai was too prone to emotion to think clearly at times. John Loftus, on the other hand, never lost sight of the fact that he was the only one who mattered. He'd come up out of the tunnel with the intention of warning the others, but when he'd arrived on the first floor he'd found too few men there to wage a successful counterattack. So instead he'd slipped aside and let the mob pass him by. He had thought about following them up the stairs and attacking from behind, but again he had no support troops. To hell with them all, he'd decided instead. When it came to gook against gook, he didn't much care who won this battle.

He was outside now, having slipped out a window. He saw some few of Khai's men far out near the fence, scuffling along, head down in the pouring rain. Lightning split the sky, followed by deafening thunder. He'd have no trouble slipping away in

this storm. He lingered. He hadn't forgotten Carol. Now that he
knew he was safe again Loftus gave up his singleminded pursuit
of escape and let his thoughts slip back to the woman who
obsessed him. If she had gone back inside the house with that
mob she was still within his reach. Loftus waited. He would take
one more chance on finding her. He should have stolen her
driver's license when he'd had the chance, but of course then he
hadn't thought he'd ever need her home address. But he needed
it now. It wasn't over between them, not by a long shot. It would
be unbearably sweet to find her again after all this, after she
thought she was safe.

He sank back into the shadows and wrapped his arms
around his chest. He had snatched up his pants as he'd run back
out of the tunnel, and put them on again before coming outside,
but the rain was cold. It kept him alert.

Long moments passed. Loftus paced around the perimeter
of the house, looking up at the second-floor windows. The noise
was dying up there. It might be safe to creep back into the house
and find out who had won. He had Chui's gun, he didn't fear
running into a few stragglers from the fight. Besides, surely a
mob of clerks, crazed as they'd been, hadn't defeated Khai's
armed soldiers. Loftus was at the back of the house, out of sight
of the front gate. He backed away from the house, staring up at
the windows. There was an open one on the second floor. He
saw a figure pass by it, but too quickly for him to identify. He
just wanted to see who was still standing. He might even get a
glimpse of the woman if he backed a little deeper into the
darkness.

"You slime," said a voice at his back.

It was Steve Rybek. The sirens Daniel had thought he
heard had been real. While uniformed officers had burst through
the front door of the house, Rybek had slipped around the back
to make sure no one escaped that way. Finding John Loftus was
as good a bonus as he'd hoped for. Rybek knew him. Knew he
was a fellow Vietnam vet but in the service of Khai now.

"You're worse than any of them," he said in a low, scathing

voice. "You should be shot just like a traitor in war. How could anybody—"

He had more to say, but Loftus turned and shot him first. Loftus was firing from the hip and the bullet went low, but well enough. It hit Rybek in the thigh and knocked his legs out from under him. Rybek fell into the mud and his own gun fell out of his hand.

Loftus didn't even know who he'd shot. Pure instinct had saved him again. He stepped closer, heard Rybek groaning, and remembered the cop. And obviously the cop remembered him. Loftus pointed the gun at his head. No one would ever pin this one on him. There'd be plenty of corpses laid to the account of the war inside the house. This would just be another one.

Rybek turned over and looked at him. Loftus gave an apologetic little shrug.

In the next instant he thought he'd been struck by lightning. It wasn't that painful, of course, but it was as unexpected as a thunderbolt. And it came from above. Something crashed into the back of his head and shoulders and shattered. Loftus turned, dazed. Something was dangling down his back. An electrical cord. It was a lamp. God had dropped a lamp on him.

He looked up at that open window on the second floor. The woman was leaning out of it. She looked like she was screaming, but Loftus could hardly hear her. He looked past her and saw that her husband was there, holding her to make sure she didn't fall. Loftus couldn't read his expression.

But they didn't have guns. They didn't matter for the moment. He'd have time to—

He couldn't make out the screaming from above but he did hear the *click*, because it was much, much closer at hand. And he felt the pressure.

Rybek had recovered his gun. He couldn't rise from the mud because of his leg, so he just laid there and stuck the gun right into John Loftus's crotch.

"That sound was me cocking the hammer. If what I've got the barrel on is important to you, drop your gun."

For emphasis Rybek pressed a little. Loftus moved only his

eyes, being very, very careful not to move his hand that was holding the gun. He looked down and confirmed Rybek's claim. Rybek had a very mild, almost amused expression. He was twisted on the ground, but his hand was rock steady.

Now Loftus could make out what Carol was shouting from above. "Shoot!" she was saying. "He's moving! His hand is moving!"

Loftus hastily dropped the gun. Rybek kept his own in place. He held it there even after he saw two uniformed officers coming toward him with their own guns drawn. He held it there while he put his thumb on the hammer and slowly lowered it back into place. Loftus watched him do it. Rybek enjoyed watching his face as he did it.

There was surprisingly little damage. Half of Khai's men had run off into the night before the police arrived. Of the ones left behind, none was unbloodied but very few dead. The ugliest thing the police found was the body of the rat-faced man, the sight of which caused one officer to turn quickly away and go looking for a bathroom.

They also found an old man cowering in one of the bedrooms. He didn't speak English and he appeared frightened by the uniforms. The old man offered no resistance. He seemed to be just a mild-mannered, nervous old man until they brought him into the same room with Khai. Khai addressed two sharp syllables to him, and when that didn't stop the flood of the old man's abuse Khai ignored him.

Daniel and Linh passed each other in the upstairs hall, each with his wife. The women hugged each other. Daniel and Linh just looked at each other. If they'd both been Americans they might have shaken hands, which would have been a pitifully inadequate gesture. They were the oddest of allies. In the moment when they'd acted together, trusting each other with their lives, they had been strangers. Linh would never have agreed to Thien's scheme if he hadn't been suicidal already. He had let the American point a gun at him not out of trust but because he didn't care what happened to him. Now here they were, triumphant, co-workers, yet still strangers. They nodded to each other as if being formally introduced for the first time.

In the living room Daniel and Carol found cops, Khai and others, and Thien. The boy was standing quietly against a wall, listening to the old man.

"What's he saying?" Daniel asked.

"'Why couldn't you be satisfied with what we had?'" Thien said without preface, picking up the translation in midstream. "'Would that I'd been unmanned before I ever fathered such a thing as you. An old man destroyed by his son's idiocy.' And so on in that vein."

The sound of Thien's voice drew Khai's attention as his father's did not. He looked down at Thien with a blank expression that nevertheless made his eyes appear deeper black. His eyes moved to Daniel and he looked almost friendly.

"Look out for that one. Baby Mao. He'll be the next boss of Little Saigon."

"Why not mayor of Houston?" Daniel replied. He put a hand on Thien's head and moved on.

On the porch he found Steve Rybek in a chair still directing operations. Ambulance attendants stood by but Rybek wouldn't let them take him away yet.

"You kept a little from me," Rybek said to Daniel, but not threateningly.

"You can see I had to."

Rybek nodded. "You certainly put on a big finish, I'll say that for you. It all looks justifiable to me, but of course I'm not a judge. All we gotta do now is sort out which gook was on which side—"

Daniel knelt beside him so they were on an even eye level. "Do me a favor," he said quietly. Rybek looked at him accommodatingly. "Don't ever say anything like that around me again." Daniel looked at him levelly. He hadn't raised his voice.

"Hey, I don't mean anything by it. You know, I just—"

"I don't care," Daniel said just as quietly. "Don't even let me hear it."

"Sure thing," Rybek said, managing not to look terrified. "I didn't know you were so sensitive."

Daniel just nodded and stood up again.

Rybek cleared his throat and said, "How'd you manage all this, anyway? How do you rate so much support from the—Vietnamese?"

"I don't. But I'll tell you how to find out. When you finish sorting through the—Vietnamese—and you come to the smallest one you can find, ask him."

Rybek tried to look as if he understood that. When Greer turned away, arm around his wife, Rybek said, "I need statements from both of you."

They ignored him.

Back inside the house, Thien passed slowly through the throng. He was so young no one seemed to see him. He found Khai's study and sat behind his desk. It was a very comfortable chair. Idly Thien glanced through the papers on the desk.

He thought about what Khai had said of him and about what Daniel had replied. Boss or mayor. Those were not the only possibilities, of course, but they were the two on which his mind lingered. First there was school to finish. And it was possible the years and circumstances might change his goals. But he doubted it. He was a very singleminded young man. In fact, there were steps he could begin taking now, while still in school. His father was a small businessman. Thien could help make him bigger. And someday . . .

He sat in Khai's chair and thought long, long thoughts about America. The future had never seemed so open.

As they walked away Carol saw Linh and his wife being questioned by a uniformed police officer. Linh looked up at them but his face was blank again, the expression he offered strangers.

"You know what you might consider?" Carol said, looking at Linh.

"What?"

"Becoming partners with him."

Daniel turned his head to look at Linh as well. Linh nodded, ever so slightly. The cop's head was down, writing, so he didn't see the movement. Daniel returned the nod. "I think I already have," he said.

As they neared the front gate, Carol's steps slowed. It was the way she left a party, slowly, afraid she might miss something. He was holding her hand. Since they had found each other they hadn't stopped touching.

"Where're Mother and Dad?" she asked. She sounded like a woman being met on the docks after a long trip abroad.

Daniel hesitated. He wondered how long it would take Carol to find out that her father had used her as a bargaining chip. He wanted to be there when Hecate saw his daughter had been delivered safe and sound. He'd probably give himself away by trying to take credit for her delivery.

"I haven't talked to them about it," he said truthfully, and continued: "Jennifer knows something, but she doesn't know what she knows. Either that I killed you or you ran off with someone."

"Jennifer," Carol said, like a name she remembered from childhood.

Carol seemed to him physically unhurt. He felt very light-headed himself. Everything was drifting away from him. He hadn't asked her any detailed questions yet, nor she him. They would talk about what had happened, talk about it for years, but not yet. The best attitude for them at the moment seemed to be to act, not as if it hadn't happened, but as if it had been something else—an event. An adventure. So he was surprised at the bluntness of her next remark.

"You know the worst thing they did to me?" He steeled himself for the answer. "They made me think you were dead."

He turned and hugged her. She was crying. He was probably crying too. It was hard to tell in the rain. "It's okay," he kept saying, or something inane like that.

They went out the front gate. Uniformed police there didn't stop them. Now that they were clear of the trees there was a view of downtown. Carol stared at it. "My city," she said. On the way home she would ask Daniel to drive through the heart of it.

Daniel was looking back at the house, where the tiny figures of people still moved. He was thinking how displaced they all were. Even Rybek, who had never managed to leave Vietnam behind. Of the whole crowd, only he and Carol were free to walk away from it all and go home.

So they did.